A Three Book Problem

Sherlock Holmes Bookshop Mysteries

A Curious Incident
There's a Murder Afoot
A Scandal in Scarlet
The Cat of the Baskervilles
Body on Baker Street
Elementary, She Read

Lighthouse Library Mysteries
(writing as Eva Gates)

Deadly Ever After
A Death Long Overdue
Read and Buried
Something Read, Something Dead
The Spook in the Stacks
Reading Up a Storm
Booked for Trouble
By Book or By Crook

Ashley Grant Mysteries

Coral Reef Views
Blue Water Hues
White Sand Blues

Year Round Christmas Mysteries

Dying in a Winter Wonderland
Silent Night, Deadly Night
Hark the Herald Angels Slay
We Wish You a Murderous Christmas
Rest Ye Murdered Gentlemen

Constable Molly Smith Mysteries

Unreasonable Doubt
Under Cold Stone
A Cold White Sun
Among the Departed
Negative Image
Winter of Secrets
Valley of the Lost
In the Shadow of the Glacier

Tea By the Sea Mysteries

Murder in a Teacup
Tea & Treachery

Catskill Summer Resort Mystery

Deadly Summer Nights

Also Available By Vicki Delany

More Than Sorrow
Burden of Memory
Scare the Light Away

A Three Book Problem

A SHERLOCK HOLMES BOOKSHOP MYSTERY

Vicki Delany

CROOKED
LANE

NEW YORK

Copyright © 2022 by Vicki Delany

Published in the United States by Crooked Lane Books, an imprint of The Quick Brown Fox & Company LLC.

Crooked Lane Books and its logo are trademarks of The Quick Brown Fox & Company LLC.

Library of Congress Catalog-in-Publication data available upon request.

ISBN (hardcover): 978-1-64385-798-5
ISBN (ebook): 978-1-64385-799-2

Cover illustration by Joe Burleson

Printed in the United States.

www.crookedlanebooks.com

Crooked Lane Books
34 West 27th St., 10th Floor
New York, NY 10001

First Edition: January 2022

10 9 8 7 6 5 4 3 2 1

To Mom

Chapter One

"You're sure we didn't go through a warp in the space-time continuum and end up in Jolly Old England?"

"Not according to the GPS." Jayne Wilson peered at her phone. "Still Cape Cod. Still West London, Massachusetts."

"Still the twenty-first century?" I asked.

"So this says."

I steered the Miata down the long driveway, passing rows of towering oak trees, their leaves turning yellow with the season. Between the flash of tree trunks I could see green lawns stretching into the distance, hedges and low stone walls, curving flower-beds, a line of oaks and maples, bursting with autumn color, and the azure sea sparkling on the far horizon. "You must be right," I said. "Too sunny to be England."

The driveway took a wide turn, the house came into view, and Jayne sucked in a breath. I might have gasped myself. The house was three stories tall, made of weathered golden stone, with tall curtained windows, numerous brick chimneys, and a grand portico waiting to greet guests. The driveway opened into a spacious courtyard and then it narrowed again to curve around the house, slipping between it and the detached four-door garage with dormer windows above which had probably once been staff accommodation. Those doors were closed now and two cars stood in the courtyard: a gleaming, recently washed and polished silver Lexus and a Honda Civic that seemed to be primarily constructed out of mud and rust.

A man stood to attention under the portico, next to one of giant iron urns on either side of the great oak door. The urns were empty, and the man wore a black suit, stiffly ironed white shirt, black waistcoat, and black bow tie. His shoes were so highly polished the sunlight bounced off them. His black hair was slicked to one side with hair oil, but he'd missed a bit and a curl escaped from behind his right ear.

"Is that Mr. Masterson, do you suppose? Jayne said.

"Oh no. The gentleman of the house would never greet the paid workers. That, my dear, can only be the butler."

Jayne giggled.

I pulled the Miata to a halt next to the front steps. The butler rounded the car and dipped his head, just a fraction. He was considerably younger than the norm for a properly trained and experienced butler, being in his early twenties. The escaped curl indicated this wasn't his regular role in life. "Good afternoon, Ms. Doyle," he said in a deep, sonorous voice. "Precisely on time. Mr. Masterson appreciates punctuality." Something approaching an embarrassed smile touched the edges of his mouth and he shifted his shoulders and stretched his neck slightly, trying to loosen contact with the tight collar.

"So I've been told," I said.

He glanced at Jayne. "Ms. Wilson?"

"Hi," she said.

The van that had followed us out of town lumbered down the driveway and pulled in behind us.

"I am Smithers," the butler said.

"You're kidding?" Jayne said. "Oh, sorry."

A flash of humor touched his eyes, and he said, "This weekend anyway. I will instruct your staff to carry on around the house to the kitchen entrance at the back. You may park over there."

"That's okay," I said, matching his tone. "My staff need supervision."

"Very well. I'll give you time to unload and have Mrs. Higgins meet you in the kitchen to show you to your rooms in half an hour."

He dipped his head and stepped back. I waved to the driver of the van to tell him to follow and we drove slowly around the house. At the rear, the façade of a nineteenth-century stately home nestled deep in the Home Counties fell away, and the house became just a big mid-twentieth-century American house on a huge lot.

"This is so exciting." Jayne clapped her hands. "I've lived in West London most of my life and always wondered what this place is like. People talk about it, but no one's ever been invited inside. No one I know, anyway. Not even my mom. She's insanely jealous that we're spending the whole weekend here and she has to miss it."

I parked close to what I took to be the kitchen door and the van pulled in beside me.

The weekend catering staff, otherwise known as Detective Ryan Ashburton, jumped down from the van. "Impressive place," he said.

"I've seen better," I said.

Jayne and Ryan both laughed. "Gemma Doyle, you can be such an English snob sometimes," Jayne said, and I grinned at her.

"We have half an hour to take the food in and get it put away," I said to Ryan, "before the housekeeper shows us to our rooms."

"The housekeeper? Was that guy who spoke to you out front the organizer of this shindig?"

"Of course not," Jayne said. "That was the butler."

"A housekeeper and a butler," Ryan said. "Fancy."

"Fancy," Jayne said, "is the word for this gig."

I opened the unlocked kitchen door while Ryan and Jayne started unloading the van. We (meaning Jayne) were here to cook and serve six meals, plus drinks, snacks, and nibbles, and so we'd brought a lot of stuff. In addition to what we'd need to feed the weekend house guests, the van was packed with assorted paraphernalia I'd grabbed off the shelves at my store, the Sherlock Holmes Bookshop and Emporium.

Jayne didn't run a catering business; she was busy enough as the head baker, part owner, and manager of Mrs. Hudson's Tea Room. Ryan Ashburton didn't normally work as sous-chef and dishwasher, and I didn't make a habit of combining my own meager cooking skills with the role of Sherlockian expert. Because I'm neither a cook nor a Sherlock expert.

But Donald Morris, who is a Sherlock expert, a regular patron of my shop, and a good and loyal friend, had sung Jayne's and my praises to the organizer of this weekend. We were being paid for our troubles, and paid very well indeed.

Well enough for us to leave our businesses in the hands of our assistants for the weekend after Columbus Day, when most of the tourist hordes had left the Cape and the slow season began. Jayne's mother, Leslie, was looking after my dogs, Violet and Peony, as my great-uncle Arthur (also a Sherlock expert) would be joining the house party as a guest. This house is no more than a ten-minute drive from my place, but we'd been offered overnight accommodation, so why not take it? Particularly as we were expected to be on hand to serve late-night drinks and hearty hot breakfasts.

This weekend would be all Sherlock Holmes, all the time. Our host David Masterson was a prominent, not to mention rich, Sherlockian. He'd been wanting to organize a special weekend for his fellow followers of the Great Detective for a long time, but a suitable venue hadn't presented itself. Last year the owner of Suffolk Gardens House, a twentieth-century replica of an English stately home, died, and his heirs immediately put the house up for sale. They weren't getting a lot of offers, if any, so in order to bring in some income the house was rented out for special occasions. Donald told David about it, David realized the property was perfect for what he had in mind, and here we were today.

The English stately country home feeling fell away when we walked into the kitchen. Instead of a warm Aga, heavily trod and creaking floorboards, scrubbed pine workbenches, brick walls, elderly wet dog snoozing under the rocking chair next to an open fireplace, there were two top-of-the line ovens, a huge gas range, stainless steel freezer and fridge, a white marble-topped island about the size of a small Caribbean country, rows of bright orange cabinets, and a glass and chrome table surrounded by six orange leather stools. Everything was clean and tidy except for two wide-bowled glasses containing the residue of red wine in the sink, and the trash bin by the kitchen door. It was missing its lid, and I peeked in to see a handful of crumpled white napkins, an empty pizza box, and two empty bottles of a good Oregon pinot noir.

Ryan and I carried in boxes while Jayne started poking in cupboards, getting the lay of the land, so to speak, and issuing orders. "Gemma, you can start stacking the nonperishables in the pantry. Ryan, get all that cold stuff out of the coolers into the fridge. Anything that's frozen needs to go into the freezer."

"Yes, ma'am." He gave her a salute and me a wink.

"I love this kitchen." Jayne sighed happily. "It's my dream to have a kitchen as big and as well-equipped as this one someday."

"The house is for sale," I said. "Contents included. Maybe you and Andy can buy it."

She smiled at the thought and absentmindedly twisted the engagement ring on her finger, but she said, "Fat chance." Jayne had recently become engaged to our friend Andy Whitehall. Summer and early fall had been so busy for the both of them, they hadn't had the chance to set the date, make any plans for the ceremony and celebration, or even talk about where they were going to live. I was starting to fear I'd have to lure them to my house one day and lock them in the basement until they got on with it. "It would be nice, though," she said dreamily. "Imagine having all this cupboard space." The kitchen at Mrs. Hudson's Tea Room was about a quarter the size of this one.

A floorboard creaked in the hallway and a young woman came into the kitchen. "Hi. I'm Annie, aka Mrs. Higgins. You must be Gemma and Jayne."

In another break from English stereotypes, the housekeeper wasn't a stern-faced woman with a pronounced accent and a stiff bun, but a tall woman in her early twenties with short blond hair, rows of piercings through both ears, a tattoo of a dragon curling up her right arm, and a welcoming smile. She wore white shorts and a red shirt under a denim jacket. Sturdy Doc Martens were on her feet.

"We are," I said. "Nice to meet you." We all shook hands, and I introduced Ryan. I couldn't help but notice her checking him out. Ryan is always worth checking out, but particularly so today in casual jeans and a loose T-shirt, with his black hair uncombed and the dark stubble coming in on his strong jaw and beneath his high, sharp cheekbones.

Annie tore herself away from admiring Ryan and turned to Jayne. "You finding everything okay?"

"Pretty much. We brought most of what we'll need, as per the instructions Mr. Masterson sent me."

"Good, because I'll try to help you if I can, but I only got here this morning myself, and I've been busy getting the bedrooms ready."

"Shall I assume you aren't a professional housekeeper?" I said.

She grimaced. "Got it in one. My name's Annie Masterson, but for this weekend, I'm not supposed to be related to David so I'm to be called Mrs. Higgins. David insists on having his pretentions and we all find it easier just to go along with him. In real life I'm in show business, but I'm temporarily between gigs."

She didn't, I thought, look entirely happy about playing the servant role, but she'd decided to make the best of it. "It's a hard time, I've heard, on Broadway these days."

She looked at me quickly, and then she grinned. "I'm not on Broadway, but you recognized me! What did you see me in?"

"Gemma notices things," Jayne said before I admitted I'd never seen this woman before, on stage or off. She was young, tall, and pretty, and not at all overweight by normal standards, but her body was softer and plumper than was acceptable for American actresses, so she was unlikely to be in film or TV. I also guessed (although I always insist I never guess) she appeared on stage rather than film, as she had a deep voice and a certain presence, a way of walking and holding herself that indicated she'd been trained to be observed. Mr. Masterson, the organizer of this weekend, lives in Manhattan. Therefore, Annie most likely lives in New York City also. Meaning she either works in commercials, soap operas, or the stage, and I settled on the latter.

"I've never quite made it to the big time," she admitted. "Not yet anyway, but I've been in some off-Broadway shows and I recently toured in the Midwest. Unfortunately, that ended not long after it began, because it turns out that people in Kansas farming communities are too busy in the summer months to come out for a live show in the high school gym. But," she held up her right hand, showing me crossed fingers, "I'm eternally optimistic, and I'm young enough to still have time to get that big break. As for this weekend: I'm your housekeeper, David's not my uncle, and I'll show you to your rooms. David and the first of the guests are here already, and the rest are due to arrive at five."

"Cocktails and canapés at six in the drawing room," Jayne said. "Dinner at eight. Is that still the plan?"

"Right." Annie pulled a slip of paper out of the pocket of her short white shorts. Definitely not an outfit you'd ever find an English housekeeper wearing. "I see you have two rooms. Oh, you're together." She glanced between Ryan and me, trying to hide her disappointment.

Ryan put his arm around my shoulders. "Yup."

* * *

We followed Annie out of the kitchen and up the rear stairs. The servants' stairs: narrow, curving, ill-lit. As we were here to work, our rooms were on the third floor and at the back of the house. They were, Annie told us, originally staff quarters, but over the years, as the need for rooms for live-in maids and kitchen workers declined, the rooms were upgraded and turned into additional guest accommodations. Ryan immediately hit his head on the sloping ceiling; he cursed and I smothered a laugh. Our room wasn't large, and it was plainly and practically furnished, but it had a fabulous view over the pool, closed for the winter, and the now-empty patio, across the lawn and ornamental gardens to the woods lining the back of the property. It was mid-October and the trees were a riot of color.

"Nice digs," Ryan said after Annie had left, testing out the bed by bouncing on it. "Long as I don't stand straight."

I turned away from the window. "It's nice of you to do this for us."

"You don't have to thank me for spending a weekend at Suffolk Gardens House. This place has always been the talk of the town, and so far I'm not disappointed."

"This isn't a holiday. You're supposed to be working, remember."

"I'll look at it as though I'm on one of those cooking vacations in Tuscany. I don't mind helping Jayne in the kitchen, and I don't mind spending time with you. Speaking of which . . ." He patted the bed.

"We should unpack."

"There'll be plenty of time to unpack later." He gave me a wicked and totally irresistible grin, and patted the bed again.

I stepped away from the window.

A knock sounded at the door. "Come on, you two," Jayne called. "No time for lollygagging around. I have to finish putting all my food away and check what's available in the way of linens and dishes. Ryan, I need you to prepare the vegetable tray while I arrange the cheeses."

"No one ever eats those vegetable tray things," he called.

"Perhaps not at police functions," she called back. "Maybe not Sherlockians either, but it's expected."

"A man's work," Ryan said, pushing himself reluctantly off the bed, "is never done."

Chapter Two

"Splendid, Gemma, absolutely splendid." Donald Morris beamed at me. Barely able to contain his excitement, Donald had arrived at Suffolk Gardens House half an hour early and joined me in the drawing room as I was putting the finishing touches on the display.

I straightened a life-sized cardboard cutout of Benedict Cumberbatch and Martin Freeman as Holmes and Watson. I had another one of those back at the store, signed by Benedict himself when he'd visited the Emporium over the summer as a favor to his parents' friend, my great-uncle Arthur.

"I don't think Holmes's head should be at that angle, Gemma," Donald said, not at all helpfully. He tilted his own head and peered at the images.

"Ryan had trouble fitting this into the van with all Jayne's supplies and so poor Benedict has a droopy neck. Pass me that tape will you, please?" I did my best to straighten the offending piece.

As the part owner and manager of the Sherlock Holmes Bookshop and Emporium, I would never say so out loud, but I tend to fall on the side of those who think you can have too much tacky Sherlock stuff. David and his friends, I had been assured, did not.

I arranged pipes and deerstalker hats and magnifying glasses, maps of London as it would have been in Holmes's day, and copies of nineteenth-century railway timetables around the room. I picked up the box at my feet. "One more room to do. You can help me." Annie had shown me around earlier so I knew my way to the library.

It was a lovely library, as befitted a pretend grand old house. Two walls were lined with built-in, floor to ceiling bookcases, stuffed with books with brown, black, or red binding, most of them old, dusty, and slightly tattered. A huge plastic, and very dusty, philodendron loomed next to a small alcove tucked into the far wall containing a large wooden desk, the surface bare now but showing signs of use and considerable age, and a standard office chair. A sliding door opened onto the patio and swimming pool. The fourth wall contained an enormous fireplace. Crumpled newspapers and kindling had been laid in the hearth and a stack of logs rested in a U-shaped iron container next to it. I studied the wallpaper above the mantle. "I can't shoot holes into the wall, unfortunately, so I brought something to fake it. Hold that chair."

Donald obediently held the chair while I climbed onto it and arranged decals resembling bullet holes into the shape of a "patriotic VR." The wallpaper was beige and gold, not red, but not much I could do about that.

I placed three hardcover books on the desk: later-edition copies of *The Hound of the Baskervilles*, *The Sign of Four*, and *Valley of Fear*. I arranged them as though the occupant of the chair would soon need to consult them.

I then scattered more props as well as reproductions of the *Times* and other London newspapers of the era around the room along with some biographies of Sir Arthur Conan Doyle I'd brought from the bookshop. I piled a stack of Holmes-related puzzles and brain teaser games onto the side tables and laid out a Sherlock Holmes jigsaw puzzle on the round table in the center of the room for the amusement of guests. Earlier, Ryan had brought in the DVD player and portable screen onto which we'd project the movies I'd brought and tucked them into a corner.

I stepped back to admire my handiwork.

"Perfect," Donald said. "I might almost believe I'm in the sitting room at 221B."

"As are you," I said, referring to his outfit.

He smiled shyly. Donald was dressed in a brown tweed suit with a bright red waistcoat and a stiffly starched white shirt. A red cravat was tied at his throat and a gold watch dangled from his waistcoat by a thick gold chain. The gold itself was fake; Donald doesn't have the money for such frivolities. A deerstalker hat was on his head.

"You look as though you're about to bound across the moors in pursuit of the great spectral hound," I said.

"Precisely the mood I'm hoping to achieve at cocktails. I have a dinner suit ready for tonight, and formal wear for tomorrow evening." His eyes narrowed as he studied me. "I, uh . . . trust you're going to change, Gemma."

I looked down at my T-shirt, jeans, and scruffy trainers. "This won't do?" I said seriously, before laughing at his expression. "Don't worry, Donald. We're here at your recommendation, and I won't embarrass you."

"You could never do that, my dear," he said. "You should have brought a violin and some sheet music with the sort of tunes Holmes would have played."

"I don't sell violins or music. Everything I brought, I pulled off the shelves of the Emporium." I glanced around the room. "Don't you think it's enough?"

"Sufficient for the library and the drawing room. I was thinking of appropriate items for the music room."

"This house has a music room? Annie didn't show me that."

"David's invitation letter said some of the weekend participants had musical talents. I popped my head in earlier and saw a grand piano."

Even though the library door was closed, we clearly heard the sound of Smithers's voice, and a man answering.

Donald clapped his hands. "The guests will soon be arriving! Talk to you later, Gemma." He bustled out.

I smiled after him, gave the room one more look over, and then went upstairs to change. Nice to have a house with a back staircase, so I didn't have to run into anyone before I was ready.

I stopped at the kitchen on my way. The delivery from the liquor store had arrived and been unpacked, and the empty cardboard boxes were stacked by the door. Jayne was taking a tray of pastries out of the oven as I came in. "Those smell good," I said. Ryan was chopping a mountain of vegetables.

"There is nothing," I said, "sexier than a man in an apron."

He growled at me. The apron was pink and frilly. Jayne wore a matching apron over a loose-fitting black skirt and crisp white blouse. Her shoes were black flats and her only jewelry a pair of small hoop earrings. She always took off her engagement ring when she baked. By rights Jayne, as the head cook, should stay in

14

the kitchen and Ryan, as the assistant, should be the one circulating with drinks and serving the food. But, as he was the lead detective in our town's police department, he put his foot down at being seen in public acting as a waiter.

I was here to provide the Sherlockian touches, but I'd also be helping Jayne in the kitchen and acting as a waitress when needed.

We should have had more staff, but my shop assistant Ashleigh was needed to keep the store open, and Jayne's two helpers would be working at the tea room. Jayne had been putting in overtime for weeks (meaning even longer hours than usual) to get food in the freezer for them to serve when she was away. Jayne's mother, who was originally supposed to help out, had come down with a cold at the last minute. In one way, that wasn't entirely a bad thing as now she could take care of Violet and Peony, whereas the original plan was for my neighbor Mrs. Ramsbatten to pop in and refresh the dogs' dishes and let them into the yard. Mrs. Ramsbatten loves the dogs and is happy to look after them, but she's too elderly to take two lively animals out for a walk.

If worst came to worst, I'd corral Donald and even Great-Uncle Arthur into washing dishes, chopping vegetables, or serving cocktails.

"Everything under control?" I said.

"What would you do if it wasn't?" Ryan asked.

"Tell you two to get it under control while I carry on with what I planned to do," I replied.

"Under control." Jayne arranged the fragrant, piping-hot pastries on a platter. It took a lot of willpower, but I managed to resist snatching one up.

I passed Annie in the third-floor hallway. She'd changed out of her shorts and Doc Martens into a calf-length black dress with a white collar and white cuffs. A black cap with lacy white trim covered her short blond hair and the long sleeves of the dress hid her tattoos. She'd removed all her earrings and slipped her feet into sturdy, lace-up black shoes.

"Goodness," I said, "you do look the part."

She glared at me and tugged at the collar. "This thing itches and my feet hurt already, but I'll do what I have to do. I'll consider it a performance and this getup my costume. It's almost five and the guests will be arriving in a few minutes. I'm to meet them at the door with Billy . . . I mean Mr. Smithers, and show them to their rooms." She continued down the hall, muttering darkly.

I smiled to myself as I went into my room. Annie might not know it, but the dour, sharp-faced housekeeper was a staple of historical fiction and she was playing the part perfectly.

I don't normally wear any sort of costume to Sherlock events, but I'd been asked to "fit in" this weekend, and so I would. For tonight, I'd found a dress in a vintage clothing store. Not quite of Holmes's era, it was peach satin, very 1920s, coming to just below the knee, with straight lines, a dropped waist, and a tasseled hem. I paired the dress with a long double strand of fake pearls, my own pearl earrings, and above-the-elbow white gloves. I studied myself in the mirror, and decided I'd do. At five foot eight, I'm tall enough to wear this style of dress, but not thin enough to do justice to the sleek lines, and my mop of dark curls is nothing at all like a smooth '20s bob, but it was a costume, not an attempt at an imitation. Satisfied, I returned to the kitchen.

I wheeled the bar cart—already loaded with a bucket full of ice, glasses, bottles of wine, gin, vodka, whiskey, mixes, and little plates of olives and slices of lemon and lime—to the drawing room, while Jayne carried in a tray of cocktail nibbles. Mr. Smithers, we'd been informed, would act as bartender.

I doubted Smithers was his real name as much as I doubted he was a real butler. Judging by his age, he was probably also an out-of-work relative of our host, same as Annie.

Of our host, there had been no further sign. So far, other than the brief encounters with the butler and the housekeeper, we hadn't met anyone, but it was obvious that people were in the house. Voices came from behind bedroom doors, leaked through walls, drifted down the stairs, a phone rang and was answered, floorboards creaked overhead. The walls and doors of this house were surprisingly thin and sound carried. Everything looked authentic and impressive, but, I'd soon realized, beneath the surface this house had been built quickly and on the cheap.

That didn't matter. It was all a pretext: it wasn't two hundred years old and nestled deep in the rolling green hills of the Home Counties either.

In addition to my great-uncle Arthur and Donald Morris, five guests were expected, plus the host David Masterson, here to re-create the atmosphere of an English country house weekend in the era of Sherlock Holmes. Rather than riding to the hounds or venturing out on shooting parties, the group would discuss the minutiae of the Canon, toss around outlandish theories, and play Holmes-related games and puzzles. They'd do all that between lavish meals and plenty of cocktails. It was to contribute to the atmosphere that I'd been invited, and to provide the food that Jayne had.

"I hope we get a chance to have a look around the house," Jayne said. "What I've seen of it so far is marvelous, but I'm not surprised this place hasn't sold. It must be worth a heck of a lot, never mind the upkeep on the grounds and the inside."

"A rich man's folly," I said. "And now his heirs can't get rid of it. They can't stop maintaining it either, or it'll never sell."

"Do you suppose it has any secret rooms, priest bolt holes, or the like?"

I smiled at my friend. "Your imagination's running away with you. This house was built in 1965, not the seventeenth century. No need to hide priests."

"It might be a modern house," Jayne said. "But they've gone all out decorating it as though it isn't." Paintings of English pastoral scenes hung on the pale green walls of the drawing room, the sofa was covered in pink flowered damask, the armchairs in cream touched with pink. The heavy drapes matched the sofa and a dark wood coffee table was centered on the thick green and pink rug.

At first glance the room was lovely, but when I looked closer, I could see that the carpet had a stain in the center and the edges were fraying. Dirt was ground into the arms of the armchairs, the tops of the drapes and picture frames were thick with dust, and the paintings were tourist-shop prints.

This room, this house, this setting, was a fantasy. No matter: the guests would enjoy it and that was what this weekend was all about.

I glanced at my watch. Five minutes to six. Almost show time. At that moment, the door opened and a man came in. Like Donald, he was dressed for the occasion.

"Mrs. Wilson and Miss Doyle, I presume. Pleased to meet you. I'm David Masterson." He was quite short at five foot five and almost as round as he was tall. His brown hair was thin on the top and he blinked rapidly at me from behind Coke-bottle bottom lenses. I estimated his age as early fifties, slightly younger than I'd expected. The small amount of information I'd found on the internet concerning our host hadn't mentioned his age.

We shook hands. His grip was limp, his hands soft and moist with lotion. He glanced around the room and gave a brief nod of approval. Jayne slipped out, back to the kitchen to get started on dinner prep. Smithers arrived, suitably dressed all in black, and took his place behind the bar, back straight, hands folded behind him, feet slightly apart, eyes straight ahead.

"May I offer you a drink, Gemma?" David asked. "If I may call you Gemma?"

"You may, and a glass of white wine would be nice."

"I am paying you to be here this weekend, but I want you to consider yourself one of my guests. Please feel free to take advantage of all the amenities this house has to offer. When your attendance is not required, of course."

His accent was upper-class New York City, and he spoke formally, far more formally than any middle-aged American should. I wondered if that was put on for the weekend or if it was the way he always spoke. He was obviously to the manor born, what Americans would call a trust fund baby. His soft pale hands were recently manicured, he was close-shaven, his cheeks slightly rosy, his small teeth blindingly white. He smelled of expensive aftershave and hand lotion. His face was lightly tanned, not a deep summer or Caribbean-vacation tan but the coloration a resident of the Northeastern United States would get by walking from the house to the car, maybe sitting outside at a restaurant patio in the summer.

I never go into a new situation blind, and I'd done my research into David Masterson. Outside of the world of the devotees of Sherlock Holmes, where he was very well known, there wasn't much to find, and I hadn't seen a picture of him other than standing at the back of a group. David's maternal grandfather had made a fortune in New York City development and real estate, and his son, David's uncle, had piled an additional fortune on top. The uncle had given up control of the company a number of years ago, and it was now publicly traded and managed by a board of directors. David himself didn't, according to what I could find, seem to do much at all except study Sherlock Holmes. He'd self-published a handful of scholarly works on the subject. When I heard about this weekend, I'd ordered copies for the store and read one of them, as much as I could get through before falling asleep. His writing was pedestrian, his topics unoriginal and uninspired.

David's mother had been well known as a supporter of classical music. She made hefty donations to, and often served on the board of, the Metropolitan Opera and the New York Philharmonic, as well as smaller and lesser-known classical music companies. My research showed that following his mother's death, David had maintained her monetary contributions to her favorite organizations, but he himself played no active part in the arts community. Those hefty donations had abruptly stopped about a year ago, with no explanation given. To the public at any rate.

David gave Smithers a short, sharp nod, and the butler took a bottle of mid-priced New Zealand sauvignon blanc out of the ice bucket and poured my drink. Jayne had been given a free hand with the food for the weekend, but David had taken care of ordering the booze. Unasked, Smithers then prepared a whiskey with a splash of soda and one ice cube for his employer.

Precisely at six o'clock the guests began filing into the drawing room. The men were in suits and ties, the women in cocktail dresses, one historic and one modern.

I put a smile on my face and circulated. The guests were a mixed bunch indeed. Two women, both in their fifties, one as tall and slim and sharp-boned as a former fashion model, one round of body, frizzy of hair, heavy of bosom, and pudgy of cheeks. The three men varied from a handsome chap in his mid-thirties, to a man in his forties with a heavy unkempt black beard and round belly, to a buzz cut–bearing gentlemen in his sixties with the tone and bearing of a former military man. I wouldn't have been surprised if his pajamas were stamped "Semper Fi." They were all Americans and all from the East Coast. The younger man gave me a long look followed by what he might have intended to be a wink, as he accepted a beer from Smithers. Beer in hand, he took a step toward me, but David stopped him and asked him if his accommodations were satisfactory.

At six fifteen, I slipped up to Donald. He and the frizzy-haired woman, stuffed into a gorgeous floor-sweeping blue and silver dress dotted with black beads, were examining the railway timetables and discussing what route Holmes and Watson would have taken to get from Charing Cross Station to Devonshire, the location of the fictional Great Grimpen Mire.

"Sorry to interrupt," I said. "Can I have a moment, Donald?"

"Oh, Gemma." He blinked at me, coming back to the twenty-first century. "Have you met Jennifer Griffith?"

"Not yet. Pleased to meet you." Jennifer briefly came out of the nineteenth century to greet me, and then immediately returned to her study of the railway schedule.

"Have you heard from Arthur?" I asked Donald when we'd stepped away. "It's not like him to be late, not for something like this."

"Not today. I spoke to him earlier in the week. I asked if he wanted a lift this afternoon, but he declined."

"I'd better give him a call." I'd left my phone upstairs and prepared to run up and get it. My uncle was fit and hearty and more than capable of looking after himself, but he was approaching ninety and it was natural for me to worry.

I hesitated when the drawing room door opened, and Annie ushered in my friend Irene Talbot. It was immediately obvious Irene hadn't come to give me any bad news. Not only was she smiling and looking around her with shining eyes, but she was dressed in a stunning one-piece evening jumpsuit of wide-legged black trousers, three-quarter-length sleeves, deep neckline trimmed in black satin, and a matching black satin belt. A tiny black bag on a metal chain hung from her shoulder. Her hair was piled high on her head, and her mouth was a slash of deep red. She saw me watching and gave me a wiggle of her fingers. Annie pointed toward the bar, where David Masterson was chatting to the former fashion model, and Irene thanked her and came into the room, almost floating in her uncharacteristically elegant clothes and stiletto heels.

I hurried to join her. "Irene, what are you doing here? Do you know where Arthur is?"

"Just a minute, Gemma. Let me introduce myself to my host first."

"Your host?"

"Mr. Masterson, sorry I'm late. I'm Irene Talbot." David turned to her with a smile and extended his hand. "Delighted to make your acquaintance, Ms. Talbot. May I call you Irene? I'm David. We don't stand on formalities here."

I glanced around the room. I'd seldom been to a more formal gathering. Then again, this might have passed for informal in Holmes's day.

"No apologizes necessary," David continued. "Please, make yourself at home. Can I offer you a drink?"

"Do you have a gin and tonic?"

"Of course. What country house party would be complete without a properly made G&T?" He half-turned and snapped his fingers at Smithers. Smithers rolled his eyes, but he prepared the drink without a word.

Irene accepted her drink, full of ice and a slice of lemon, and took a sip. She sighed with pleasure, thanked David, and joined Donald and me. "Arthur called me this morning. You'd already left for the store, and he didn't want to bother you."

I shook my head. "Instead he's given me a heck of a fright. What's happened?"

"He's gone to Spain. The Costa del Sol."

"You can't be serious. Today?"

"Yup. An old navy pal of his had a heart attack. He lives in Spain and he's summoned Arthur to his side for one last hurrah."

"Oh, dear. That's terrible."

"Not according to Arthur. The friend had the heart attack a week ago. It was mild, but it made him realize that time's running out, so when he rose from his sickbed he decided to throw a big party and summoned the old crowd."

"But . . . but what about this weekend? It's been planned for ages."

"I guess Arthur decided Spain would be better." Irene took another sip of her drink. "As nice as this place is, I would have too. He called David to say he wasn't coming, and asked if I could take his place. David said sure." She spread her arms. "And here I am. I tell you, Gemma, I've had quite the day trying to pull together formal clothes at the last minute. I found this little number at the secondhand shop."

"But . . . but. Irene, why would Uncle Arthur ask you to take his place? You have absolutely no interest in Sherlock Holmes."

She put her index finger to her lips. "Keep your voice down. I've been thinking maybe I'd like to learn, and I told Arthur that when I was at your place for dinner last week."

"I don't remember you saying anything of the sort."

"You were in the kitchen, trying to save the chicken. It wasn't too bad either, Gemma. Not once you'd scraped the burnt parts off."

"Thanks. I think."

"The potatoes were lumpy, though. I'll get you a proper potato masher for Christmas."

"Let's return to the original subject, shall we? This weekend David Masterson has invited a circle of Sherlock experts to exchange knowledge and participate in informed debate. You, Irene, don't have any knowledge to exchange."

"I'll listen intently and agree with everyone." She grinned at me. "Come on, Gemma. Do you think I was going to pass up the opportunity to spend a weekend at Suffolk Gardens House? Everyone in West London is dying to see this place. The owners almost never invited anyone here, and now that it's for sale you have to prove to the realtors you can afford it before you get a showing."

"You checked on that?"

"Sure I did. Tell me you didn't?"

I didn't answer. Of course I had. "Try the mushroom tarts. They're fabulous."

"Don't mind if I do," Irene said. "Another reason I came is because Arthur said Jayne's doing the catering." She helped herself to a cocktail napkin and one of the flaky pastries.

"Did Arthur tell you that because Jayne doesn't have any helpers with her, the plan is he and Donald will work in the kitchen when required. Doing the dishes and the like."

"No, he didn't mention that."

I smiled at her. "You'll like the kitchen. All the modern conveniences."

* * *

The cocktail party passed uneventfully. I amused myself, between telling the guests what my role here was, by studying their interactions. It soon became obvious they didn't have much in common. Not even an interest in Sherlock Holmes, which was ostensibly the reason for this gathering.

The frizzy-haired woman, Jennifer, the bearded man, and the older man, who went by the names Cliff and Steve, chatted comfortably with Donald about the Great Detective and discussed the props I'd brought. The former fashion model, Miranda, drank steadily and sat by herself most of the time, a carefully arranged look of total boredom on her face. Eventually, she left the room, drink still in hand, without a word to anyone. The young man, Kyle, gave up on me and tried to charm Irene. Irene didn't seem entirely averse to his attentions. "I'm from New York City," I heard him say to her. "A musician."

David didn't interact with his guests very much. I noticed the occasional little smile Jennifer threw in his direction, and the way he stiffly pretended not to notice. Kyle, Steve, and Cliff avoided speaking to David or even looking at him. In turn, he stood by himself, sipped his whiskey, and watched everyone with a sly smile on his face.

Was he, I thought, pretending to be the Great Detective? Observing everything and everyone while not getting involved? If so it was an odd approach to hosting a weekend.

"Nice party." The bearded man came up to me and offered me a huge smile. "I'm Cliff. Cliff Mann. How do you know David?"

Our host's head turned at the sound of his name, but he made no move to come and join us.

"I don't," I said. "I haven't had the pleasure until today. I'm one of the hired help. I brought all the props you see around you."

Cliff looked confused. "You mean the hat and pipe and stuff?"

"Yes. I own a shop in West London. The Sherlock Holmes Bookshop and Emporium. If you're a Sherlockian you might have heard of it."

"I . . . uh . . . yes, yes, I think I have. You sell books, do you?"

"Anything and everything to do with the Great Detective. Do you collect yourself?"

David took a step toward us. "I . . ." Cliff said. "No. No, I don't. Excuse me." He scurried away.

That was odd, I thought, but I put it out of my mind. I was supposed to be working. The platter of mushroom tarts hadn't lasted long, and I whisked it off the table and took it into kitchen. We'd be serving dinner at eight, so the canapés wouldn't be refreshed.

The morning room, where breakfast would be served, was next to the kitchen. As I passed I heard the squeak of a drawer. I peeked into the room to see Miranda closing one drawer and opening another. She put a hand in and rifled through the contents. She didn't hear me, and I slipped away. This wasn't my house, and it wasn't any of my business if Miranda was admiring the furniture.

In the kitchen, Jayne was seasoning the soup and Ryan chopping tomatoes and cucumber for the salad. I took a moment to admire him. Nothing more attractive than a man preparing food.

Ryan heard the creak of the floorboards and looked up. He gave me a grin. "How's it going out there?"

"Well enough. The guests have all arrived, with one exception. Uncle Arthur isn't coming. He's gone to the Costa del Sol instead."

"Sounds like Arthur," Jayne said. "My goal in life, should I be fortunate enough to live so long, is to be an Uncle Arthur. Old and fancy free. Taste this and tell me if it has enough salt." She scooped a spoonful of thick orange liquid out of the pot and held it out to me. I tasted. I sighed with pleasure. "Yummy. What is it?"

"Carrot and ginger."

"Where's the Costa del Sol?" Ryan asked.

"Spain."

"Arthur went to Spain with a day's notice?"

"You know Arthur," I said. "He comes. He goes. The food's almost finished, so I'll start clearing up. Oh, Irene's here in Arthur's place."

"Irene Talbot?" Ryan asked.

"Yup."

"I've never known her to be interested in Sherlock Holmes. Is she planning to do a piece for the paper?"

Irene was a reporter—the only full-time reporter left in these days of dwindling newspaper revenue—at the *West London Star*.

"If she is, she's undercover and I don't think that would be such a good idea," I said. "No, she's here to see the house and eat Jayne's food and wear fancy clothes."

I picked up a tray and headed back down the long dark hallway, past the rows of stern-faced gentleman with enormous whiskers and pale ladies with feathers and lots of jewelry glaring at me from their dusty gilt frames.

". . . most preposterous theory I've ever heard," the bearded man was saying as I came into the drawing room. His face was turning red and his eyes bulging. "A disgrace to the memory of Sir Arthur."

The former soldier faced him, braced for combat. "I'll have you know, Cliff, that respectable scholars—"

"Respectable! Ha. You mean people like you, Steve Patterson. Pack of dilettantes, the lot of them."

David wasn't in the room, but Miranda had returned. The others clutched their drinks and the last of the canapés, awkwardly watching the exchange. Smithers passed Irene a fresh drink.

Donald approached the arguing men, trying to smile, wringing his hands in front of him. "Now, now, gentlemen. Let's remember that we're all friends here."

Steve turned on Donald. Spittle flew. His small eyes were dark in a dark face. "What makes you think that?"

"I . . . I . . ." Donald floundered. "Aren't we?" he finished weakly.

I stepped forward and spoke loudly, trying to sound as though I was in command. Someone had to be in the absence of the host. "It's time to freshen up before dinner. Drinks will be served in the library at seven forty-five, and dinner promptly at eight. Please don't be late. At eleven we'll be showing *The Scarlet Claw* starring Basil Rathbone in the library."

"Excellent!" Donald exclaimed. "One of my absolute favorites."

"Rathbone is *so* overrated." Miranda suppressed a yawn. "People only like him because they're expected to. Don't you agree, Jennifer?"

"What? Uh . . . Don't be ridiculous," the frizzy-haired woman stammered. She took a long glug of her drink.

"You don't know what you're talking about," Cliff said.

Miranda turned on the bearded man. "And I suppose you think your taste is so much better, Cliff? As if."

The others began chiming in and soon the argument had moved on to a discussion of who was the best of the old-time Holmeses on film.

I put my tray on the table and piled it with used dishes, dirty glasses, and crumpled cocktail napkins. Smithers began closing the various bottles and placing them under the cart in an unmistakable signal that the bar was closing. Kyle snatched the wine bottle out of the cooler before Smithers could put the top back on it.

The guests filed out of the drawing room. A sub-argument had broken out over the virtues (or lack thereof) of the various Watsons.

The young man approached me and held up the wine bottle. "We weren't properly introduced. Kyle Fraser."

"Gemma Doyle."

"I'm not entirely sure what your role here is this weekend, Gemma. Why don't we find a quiet spot where we can finish off this bottle and you can tell me?"

"Sorry. One of my roles is to help the cook. Right now, I suspect I'm needed in the kitchen."

"You're English!" His eyes twinkled. He was a good-looking man. And didn't he know it. "I love English people. Come on, sneak away with me. Let's have some fun. Let those old fogies argue about Sherlock this and Holmes that."

"I have enough fun in my life, thank you." I picked up my tray, turned, and walked away.

"Hey!" I heard him say. "Irene, what's your hurry? Let's find a quiet corner and finish this bottle."

I headed toward the kitchen, feeling that I was again being watched over by someone's disapproving ancestors. As I passed the library, low and angry voices came out of the not-quite-closed door. I slowed. What can I say? I'm naturally curious.

"You should have told me," a voice said. I couldn't make out who it was. "I never would have come, not if I'd known he'd be here."

"You can always leave," David replied.

". . . pest . . . I don't know why you aren't . . ."

"Because I don't want to."

The voices trailed off as they walked away from the door.

Chapter Three

A proper formal Victorian dinner party might have consisted of twelve or more courses. Each course would have had its own cutlery and been accompanied by a specific wine, which would have been served in its own glass. The napkins would have been elaborately folded and the table laden with candlesticks, flowers, plants, stands of fresh fruit, and maybe even an ice sculpture. The entire meal would have taken hours to get through, with time provided for each course to be digested. The kitchen staff would have been working from early in the morning to early the next morning.

We might have been playing at being Victorians, but we definitely were not Victorians. Jayne adapted a nineteenth-century menu for modern tastes and served a marvelous dinner beginning with carrot and ginger soup and a salad bursting with locally sourced Cape Cod produce. The main course was roast of beef with roasted potatoes and root vegetables, Yorkshire pudding and gravy. Two choices were offered for dessert: a chocolate cake decorated with a thick topping of chocolate ganache and piles of fresh raspberries or a lemon meringue pie. Unable to decide, I chose both. Ryan had absolutely refused to act as a footman, so Smithers waited on the table and served the wine. A lot of wine was served.

The heavy drapes were closed against the night, the chandelier above the table turned low. A row of white pillar candles in heavy glass candlesticks ran down the center of the table on either side of a vase bursting with red roses; masses of votive candles flickered on the sideboard, and a fire crackled behind the grate. The dishes left in the house for the use of renters were cheap and mismatched, and so Jayne had borrowed the crystal glasses, fine china place settings and serving dishes, and silver flatware from her mother. Leslie had been thrilled to get all the old pieces she and her own mother had collected over the years out of storage and washed and polished. The linens, white tablecloths, and dark green place mats and napkins, came from Mrs. Hudson's, as would the china for tomorrow's traditional afternoon tea.

Everyone, with the exception of Miranda, who had nothing but a half a spoonful of soup and a small serving of salad, along with plenty of wine, ate and drank with gusto, but it was a wonder to me that they managed to do that with all the squabbling they engaged in.

It didn't sound like good-natured arguing or reasoned debate. As I'd observed earlier, there was an underlayer of genuine hostility between some of these people. I listened without participating, enjoyed my dinner very much, and tried not to feel too guilty at the thought of Ryan and Jayne laboring away in the kitchen.

I was seated between Jennifer, who barely said a word all through the meal, and Kyle, who kept trying to refill my wine glass. In that he was unsuccessful as I confined myself to one. Miranda, seated on the other side of Kyle, eventually wrested control of the bottle from him and kept it to herself.

I'm no Sherlock Holmes expert, but in the five years since I moved from London to Cape Cod to run the bookshop that Great-Uncle Arthur started on a foolish whim I couldn't help but learn a lot. Not to mention that Arthur himself is a Sherlockian and he surrounds himself with the like-minded. The saltbox house we share is often a gathering place for debate and discussion and, whether I wanted to or not, I've picked up a great deal.

Nevertheless, I'd been worried about holding my own in this company, but I needn't have bothered. As early as the beginning of the cocktail hour I realized that, other than Donald and David, only Jennifer and Steve had any true depth of knowledge. Cliff knew little more than what the average customer in my shop did; Kyle was obviously not interested in the least, and I wondered if Miranda had even read any of the Canon. She was an enthusiastic fan of Benedict Cumberbatch, and when David commented that, in his opinion, Cumberbatch's interpretation verged on blasphemous parody, she dared to tell him that it was ridiculous to believe anyone could actually be that observant or quick-minded.

While David and Steve sputtered, Jennifer protested, Cliff laughed, Kyle called to Smithers to bring another bottle, and Irene studied the details of the furniture and the paintings on the wall, Donald said, "As it happens, I myself know someone with a mind like that."

"Really," I asked. "Who's that?"

"You don't know?" Irene said.

"If I knew, I wouldn't have asked, now would I?" I said.

Irene and Donald exchanged a look I couldn't decipher, but they seemed to be highly amused about something.

"For your information, madam," David said to Miranda when he'd recovered his wits. "It's generally believed that Sir Arthur based Holmes on a professor of his at Edinburgh University, one Doctor Bell, who was able to ascertain intimate details of a person's life and character simply through observation."

"Okay," Miranda said. "Whatever. I guess." That cemented it. Anyone with anything beyond the most basic knowledge of Sir Arthur knew the story of how Holmes had been inspired by Dr. Bell. I wondered why Miranda was here. I hadn't noticed any sort of affection or secret glances between her and David, or her and anyone else. They barely seemed to be on speaking terms.

"Why's Mr. Doyle a sir, anyway?" Miranda asked. "Was he really rich, or like a relative of the queen or something?" Her eyes widened and she leaned across Kyle to address me. "Hey! I've just realized. Your name's Doyle. Are you a relative of this Sir Arthur guy?"

"No," I said.

"Yes," Donald said.

"No," I said.

"Gemma's being coy," Irene said. "She's like a seventh cousin five times removed."

"I'm nothing of the sort," I said.

"Cool," Kyle said. "You have got to tell me all about that, Gemma. Why don't we go for a walk in the garden after dinner and talk about your . . . uh . . . cousin."

I smiled at him. "Never mind me, I'd love to hear your interpretation of Kitty Winter. Villainess or righteous feminist avenger? Where do you stand?"

He lifted his glass to me in a salute. "I'll trust your judgment."

"An excellent question," Donald said. "I myself have changed my opinion of Miss Winter over the years. Wouldn't you agree, David, that one of the delights of Holmesian scholarship is how one can reinterpret much of the Canon as one's knowledge of the world expands and grows."

"Absolutely!" David agreed. "Why I recently read . . ."

And the conversation carried on.

Eventually, David scraped his dessert plate clean, cleared his throat, and said, "Brandy and coffee in the library, gentleman, prior to the movie. And, in a nod to modern and occasionally better times, ladies are welcome to join us."

Napkins were folded, chairs shoved back, and people pushed themselves to their feet. Cliff patted his ample stomach. "Delicious dinner. My compliments to the chef. I can't wait to see what's served tomorrow."

"Oh, my gosh, Gemma," Irene said. "We're having brandy and cigars in the library. It's like a real-life episode of *Downton Abbey*. I'll play Lady Mary. Who are you? The spirited Lady Sybil, I bet."

"I'm Daisy, the lowly kitchen maid, and so are you. Remember what I said about helping out?" I linked my arm through hers. "Come along, Daisy."

"But . . ."

"No buts."

* * *

I should have known better. I'd told Ryan and Jayne I'd see to the cleaning of the kitchen as they'd made the dinner. Ryan might have wanted to escape to our room the first chance he got, but Jayne couldn't leave a kitchen mess for someone else to handle, so she'd started on the dishes. And Ryan, who would usually be more than happy to leave a kitchen mess for someone else to handle, felt guilty and stayed.

After the others headed for the library, Irene and I helped Smithers blow out the candles and clear the table of the dirty linens, the last of the glasses, and the dessert plates.

When we carried everything into the kitchen, we found Jayne loading the dishwasher and Ryan scrubbing pots.

"I have got," Irene said, "to take a picture of this for the paper. You look absolutely adorable in that apron, Ryan."

He muttered something about laying charges for disrespecting the police.

"What's that mean?" Annie sat at the big island cradling a cup of tea.

"Never mind," Ryan growled.

"Okay. How'd it go, Gemma?" Annie asked.

"It went well," I said. "Everyone raved about the food, Jayne."

"I always like to hear that," Jayne said. "Why don't you pour yourself a cup of tea? Or even a glass of wine." This wasn't exactly the kitchens of *Downton Abbey*: Ryan had a bottle of beer open on the counter next to him. He put the last of the heavy pots on the drying rack and took a swing from his bottle. "I'm beat. I'm going up. Gemma?"

"I'll be a long time yet. They've gone into the library. I need to check on the display I've laid out there, and set everything up for the movie. I'll come back and finish here before the movie starts." I looked around the tidy, sparkling kitchen. "Not that there seems to be much finishing required."

"Other than the dinner, how'd it go?" Jayne asked.

"Strangely. Several of these people are not genuine Sherlockians. I'm not entirely sure why some of them are here."

"Does it matter?" Irene asked. "I'm here. I like to think I engaged in sparkling, witty, yet deeply significant conversation for the edification of my fellow diners."

"Someone once told David that the most interesting gatherings are not with like-minded people but those who are completely different," Annie said. "David likes to think of himself as a collector of people. Putting the right combinations together for maximum effect. In reality he just enjoys watching people leap to his tune." Her tone verged on bitter and I gave her a quick glance. She saw me watching her and dipped her head to stare into her teacup. "He doesn't entertain often, and he doesn't go to parties much himself, so he doesn't have a lot of experience with groups of people. But he does like to go all out when he does."

"He's married, isn't he? His wife isn't here this weekend," I said.

Annie's laugh was bitter. "Her. Rebecca. Talk about opposites. She lives for parties, the wilder the better. This wouldn't exactly be her scene, and I say thank heavens for that, right, Billy?"

The "butler" put an opened bottle of white wine into the fridge. "I have no comment."

"Your name's Billy?" I asked. "I'm glad to know that. I'm uncomfortable calling you by your surname."

"Is Smithers your real name?" Irene asked.

"Are you kidding me?" he snorted. "I'm Billy Belray, and Uncle David talked me into renting a stupid costume and doing this stupid weekend. Me and Annie. Before you ask, we're cousins."

I glanced at the "housekeeper," who gave me a shrug. "Uncle David pays my expenses when I'm temporarily between gigs. I couldn't say no. Say, I don't suppose any of you speak Italian, do you?"

"Sorry, no," I said. "Why do you ask?"

"I'm planning to go to Italy next year. I've been trying to learn some of the language, but I'm having a heck of a lot of trouble doing it on my own. Uncle David was going to find me a tutor, but . . . sometimes he forgets to do things he said he'd do. Oh well. I suppose everyone in Italy speaks English. Morning comes early around here. Night all." She gave us a nod, pushed herself to her feet, and left.

"Early for me, too." Jayne closed the door of the dishwasher and set the buttons. "Breakfast in the morning room at seven. Good night." She followed Annie to the back stairs.

Ryan picked up his beer bottle, gave me a wink, and said, "Don't be too long, Gemma."

"I'll make sure she isn't," Irene said.

Ryan chuckled and I gave my friend a glare. Unintimidated, she grinned back at me and left the kitchen, chatting to Billy Belray.

Ryan crossed the room and wrapped his arms around me. "What's bothering you, Gemma?"

I nestled into his embrace. "This whole thing seems off to me. A Sherlockian weekend with a bunch of know-nothings? Relatives playing the servants? Some of these people don't like each other, and I don't sense any warm and fuzzy feelings toward their host. Or from him to them. I can't imagine why most of them came."

"Maybe like Irene they just wanted to see the house."

"Maybe. Except that they're not from around here. I suppose they might have heard about the house, but still . . ."

"I've always said your instincts are good, Gemma, and they are," Ryan said. "But this time, there's nothing to it. A bunch of sycophants want to get on the right side of a rich man, and if playing to his whimsy is what it takes, they'll do it. That's all. Let it go."

I smiled up at him. "You're right. As usual. I'll try to make my escape from the library as soon as I can. I might not even stay until the end of the movie. See you upstairs?"

"I'll be there."

And, when I finally got away, he was. Sound asleep and snoring lightly.

Chapter Four

R yan woke early and gave me a nudge. "You awake?"

I buried my face in my pillow. "No."

"Glad to hear it. As I have to spend another day slaving over a hot dishwasher, how about a short stroll through the garden before we have to report to work?"

I rolled over and smiled up at him. "Now that sounds like something worth getting up for."

We were dressed and downstairs in record time. It was a beautiful fall day, the rising sun shining through trees ablaze in shades of rusty orange, yellow, and red, leaves crunching underfoot, the air crisp and cool, full of the whisper of winter soon to come. "The owners need to sell this house, and fast," I said as Ryan and I strolled along the paths, wrapped in thick sweaters and scarves. "Before the neglect starts getting obvious and out of control."

"Neglect? Isn't the place being well kept up? Look around you. The grass is cut, the . . ."

"Kept up, yes," I said. "At first appearance. Look further, Ryan. The peonies haven't been cut back, the perennials aren't dead-headed. Inside the house itself the surfaces are superficially clean, but mice have been in the cupboard under the kitchen sink and no traps or poison have been laid, cobwebs are multiplying in the far corners of our bathroom, the tops of the frames of the paintings in the hall are thick with dust, and a decidedly sour smell is coming from the powder room off the hallway. Not to mention the—"

"I get the point, Gemma. But how much does anyone want to fork out for a house they're trying to get rid of?"

"I'm simply making an observation," I said. "And as long as I'm observing, I'll observe that the position of the rising sun on the horizon indicates that it's not long after six o'clock and Jayne needs to have a full English breakfast for eight people on the table at seven."

Ryan sighed. "A man's work—"

* * *

I didn't join the party for breakfast. While Jayne flipped sausages, grilled bacon, fried eggs, heated baked beans—and Ryan supervised the browning of the toast—I laid the table and brought out tea and coffee. Breakfast was served in the morning room, and in true country house fashion, the food was laid out on the long oak buffet for guests to help themselves as they came down.

When I returned to the kitchen, Annie, again wearing her housekeeper's dress, was assembling a tray. "Can you believe it," she growled. "Her Ladyship, aka Miranda Ireland, waylaid me in the hallway last night and demanded her breakfast be brought up to her. She read somewhere that married women didn't join the family and guests at breakfast, but instead had a tray served to them in their room, and although she is no longer married, she was a couple of times, so that counts. I swear some of these people are letting this weekend go to their heads."

"Is that true, Gemma?" Jayne asked.

"Is it true Miranda has been married a couple of times? How would I know?"

"Not that. I mean that a married woman doesn't have breakfast at the breakfast table."

"How on earth would I know that?"

"You're English."

"Believe me, the Englishwomen I know not only have their breakfast at the kitchen table, they make it first. Except for my mother. She orders her croissants and pastries from Paul's Boulangerie in South Kensington."

"Oh, yeah." Ryan sighed happily at the thought of our brief holiday in London in January. "Best chocolate croissants I've ever had."

The toast popped and Annie dodged around him to grab two slices for Miranda's tray.

Jayne cleared her throat. "I beg your pardon."

Ryan changed color. "Your croissants are okay, but the cakes and tarts, not to mention the cookies, at Mrs. Hudson's can't be beat."

"Try harder, buddy," Jayne said.

I intervened before things could get out of hand. "Let's review what's on the schedule for today. After breakfast, they're going for a walk on the moors, otherwise known as the back yard. Then they have private time followed by a light lunch at noon, some sort of games in the afternoon. Afternoon tea—"

"My specialty," Jayne said.

"At four, followed by a showing of *Murder by Decree*, which I will modestly mention was my suggestion in a feeble attempt to contribute something of importance for the weekend. Turns out

David loves the movie, but Cliff has never seen it, so that gives David a leg up on Cliff."

"That sounds rude," Ryan said.

"Followed by dinner at eight. You are, I trust, pulling out all the stops, Jayne?"

"Do you doubt it, Gemma?"

"No," I admitted. "This dinner is going to be super formal, as Holmes might have enjoyed at Baskerville Hall or Merripit House."

"Except," Jayne said, "rather than twenty courses, including fish and game caught locally by the grounds staff this very morning, I'm doing four courses with stuff I bought at the supermarket." She glanced at Ryan. "Seeing as how my kitchen maid can't peel a potato."

"Hey," he said. "I'm trying."

"Just wear the apron," I said. "And everyone will forget your culinary shortcomings."

He growled. Jayne tried to hide her laugh.

"After dinner," I continued, "the guests will return to the library for coffee, brandy, and hopefully not cigars, and David will read from a paper he spent the entire summer writing."

"What's the paper about?" Jayne asked.

"I don't know. He's keeping it to himself. Considering the quality of the couple of books he self-published, I do not have high hopes." I was suddenly aware of Annie, taking a long time to assemble Miranda's breakfast tray. "Sorry, forget I said that. I'm sure other people have different opinions."

"Everyone raved about those books," Annie said. "To David's face. What they said behind his back was another matter entirely." She left the kitchen with Miranda's tray, still grumbling.

"Donald, on the other hand," I said, "is excited about hearing David's paper."

"Donald gets excited over everything," Ryan said.

"Okay, so we have a full schedule." Jayne clapped her hands. "Let's get to work, people. Chop chop."

"Irene seems to have mistaken this for a holiday," I said. "I'll go to her room and drag her out of bed."

"You most certainly will not," Jayne said. "If you wander off you'll find yourself studying the Chinese porcelain or some such thing and never return."

"I haven't noticed any Chinese porcelain," I said. "A few rough imitations are scattered about in the downstairs corridor and the front hall, but nothing worth examining. Have you seen some genuine pieces?"

"I was speaking in general terms," Jayne said. "I can barely distinguish Chinese pottery from Navaho. Are you telling me you can?"

"An extra course I took at university when I was bored with my regular classes." I noticed the glance Jayne and Ryan exchanged. "What?"

"Nothing." Four slices of perfectly browned toast jumped out of the toaster, and Ryan put them into the silver rack. As Jayne flipped sausages, she said, "Can you start dishing up the platters and take the things out, please, Gemma. It's almost seven."

I did as instructed. Jayne's phone rang and, spatula busy in one hand, she dug in the pocket of her jeans with the other. "Hello? Oh, David. Hi. Yup, almost ready. Yes, we can do that. Eleven in the library? Sure."

"What's that about?" I asked when she'd put the phone away.

"David wants to meet with me in the library later. Something about going over the dinner menu. I sure hope he doesn't expect me to change it at the last minute. I've done all the prep I can and I brought the necessary groceries." The timer on the stove dinged and she took the bacon out of the oven.

*   *   *

I didn't join the party for breakfast, but at nine o'clock I met them by the front door to go on the walk. The air was warming as the sun came up, and I wore jeans, a favorite wool sweater, and sturdy hiking shoes.

Irene slid up to me and whispered in my ear, "I didn't get the memo about dressing the part." Her clothes were much the same as mine—thoroughly twenty-first century.

Donald, David, and Steve were dressed as though they were extras in a historical movie, in checked Harris Tweed or brown wool jackets, with waistcoats and cravats and tall hats. They even carried sturdy walking sticks. Cliff was more casual, in a white shirt and blue tie under a cashmere cardigan. Miranda's sage green skirt came to just above her ankles. She wore leather boots with heels and carried a pale peach parasol. Jennifer's lilac dress was long and full, tight at the bosom, worn under a waist-length purple velvet cape adorned with gold embroidery.

Kyle, also in his street clothes, came to join Irene and me. "Good morning." He smiled at Irene. "Sorry I missed breakfast. Did you sleep well?"

"I did," she said. "There's nothing like this lovely country air."

"We're still in West London," I reminded her.

"Yes, but this property's so big it seems like we're in the distant countryside."

I was surprised to see Annie and Billy join the walking party. Annie had pulled her Doc Martens on under her housekeeper's dress and a slightly tattered oatmeal sweater over it, and Billy was in the black suit, although he'd dispensed with his tie.

"Now that we're all here," David said, "shall we begin? A brisk walk in the garden to get our day off to an excellent start."

"Why are we doing this?" Steve said. "Sherlock Holmes wasn't a gardener."

"Hard to be," Cliff replied, "as he lived in the city."

"So did Nero Wolfe," David said, "but he had his orchids."

"Who's Nero Wolfe?" Miranda asked. No one answered.

"Holmes would have made a point of knowing his surroundings, wherever he might be," David said. "As shall we. Let's be off. If anyone needs anything fetched from the house, Mrs. Higgins and Smithers will be happy to run and get it for you."

"Absolutely thrilled," Annie mumbled. "Not."

"As we admire our surroundings, Jennifer will educate us on the country house party habits of the ladies and gentlemen of Holmes and Watson's era. Jennifer . . ."

Jennifer blushed and said, "Thank you, David. The social customs of Sir Arthur's day are of particular interest to me and . . ."

"I say, Gemma," Donald said. "Rip roaring old day, wouldn't you agree?"

"Absolutely rip roaring, Donald," I said.

"I trust you're having a marvelous time."

"Marvelous."

"Excellent, excellent."

Jennifer clapped her gloved hands to get our attention. "It is irrelevant whether or not Holmes would be interested in the details of a garden such as this one," she said. "He, as Doctor Watson informs us, did not approve of physical exercise for its own sake, but the typical Victorian gentleman, no doubt including Doctor Watson himself, was a keen practitioner of what they called the daily constitutional."

"Sounds rude," Kyle said to Irene. She laughed.

David threw them a warning look. Irene snapped her lips shut and folded her face into a serious expression.

"That means," Jennifer continued, "a walk. Upper- and middle-class Victorians were keen on the health benefits of exercise and good country air. As they would never dare be seen in public not fully dressed, about all the exercise they could participate in was walking. Those of a more daring nature, women in particular, would bicycle."

"Like in 'The Adventure of the Solitary Cyclist,'" David said.

"Exactly," Donald said. "The point is made in the story that Miss Violet Smith . . ."

Jennifer coughed. "If you're ready, shall we begin?" She led the way, prattling on about the customs of an English country house weekend. Yesterday. during cocktails in the drawing room, dinner, and then brandy in the library, Jennifer had been quiet. She kept to herself, her head down, her fingers twisting together. She didn't talk much, and only when spoken to, but when Donald drew her into conversation about the world of Sherlock Holmes, she proved to be extremely knowledgeable. Now that she had center stage, to talk about something that clearly interested her, her voice strengthened and her face shone with enthusiasm. David gave her a soft smile, and she blushed and turned away. David and Donald swung their sticks as they walked, and although at first they paid attention to Jennifer, they soon fell into a discussion of Dr. John Watson's confusing marital relationships. Miranda strolled beneath her parasol; Kyle continued his attempt to chat up Irene; Steve tried to lead us in a brisk pace, but no one was interested in keeping up and he soon was far ahead, disappearing between the hedgerows. Cliff stifled a yawn, and Billy and Annie trailed along behind.

I'm not much of a gardener, but as I walked I couldn't help but notice that many of these plants were out of place in a repro-duction English country garden. There were a lot of succulents, and quite a few plants that seemed to be suffering as the tempera-tures dipped with the approach of winter. I recognized hibiscus, which had to be brought into a greenhouse, and soon, if they were to survive. Likewise, the bulbs of the dahlias needed to be dug up and overwintered.

More signs, not that I needed to see more, to show me the property was being neglected. That was a shame. It was a beauti-ful house in beautiful surroundings.

If I had a spare twenty million I might consider buying it myself.

Even if these gardens had been kept up, they'd be well past their prime in late October, but I did enjoy the walk, and I had to agree with the Victorians that there's something about a leisurely stroll in crisp clean air to improve one's spirits. The sea was out of sight from here, but I could smell its salty traces on the air and the sun was warm on my head. The property, I estimated, was about five acres in size, much of it formally organized with curv-ing pathways, low stone walls, and once-pruned hedges enclosing private alcoves. A properly laid out rose garden, sad with weeds pushing up through the flowerbeds and spent flowers drooping brown and dead on their stalks, was surrounded by a boxwood hedge. Perennial beds, overgrown, unmaintained, weeds and grass invading the borders and poking through the remnants of red cedar mulch, curled around the eastern perimeter of the lawn.

Stone and metal statues were tucked behind the hedges or next to a dry fountain, providing interest along with benches for relaxing. One statue in particular caught my attention: a lovely bronze thing of a girl, all pigtails and short skirt, holding out a ball to a small dog. I stopped to look at the statue while the others carried on ahead. So lifelike was the girl, she reminded me of Lauren Tierney, my eleven-year-old friend. Lauren has a cat, not a dog, but she has the same loving expression on her face when she plays with her pet as does the girl in bronze.

A wooden bench was tucked next to the statue, and I imagined generations of women coming here with a book to enjoy the day and the privacy afforded by the surrounding hedge. The house, I knew, was being sold fully furnished, but I was surprised the family hadn't taken some items, like this statue, away. Sad, I thought, that the heirs hadn't wanted anything of what the original owners had no doubt painstakingly collected and dearly loved. As it hadn't been removed, this statue was probably of no significance and not much value, but I liked it. I'd like to have it in my own yard.

"Gemma, are you coming?"

"Oh. Sorry, Irene. I was admiring this statue."

"It's nice, isn't it? I wonder what it would be like to have a garden like this. Heck of a lot of work, I'd assume. I have trouble keeping a plant alive on the windowsill of my apartment."

"If you have a place like this," I said as we walked down the slight slope and through the line of trees marking the boundaries of the property, "you hire a team of gardeners to do the work for you. All you have to do is cut flowers to arrange in the dining room and front hall and admire it all."

"I can do that," Irene said.

Dead leaves and broken branches crunched under our feet, and overhead the dying, brilliantly colored leaves swayed in the light wind. Through the trees a small shallow stream ran along the chain-link fence, moving quickly toward the sea, bubbling over rocks and gravel. Tiny silver fish darted among the rocks, visible in the clear fresh water.

"Oh to be rich," Irene sighed. "Must be nice, but I'm not likely to ever know, not working at the *West London Star*."

Kyle fell back to walk next to her. "You'll have to marry a rich man. As it happens, I can help you with that. I'm a musician, like I told you, and my future's looking bright."

Irene laughed. "Gonna get that big record deal any day now, are you?"

"Doesn't hurt to hope," he said. "I have an inside track for a job opening." He glanced at David, head bent close to Donald's. "If it comes through."

Not wanting to hear Kyle brag about himself, I increased my pace as the group turned and headed back toward the house.

"No matter how large or how small, any country house worth its salt would have had a kitchen garden," Jennifer was saying when I caught up with her. "I had the opportunely to poke around first thing Friday morning, and I was absolutely delighted to discover that this one does too."

Jennifer had stopped at the back of the house, close to the kitchen door, and the group gathered around. Probably as protection from hungry deer, a thick hedge about my height enclosed a section of the yard. "While the gillie, or head fishing guide, was collecting fish from the private lake or streams running through the property, and the lord of the manor took his guests shooting grouse or partridge . . ."

"How horrible of them," Miranda said.

". . . one of the cook's army of helpers would be in here, collecting the day's vegetables and fresh herbs from the kitchen garden. They truly did have a local diet."

"While the working poor starved in the streets of the cities," Kyle said.

"Wouldn't have taken you for a revolutionary," Irene said.

"I'm not," he said. "Which is why I intend to never be one of the working poor. I'm all for having an army of kitchen helpers. Right, Mrs. Higgins?"

Annie pulled a face.

"I've had enough exercise for one day," Cliff said. "I'm going inside."

"But this is the most interesting part of our tour," Jennifer said.

"You call that exercise?" Steve said. "That little walk isn't even a decent warm-up."

Cliff waved to us over his shoulder as he walked away. Billy scurried after him.

I wasn't all that interested in seeing a rundown kitchen garden either, but I trotted after the group. A beautiful wrought iron gate, all curlicues and swirls, was set into the hedge. David slipped the latch and opened the gate and we entered the kitchen garden. As expected, the beds were laid out in neat rows, but they contained little except for a few seedy heads of lettuce, runaway kale, and dead tomato vines. Someone had harvested the last of the vegetables before leaving the place to run wild. A gravel path, quickly filling with weeds and grasses, ran down the center of the garden, ending at an iron bench.

"Fascinating," Kyle said as he theatrically suppressed a yawn. "Too bad they didn't grow grapes and bottle their own wine.

Speaking of wine, I think it's time to open the bar. Anyone interested?"

"What an excellent idea," Miranda said. "I'm in."

"Irene?" Kyle asked.

She shook her head. "Too early for me."

"I have to finish making up the rooms." Annie pushed at the gate and followed Kyle and Miranda.

"I don't suppose you found a physick garden?" Donald asked.

"No such luck," Jennifer said. "They wouldn't have needed one, not in the twentieth century in New England. By Holmes's day the physick garden was largely out of date for the same reason. People could go to the apothecary for their medicinal needs."

"What's a physics garden?" Irene asked.

"Not physics," Donald said, "but physick." He spelled the word out.

"A medicinal garden," Jennifer said. "Containing plants that would be used to treat common ailments."

"A great many of which we call, in modern times, poison," Donald said.

"They treated the sick with poison?" Irene said.

"Even in modern medicine much of what we take to cure us can kill us in a larger quantity," Jennifer said.

I added, "Which is why doctors and chemists worry about people overdosing."

Donald rubbed his hands together in glee. "By chemists, Gemma means pharmacists. You'd be surprised how many common garden plants are deadly."

"Thank you so much for leading our tour, Jennifer. Most enjoyable and highly educational." David dipped his head in a slight bow toward her. The remaining guests, including me, applauded.

She flushed with pleasure. "Not at all. I enjoyed it."

Before leaving, I turned my attention to the gate. It appeared to have been individually crafted, and it was beautifully made. I rubbed my fingers across it, enjoying the feel of the smooth, cool surface. It had been built, I guessed, by the same craftsman who made the gate at the top of the driveway, which had been standing open yesterday when Jayne, Ryan, and I arrived.

Everyone headed back to the house. Jennifer and David were the last to leave the kitchen garden, talking together in low voices. I heard the gate clang shut behind them.

* * *

After the walk, I spent a pleasant hour in the drawing room with Donald, Steve, and Jennifer discussing the modern pastiche versions of the adventures of Sherlock Holmes and Doctor John Watson. The group had broken up to go their separate ways before lunch, and I'd wandered into the kitchen to give Jayne and Ryan a hand with lunch preparation. Lunch was going to be a light meal of soup, bread, and salad as Jayne would be serving a full afternoon tea in the music room at four o'clock.

I found Ryan alone, perched on a stool next to a mug of coffee, reading his phone. I gave him a quick kiss on the top of his head. "You're not checking in with work, I hope."

"Fear not. The station knows I'm off and not to be contacted unless it's a genuine emergency. My mom's inviting us, meaning you and me, to a birthday dinner next week."

"It's not your birthday. Not mine either."

"No, it's hers."

"She shouldn't be putting on her own birthday party."

"She always does. She says that's the only way she can be sure of getting one." He pulled me close and gave me a long kiss. We separated at the sound of footsteps on the stairs.

"Is this house supposed to be haunted?" Jayne said as she came in.

"Not that I've ever heard," Ryan replied. "The house isn't old, and far as I know no one's been murdered here."

"Why are you asking?" I said.

She shrugged. "I think someone's been in my room."

Ryan sat up straight. "Is something missing?"

"No. Nothing like that. But . . . never mind. It's nothing."

"It's obviously not nothing if it's bothering you," I said. "What?"

"My ring isn't where I put it."

"Are you sure?"

"Yes. I mean, pretty sure." She held up her bare left hand. "I wore it to bed last night, like I always do, and this morning I took it off. Like I always do. I put it in its box and put the box on top of the dresser. I remember admiring the ring, and thinking about . . ." She blushed. "Never mind what I was thinking about . . . When I went up just now to put on a fresh apron I looked at the ring again. It was in the box, but not properly tucked into the satin lining. It was just . . . lying on top. I must have forgotten moving it."

"You don't forget things, Jayne." Ryan said. "Has the housekeeper been in your room?"

"No one made my bed or changed the towels, and I wouldn't expect them to do that until we leave. We aren't guests here."

"This is a private house, not a hotel," Ryan said. "The rooms don't have locks, so anyone can go anywhere. No ghosts required."

"Some people are more curious than they should be," I said. "As long as nothing's been taken, I don't think we should make a fuss, but maybe you should put your ring away."

"I did. I locked it in my suitcase."

"Good," Ryan said. "Let me know if anything else seems to be tampered with. You too, Gemma."

Jayne glanced at the clock on the stove, and began untying her apron. "It's almost eleven. Time for my meeting with David in the library."

"I'll come with you," I said. "He might have some new ideas for the entertainment."

To be honest, I was starting to feel like a spare wheel here. I wasn't really needed to help in the kitchen, I could only rearrange the puzzles, books, and props so many times, and no one was particularly interested in engaging with me in spirited Sherlockian debate. David, Donald, and Jennifer were far above my level of expertise; Steve and Cliff had some knowledge but not a great deal of interest in talking about Sherlock all the time; Kyle, Miranda, and Irene could barely distinguish Holmes from Watson.

"Do you think I should curtsy?" Jayne said.

"No, I do not."

Promptly at eleven o'clock, I rapped on the door to the library.

"Come in," David's high voice called, and I opened the door.

Our host for the weekend sat behind the big desk, brow furrowed, fingers steepled, still dressed in the Harris Tweed suit he'd worn on our walk earlier. He was reading one of the books I'd brought from the store, the other two close at hand. He closed his book, put it with the others, rested his hands on top of the stack, and said, "Mrs. Wilson. Miss Doyle. Do come in."

For a moment, I almost considered dropping into a curtsy myself, so perfect was the atmosphere. The lord of the manor in his study, tending to the serious business of the estate, the apple-wood fire burning cheerfully in the grate, the head cook (and her lowly assistant) come to consult on the menu for the dinner party. I put my hand in the pocket of my jeans and touched my phone as if it were a lodestone, linking me to my own time and my place in the world.

The fire was burning more for atmosphere than for heat as the day continued warming as the sun rose in the sky. The rich scent of grass given its final cut for the season and of the woodlands closing down for the winter drifted through the open sliding door that led to the pool and patio enclosure.

"I trust everything is to your satisfaction in the kitchen, Mrs. Wilson," David said.

I didn't bother to point out that Jayne was not married, there-fore she was not Mrs. Wilson. Cooks and housekeepers, at least in historical fiction, are always Mrs., whether married or not.

"Yes, sir. Uh, I mean David. We're good to go."

"Excellent. I simply wanted to confirm. This evening is important to me, you know."

I wanted to ask why, but I didn't.

"I understand," Jayne said.

He stood up and walked around the desk. "Things have not been going so well in my life of late. This weekend is a chance for me to get back on track. I thank you both for helping . . ." Some-thing flashed through the air in front of my face. David stopped abruptly and let out a sudden sharp cry. His eyes widened and his left hand flew to his neck. His mouth opened. It closed again. He stared at me, took a step backward, and staggered against a chair. The chair fell over with a crash and David collapsed onto the floor next to it.

Jayne gasped, and I crossed the room in two quick strides to drop to David's side. His body was stiff and he looked at me through wide, frightened eyes, struggling to breathe. His mouth opened in a silent scream, his body jerked, fell back, jerked again as though he were trying to get up, but his muscles wouldn't let him. "Call 911," I told Jayne. "We need an ambulance, fast." I lifted David's hand away from his neck, and what I saw there had me jumping to my feet. "Stay with him. After you've got 911, call Ryan and get him in here. Do not, under any circumstances, touch that thing in his neck, and tell Ryan the same."

I ran across the room. The sliding glass door had been pulled open, but the screen door was shut. The screen, I noticed, was badly torn. I grabbed it and pulled. It didn't move. I found the latch and flicked it and the door slid open a good deal slower than I would have liked on stiff and dirty runners. Behind me, I heard Jayne yelling into her phone. "Hurry, hurry!"

The door led onto a stamped concrete patio surrounding the swimming pool, its winter cover dotted with dead brown leaves. Large terra-cotta and iron pots were full of dying annuals, the soil being taken over by more hardy weather-tough weeds. The outdoor furniture had all been taken away. A quick glance showed me that no one was out here, and there was no place for anyone to hide. The pool area was surrounded by a four-foot-high chain-link fence with a gate set into it. The gate swung open on rusty hinges, and I ran through it. I emerged onto an expanse of lawn at the side of the house, near the rose garden. I glanced around me, unsure of where to go. No one was in sight, but the hedgerows and low stone walls offered places of concealment, provided the person I was after crouched in place. I'd emerged from the library closer to the back of the house than to the front, so I turned left. I ran around the house to find myself close to the bottom of the kitchen garden. The house's back door was closed, my car and Jayne's van parked where we'd left them yesterday. I stopped, stood still, and listened. Birds called to each other from the trees, but otherwise all was quiet. A section of the hedge surrounding the kitchen garden moved, more than could be accounted for by a touch of the light wind, and I ran toward it. Some of the branches were bent, and another was cleanly snapped off, indicating someone had recently passed this way. I pushed through the damaged foliage to emerge at the back of the empty vegetable garden, near the bench. Again, no place for anyone to hide. I kept moving, studying the ground as best I could as I ran. It hadn't rained for several days and the earth was dry. A few footprints marked the soft earth that had once nourished the vegetables, but the entire pack of us had walked through here a short while ago. The iron gate, which I'd heard close behind Jennifer and David as they followed us out of the kitchen garden, swung open.

I'd made a mistake by ducking through the hedge into the enclosed garden. If I'd stayed on the path, I would have seen whomever I was after come out. I ran through the garden, burst through the gate, and emerged on the cement path leading to the kitchen door. I threw open the door and ran into the house. The kitchen was empty, the stack of cucumbers and tomatoes half-chopped on the cutting board abandoned.

I stopped and listened. I could hear voices, natural enough, as this was a full house and the walls were thin. People were calling to each other, demanding to know what was happening. A woman wept, and a man shouted, "Stand back. Stand back."

In the distance, sirens approaching.

I made my way down the hallway to the library. Miranda was the one crying, as Steve ordered everyone to stand back. Not that anyone was paying any attention to him. The rest of the weekend party—Jennifer, Cliff, Kyle, Irene, Donald, and Annie—milled about in the hallway, shouting questions at each other, trying to see what was happening in the library.

Donald was the first to spot me. "Thank heavens you're here, Gemma. Smithers has gone to let the authorities in and show them the way."

I pushed through the crowd. Over the hubbub I heard the front door open, the sound of heavy boots rapidly heading toward us, and Billy saying, "This way. Quickly."

Steve stepped in front of me and held up his right hand. "No one's to go in there."

"I don't recall you being put in charge, old man," Kyle said.

Steve swung his attention away from me. "Now see here!"

"Let's get out of the way, shall we?" I said. "Help is here. Let's let them do their jobs."

"David," Jennifer yelled. "Where's David!"

Billy came around the corner, followed by two paramedics, laden with their equipment. Everyone, including Steve, stepped out of their way.

"Irene," I said. "Take everyone into the drawing room and wait there for news."

"Okay," she said.

"Why should—" Steve said.

"Thank you." I slipped into the library alongside the medics.

Jayne crouched on the floor next to David, her hands hovering in the air above him, wanting to help but knowing she was unable to. She looked up at me when I came in, and her face was very pale. Ryan stood over her, talking rapidly into his phone. He wasn't wearing his pink apron, but that wasn't the only change that had come over him. All the good-natured fun had fled, leaving only the cop behind.

He caught my eye and gave me a short, sharp nod. I put my hand on Jayne's shoulder. "Why don't we get out of these people's way?" I slipped my hand under my best friend's arm and helped her to stand.

"No one's to touch that without protective gloves," Ryan said to the medics.

When Jayne moved aside, I could plainly see what Ryan had been referring to. The same thing that had had me running out of the library. A dart was embedded in the side of David Masterson's neck.

Chapter Five

"You're not the kitchen helper then?" Annie said.

"I was the kitchen helper," Ryan replied. "This weekend only. The rest of the time I'm a police detective."

"Oh," she said.

"And, because I am the lead detective with the West London PD, I'm taking control of this case. So yes, Mr. Fraser, you will do as I tell you."

"Just making sure we know the situation here." Kyle dropped back into his chair.

I glanced at Ryan and rolled my eyes toward the ceiling. Kyle had announced that he'd suddenly remembered an important appointment in town. Ryan had told him he was going nowhere, and an argument threatened to break out.

The argument hadn't gone far, and Kyle decided his appointment could wait.

We were all gathered in the drawing room. Quickly and efficiently, the paramedics had loaded David onto their gurney and left in a great hurry, but I could tell by the look they gave Ryan and the expression on their faces, they knew they were too late. Ryan had ordered everyone to wait in the drawing room. With another silent nod to me, he'd asked me to keep an eye on them. When Kyle decided it was a good time to leave, I'd asked Ryan to join us, and he'd come in, accompanied by his hastily summoned partner, Detective Louise Estrada, and Officer Stella Johnson.

Estrada had managed to keep her face impassive when she spotted me sitting quietly on the couch, my hands in my lap, my ankles primly crossed, but it hadn't been easy for her. She and I don't exactly get along, and she's complained, loudly and often, that I seem to get myself involved in police matters more than the average citizen should.

"I'm going to talk to each of you privately," Ryan said. "I expect the rest to wait here, and not talk among yourselves."

Donald raised his hand.

"Yes, Donald?" Ryan said.

"May we discuss matters pertaining to why we have originally gathered here? By which I refer to the Canon?"

"You don't mean to tell us you bunch are collectors of historical artillery pieces?" Estrada glanced around the room as though searching for models of ancient fighting machines.

"Not cannons," Donald explained as though he were speaking to a particularly clueless child. "The Canon. The Sherlock Holmes novels and stories by—"

Louise Estrada wore her usual work clothes of black leather jacket, black blouse, black trousers, and black boots with one-inch heels. No jewelry, no makeup. Ryan's partner was a tall, lean, attractive woman in her mid-thirties, with flawless olive skin, thick black hair, and large dark eyes with which she could give a penetrating stare that would instantly silence the most ruthless of criminals. She's been known to silence me on occasion. "Oh, for heaven's sake," she said. "Not that nonsense again."

Jennifer sucked in a breath in shock. Kyle chuckled.

"I should have guessed," Estrada said. "At first glance I thought there'd been a gun battle in that room. Then I noticed that the bullet holes in the wall are fake and they're arranged in a strange pattern."

"The queen's initials," Donald said.

"The what?"

"The bullet holes form the letters VR. Victoria Regina. Not that the queen's middle name was Regina. That word means queen or female ruler. Holmes was bored and so he shot the queen's—"

"Is this directly related to the death that happened in that room today?"

"No," Donald said.

"Then I really, really do not care."

Donald sank further into his seat.

Ryan's phone rang and he checked the display. "I have to get this. One moment." He slipped out into the hallway.

He was back a moment later. His face was impassive, but I knew by the set of his jaw the news wasn't good. "I'm sorry, but that was the hospital calling. Mr. David Masterson has died."

I ran my fingers lightly across my right cheek as I studied the people in the room while they reacted to the news.

Cliff bent his head and whispered what might have been a private prayer. "Sorry to hear that," Kyle said. Miranda sobbed into a handful of tissues, but I suspected it was more for effect than grief. Her eyes and nose were clear and dry, and although the tissues she clutched in her hand were crumpled and damp, they weren't sodden.

Annie, on the other hand, was genuinely crying, loudly and copiously. She sat on the love seat next to Jayne. Jayne's arm was wrapped around the other woman's shoulders to provide what comfort she could.

Irene's eyes flicked around the room, and I assumed she was composing her newspaper copy. Steve sat in a delicate armchair that looked as though it would collapse under his weight at any moment. His posture was erect, his arms crossed over his chest, his feet placed solidly on the floor in front of him. Kyle sprawled on the couch, trying to seem blasé and oh-so-cool in the face of the drama, taking up more room than he should. But the twitch in the corner of his right eye told me he wasn't as casual about all this as he wanted us to think. Silent tears ran down Jennifer's face, and she huddled into herself in the space on the couch Kyle had left for her.

"As I said, I'll be needing to speak to each of you privately," Ryan said.

"You think someone killed him?" Kyle asked. "Well, let me assure you, it wasn't me."

"I think nothing," Ryan said. "Not yet."

"While we're waiting until it's our turn to be interviewed," Donald said, "perhaps we could start the movie. *Murder by Decree* is one of my favorites."

Jennifer's head snapped up. "You want to watch a movie? Now? Have some respect. A man," she swallowed heavily, "has died."

"I mean no disrespect," Donald said. "None at all. We have nothing better to do. In my experience, these things take time."

"Your experience?" Miranda said. "Are you a police officer too?"

"They're coming out of the woodwork," Kyle muttered.

"I am not," Donald said, "but I've been of assistance to Gemma . . . I mean Detective Ashburton, on some of her . . . I mean his cases."

All eyes turned to me.

"Not that I have cases," I said quickly. "Donald means he's helped me solve minor problems at my shop. Isn't that what you mean, Donald?"

"Uh, yes. Like the time your sales machine computer . . . thing . . . broke and I fixed it for you," said the totally computer-illiterate Donald.

"No movie," Estrada said.

"In that case," Kyle said. "How about a drink? Smithers, why don't you open the bar?"

"That would not—" Officer Johnson began, but the fake butler spoke over her. "My name's not Smithers, as you well know, Kyle. As you also know perfectly well, I am not a butler, and from now on you can pour your own blasted drink."

Smithers, who I must remember to call Billy, had been pacing up and down, up and down, across the room. Letting off nervous energy, I wondered, or did he have something specific to be nervous about? His face, until he'd turned on Kyle, had been expressionless, but his body language told me he was troubled. David had been his uncle. Was that it, or something more?

Whoever had killed David Masterson—and that person, I believed, was in this room—wasn't about to stand up and confess.

"Ms. Doyle," Ryan said, "I'll interview you first. Officer Johnson, stay here and ensure no one discusses what happened. Ms. Talbot, I hope I don't have to remind you that nothing is to appear in the papers without my permission."

Miranda perked up. "Papers? You're with a newspaper? How interesting."

Ryan and I walked out of the room, followed by Louise Estrada. As we left, I heard Kyle say, "Okay, you don't have to serve. Get the bottle out and find some glasses, will you?"

Miranda said to Irene, "If you'd like a photograph, can you wait until I've had a chance to fix my hair? I must look a total mess." She was probably disappointed that no one hurried to assure her she looked as lovely as ever.

"I'm particularly fond of the pea scene in *Murder by Decree*," Steve said to Donald, "although otherwise I didn't care for James Mason as Watson."

With the library blocked off and the group gathered in the drawing room, Ryan had appropriated the dining room as his interview space. I couldn't think of any place that seemed less suitable. The walls were covered with gold silk paper, the art consisted of a series of framed black-and-white sketches of crumbling castles. A round mirror in a gilt frame was mounted above the fireplace, and a teardrop chandelier hung over our heads. The table had not yet been set for lunch, and the shine of the dark wood of the table reflected the candelabra. The golden drapes were closed, the lamps switched on, the chairs tucked up to the table, and the fireplace contained nothing but cold gray ash. Ryan and I pulled out chairs and Estrada stood against the wall.

"Did you tell Louise why we're here?" I asked.

"I did," he said.

"Unbelievable," she muttered.

"I don't suppose I can tiptoe into the library and get some of my books and games?" I asked. "If the guests are to remain here, they'll need something to do."

Estrada gave me that penetrating stare.

"Just asking," I said meekly.

"I was in the kitchen cutting vegetables for the salad for lunch," Ryan said, "when Jayne called and told me someone had been killed in the library. I might have thought she was getting into the spirit of the weekend, except for the tone of her voice, which told me this was no joke. Less than ten minutes before, you and she had gone to the library to meet with David Masterson, as arranged. When I got to the library, you weren't there, but Jayne said you'd told her to call 911 and then me."

I nodded. "That's right. I ran after the person who did this."

Estrada groaned. I spread out my arms. "Obviously I had no luck, otherwise I would have told you who it was right away."

"Gemma," Ryan said. "I seem to recall on another occasion advising you not to chase someone you think is a killer, alone and unarmed. Maybe you should have waited for the police? Meaning, in this case, me."

"Sorry," I said, although I wasn't sorry at all. I hadn't been intending to tackle the perpetrator as though I were an American football player, but I hoped I could at least get enough of a look at them to be able to identify him or her.

"Did you see this person? The one you chased?" Ryan asked.

"No, not even a glimpse. Sorry. They moved fast, and there are all sorts of places on this property where someone can duck behind a fence or through a hedge or turn a corner."

"Take us through exactly what happened," Ryan said.

I did so. David had been seated at the desk reading when Jayne and I arrived. He closed his book, got to his feet, and walked around the desk, talking to us. Someone fired a dart through a tear in the screen door, and it struck him in the side of his neck.

Involuntarily I lifted my own hand to indicate the spot on my neck. He dropped on the spot, and I left him in Jayne's care and gave chase.

"Have a look at the screen," I said. "As I mentioned earlier, this house is not as well kept up as it first appears to be." I gestured around me. The wallpaper peeling at the edges, the watermark in the plaster ceiling, the dust gathering in clumps on the picture frames. "The screen on the library door is in particularly poor condition. Screens are intended to keep out small insects, but the hole in the center of that one wouldn't stop Moriarty." Meaning my shop cat. "Louise, you might want to check and see how recent the tearing is."

"I might, might I?" Estrada said.

"You might. If someone cut or ripped it with the intention of creating an access point for their projectile, that would indicate the attack was planned. I didn't hear the sound of screens ripping, nor see anyone lurking outside the sliding door or peering through the windows when Jayne and I came in. But I will admit I didn't look toward the door or windows because David greeted us immediately. After firing the dart, whoever did so ran across the pool enclosure, through the gate, rounded the house to the rear, and then went through the hedge into the kitchen garden. The ground's hard, so you likely won't be able to get footprints, but if they left the path and went across the lawn or through the vegetable beds, some residual prints might be visible. Unfortunately, that will probably be of no use to you. I have to mention that we all, with the exception of Jayne and you, Ryan, toured the gardens after breakfast. Even Annie Masterson and Billy Belray, who are pretending to be the housekeeper and the butler, respectively, joined the expedition. As there are no vegetables to be wary of trodding upon, we would have not minded where we were putting our feet. Our dart thrower crossed the kitchen garden and exited via the gate." I closed my eyes and thought, trying to visualize the scene. Estrada shifted but said nothing; Ryan's chair squeaked.

"Cliff Mann left the group before we went into the vegetable garden, saying he wasn't interested. Billy joined him, but the rest of us accessed it via the gate and everyone, including me, sort of wandered around. We didn't stand in one place. Jennifer and David were last to leave the kitchen garden at the end of our tour, and one of them pulled the gate shut after us. I distinctly remember hearing the sound as the latch fell into place. Their prints will be on it, but they won't be the only set. The ironwork is quite nice and some of our party examined the gate earlier. Including, unfortunately, me. By examined, I mean touched."

"Your prints are on it," Estrada muttered. "Why am I not surprised to hear that?"

"The gate was closed but not locked?" Ryan said.

"There isn't a lock, and probably never was. No reason there should be. Deer can't open gates." I continued mentally retracing my steps of earlier. "The gate opens onto a cement path leading to the kitchen door and then on to the rear parking area and the driveway. I had to decide what direction to go, and I went into the house via the kitchen."

"Why?" Estrada said. "Wouldn't this person be more likely to stay outside, to get away? People might have been in the kitchen."

"Jayne had called Ryan, and thus sounded the alarm. I assumed no one would be in the kitchen after that, and I assumed our killer would have also thought so. He, or she, would want to blend into the people in the house as quickly as possible, and not to stand out in any way. As they would have if they'd come in through the front door. That's precisely what happened. When I arrived back at the library, every one of them was there. With the exception of Smithers, I mean Billy, who'd gone to meet the police and medics at the door. They were all wearing some sort of footwear, and I didn't notice any recently deposited dirt on any of them."

"You had time to check their shoes?" the ever-suspicious Estrada said to me.

"It was a matter of seconds. Miranda was in high-heeled boots when we went on our walk, and she since changed into shoes. You might want to ask to see the boots she had on earlier."

"We will."

"Was any one of them out of breath?" Ryan asked.

"Not that I noticed. Steve's the oldest one here, but he seems in reasonably good shape, and I suspect Miranda exercises regularly to keep herself so thin. Jennifer's overweight, but that doesn't necessarily mean anything in terms of fitness. I'm not sure about Cliff. Annie, Kyle, and Billy are fairly young. Around my age, our age, and I have to point out that I'm not a regular runner, although I do like to swim in the summer months, but I wasn't out of breath when I came into the house. We didn't go very far. Annie was crying, Miranda was pretending to be, and Jennifer seemed genuinely shocked. Steve was shouting, everyone asking questions."

"Pretending to be?" Estrada asked.

"I don't mean to imply anything by that. I think she was acting as she thought she should, rather than through any deep emotion."

"You think one of the house guests did this?" Estrada said.

"Or the temporary staff, yes. Present company, and Jayne, excepted."

"Don't rush it," Estrada said, but her heart wasn't in the threat. She'd asked a good question, and I was glad of it. In the past she would have instantly dismissed anything I had to say.

"Why do you assume the perpetrator was in the house?" Ryan asked. "Why couldn't someone have come from outside? Do the deed and then take off?"

"That could have happened. The property's fenced and gated. I don't know if the gate is kept shut; it was open when we arrived yesterday, if you remember. You'll want to have people searching for signs of an intruder. This person might have been creeping about the shrubbery all morning, waiting for the opportunity to throw a dart at David, but I consider that highly unlikely. Anyone in the house could have overheard David call Jayne and invite her to the library at eleven o'clock, and thus have been lying in wait outside. How could someone not part of this group know where he was going to be, and when?

"If someone had been lurking in the shrubbery trying to see into the house, they were likely to be spotted. Remember the torn screen door. Also remember this is not David Masterson's home. He's a weekend guest as much as the rest of us are. He didn't have a regular routine that he might be expected to keep. No, one of the people invited here for this weekend killed him. And they came with the intention of doing so."

"I can't disagree with that," Ryan said. "Not many people carry poisoned darts on their person on the off chance they get an opportunity to use them."

"Poison," Estrada said. "Why do you assume it was poisoned?"

Ryan said nothing but looked at me.

"You noticed that as well," I said. "The dart's fairly small, although undoubtedly quite sharp. David dropped instantly, as anyone might when receiving a shock like that. He fell against a chair, knocked it over, and collapsed to the floor, but he didn't bleed any more than could be expected from a tiny prick. The dart didn't go into his neck deeply enough to reach an artery. Therefore, it had to have been coated with something that did him in on the spot. His body convulsed almost immediately, he appeared to be unable to breathe, and his muscles froze. Strychnine is my guess."

Estrada blanched.

"Where's the dart now?" I asked Ryan.

"I secured it and it's on its way into town. I removed it before the medics tended to him and I called the pathologist's office to let them know what we suspect."

"I'm not a dart player," I said, "but I have seen the game being played on several occasions. The thing that was used to kill David didn't look at all like the typical dart as thrown in the pubs in England. Unless you play the game quite differently in America, I suspect this one came from some sort of projectile-firing object."

Ryan nodded. "Blowgun, most likely. Yesterday and today, I spent most of my time in the kitchen," he said to Estrada. "I didn't meet any of the guests, or even David Masterson himself. You had contact with them, Gemma. Did you notice anyone showing any animosity toward Masterson?"

"No. But one thing in particular struck me. This was supposed to be a Sherlock Holmes weekend. I was invited to bring the props, the books, the games, the movies, that sort of thing, and help keep the conversation going. Donald and Uncle Arthur were invited because of their knowledge of Holmes. I expected everyone would be on the same page, so to speak."

"They're not?"

"Not at all. Jennifer and Steve seem knowledgeable, particularly Jennifer, but the others, not so much. Cliff is so-so, but Kyle and Miranda aren't even bothering to pretend an interest. You might want to ask them why they're here."

"I'll do that. Thanks, Gemma."

"I have one question before you go." Estrada pointed to the three books in a small pile on the otherwise empty desk. "You said David was sitting behind that desk when you came in, reading. Those books look old, judging by the covers and some wear on the edges of the paper. Are they valuable? I know some of those books can run in the tens of thousands of dollars."

I glanced toward the desk. "You're wondering if theft might have been a motive, but the answer is no. Not of those three anyway. They have no value to a collector. I brought them from the store to use as props for the weekend. They're not first editions and are not signed or have any other significance. They're just ordinary used books I sell in the Emporium."

"I'll talk to Jayne next and then the rest of them," Ryan said. "You two might as well carry on with whatever you were doing. I guess my stint as a kitchen maid is over." He tried not to look too pleased at the idea.

I stood up. I would have liked to stay and listen in on the interviews, but I knew better than to ask. Ryan didn't like it when I got involved in his cases. To be honest, I didn't like it either, but that's what happened sometimes. "We've got a fully stocked kitchen and bar so that'll go a long way toward keeping the guests, aka the suspects, in place. Are you going to let them leave after they've given their statements?"

"I'll decide later," Ryan said.

Estrada walked out of the dining room with me. We found the guests in the drawing room, where we'd left them under the watchful eye of Stella Johnson. Donald was reading the latest edition of *Canadian Holmes*, which I'd brought from the store. Jennifer appeared to be examining the railway timetables again, but I could tell by the tilt of her head she wasn't seeing anything. Cliff was working on a jigsaw puzzle, while Steve shifted restlessly on the couch. Miranda flipped through a fashion magazine, and I had not the slightest idea where she would have found that in this house. Irene had taken a seat on the couch, with the latest version of *Sherlock Holmes Magazine* on her lap, but she wasn't reading. Billy had opened the bar and Kyle was sitting by himself in a far corner, nursing what looked like a scotch. Annie sat with Jayne. The two women spoke in low voices, and Annie wept softly.

"Ms. Wilson," Estrada said. "If you'll come with me, please."

Jayne stood up. I took her place next to Annie.

"You okay?" I asked.

The fake housekeeper swallowed heavily, gave me a small nod, and blew her nose.

"Were you and David close?" I asked.

"I guess we were. Sorta. He's . . . He was my mother's brother. When I was in junior year of high school my mom got married and moved to New Hampshire. I didn't want to switch schools, so I went to live with Uncle David. We lived in the same apartment for a couple of years, but didn't spend all that much time together. You know how it is."

I didn't, but I nodded. My Uncle Arthur and I share a house and I'd say we're very close.

Then again, I hadn't even known he was on his way to Spain.

Donald looked up from his journal. "What do you think happened, Gemma?"

"No talking about it," Officer Johnson said sharply.

"It's obvious the cops think David was murdered," Kyle said. "Otherwise, why are we all being kept here, right? And told not to talk about it."

Miranda looked up from her magazine. "Murdered? That's absolutely preposterous. Everyone loved David. He never hurt a fly in all his life."

"I don't know about any flies," Kyle said. "But I've heard that he had his enemies. Isn't that right, Billy?"

Billy jumped to his feet, his face set into dark lines and his fists clenched. An interesting reaction, I thought, to what might have been nothing but a passing comment. "What's that supposed to mean?"

Kyle smirked. "Or should I say Smithers? You did a good job playing the obsequious butler."

"Do you have something to say to me, Kyle? If you do, spit it out."

"Beggars can't be choosers. Nor, so it would seem, can butlers." Kyle laughed and leaned back in his chair.

I wanted to hear more, but Johnson stepped between the two men. "That's enough of that. You'll both have a chance to tell your story to the detectives."

"I don't have a story," Billy said.

"Glad to hear it," she replied. "Now sit down."

He threw a poisonous look at Kyle before, grumbling, dropping into a chair.

"A coffee would be nice," Miranda said as she returned her attention to her magazine.

"Sounds good to me," Donald said.

"As long as you're making, I'll have one too," Irene said.

I was about to say I'd like a cup of tea, when I realized they were all looking expectantly at me. I got to my feet with a sigh. "Officer Johnson, can I get you something?"

"Coffee'd be great, thanks. Maybe the detectives would like one too?"

"Jennifer," I said, "would you like something?"

She started. The railway timetable trembled in her hands. "What?"

"I'm making tea and coffee. Would you like a cup? A glass of water perhaps?"

"Coffee? No. I mean, no thank you."

"While you're at it," Kyle said. "Some sandwiches or something would be good. Unless we're having lunch soon?"

"As Jayne's busy," I said, "Annie, can you give me a hand?" Johnson began to open her mouth and I added quickly, "We won't talk about what happened this morning. I promise."

"I guess it's all right then," she said.

In the kitchen vegetables were laid out on the island, abandoned in the midst of being chopped and added to the big salad bowl intended to be lunch.

I kept my promise, and I didn't talk about the events of this morning while I filled the kettle and Annie ground coffee beans. "Tell me about your uncle," I said. "I assume he was fairly well off, if he could afford to rent this house for a weekend." I already knew that, from my brief pre-weekend internet search, but I wanted Annie's take on the man.

"He took it for the whole week, but yeah, he's loaded. He's my mother's half-brother, same father, different mothers. They didn't grow up together. David's mom's family's pretty rich. His parents died in a car accident about ten years ago, and he inherited the lot."

"Didn't your mother get anything on the death of her father?"

"Not a penny. It wasn't his money to give to her. Look, Gemma, don't get me wrong. Uncle David was good to me. He helped me out when I needed a place to stay when I was trying to make a go of my career." Her face twisted. I turned away from her and began getting down mugs and cups. "I'm still trying to make a go of my career, and I'm still needing handouts. Like this ridiculous housekeeper gig. It's just that . . . well, sometimes he liked to see me beg for his help. I tried not to let it bother me. That's just the way he was."

I arranged things on a tray while Annie took milk and cream out of the fridge.

"What's Billy's relationship with David?"

"Not a good one, believe me. Billy's mom's a sister of David's mom, so he and I aren't actually related. I don't know the whole story, but his mom was estranged from her family a long time ago and disinherited. Billy sniffs around looking for handouts and feeling hard done by because David inherited all the family money, via his mom, and Billy's mom didn't get anything. David talks about letting bygones be bygones and how blood is thicker than water and all that stuff, but he treats Billy like a toy. Like making him answer to the name of Smithers this weekend?"

I didn't recognize the name. "Why is that significant?"

"You don't know?"

"Smithers? Is it supposed to mean something?"

"You don't know who Smithers is?"

"Should I?"

"Gemma didn't know who Clark Kent is." Jayne came into the kitchen.

"Really?" Annie said. "How can anyone not know who Clark Kent is?"

"Gemma managed."

"Thank you so much for pointing that out, Jayne. I now know that Clark Kent is the adoptive name of Superman. In the same way I will soon know who Smithers is, if anyone bothers to enlighten me."

"The assistant on *The Simpsons*."

"Who are the Simpsons and why should I know who their assistant is?"

"He's not the Simpsons' assistant. They don't have one. Smithers is Mr. Burns's overly obsequious PA."

I threw up my hands. "If I need know who Mr. Burns is, never mind Mr. Simpson or Mr. Smithers, please tell me. Otherwise, the tea is almost ready."

Jayne was laughing so hard, at my expense, I hoped she'd get a stitch in her side.

"*The Simpsons* is a TV show," Annie explained as she filled the coffee carafe. "Expecting Billy to be called Smithers all weekend wasn't meant to be polite. David said I was to be known as Mrs. Higgins because the housekeeper having the same name as the host wouldn't look right. Not that it matters, but my mom and my dad were never married, thus my name's Masterson, same as Mom and David's."

I poured coffee into mugs for Ryan and Louise while Jayne and Annie arranged the teapot and coffee carafe on a tray next to cups and mugs.

"What about the others?" I asked Annie. "Did you know any of them before this weekend?"

"Other than Miranda, who was a friend of David's mom and came around to his house a few times when I was living there, I've never seen any of those people before. Doesn't mean anything. Uncle David and I never socialized. Different lives, completely different interests."

I found a smaller tray and arranged the two coffees on it. "I'll take these to the dining room. Jayne, would you mind waiting here until I get back?"

"Sure," she said. "I wonder if I should throw something together for lunch. Ryan never did finish the salad." I left her peering into the fridge.

I knocked at the door to the dining room. Estrada opened it, and I gave her a broad smile. "I thought you'd like a coffee."

She moved to take the tray from me and I slipped around her. "I'll put it down over here, shall I?"

At the moment, Steve was the one in the hot seat. He didn't look particularly bothered to be there. He sat ramrod straight in his chair, arms crossed over his chest, smirk curling around the edges of his mouth.

I put the tray on the sideboard and Ryan said, "Thank you, Ms. Doyle."

"Cream, Detective? Sugar?"

"We'll serve ourselves, thank you."

I glanced at Steve again. He was studying his fingernails. I could think of no further excuse to linger, so I left and returned to the kitchen.

Jayne was bagging the vegetables. "I want to get these put away while they're still fresh. We've got a heck of a lot of food in here, and I don't suppose I can take any of it back to the store. I was paid a deposit to do the shopping but we're still owed for our time and effort."

I took a cucumber out of her hand and dropped it on the counter. Then I turned her to face me and took her hands in mine. "You okay, Jayne?"

She smiled at me. "I'm okay. It was upsetting, yes, but I didn't know the man well."

"More than upsetting. I left you alone with him. You were with him when he died."

The smile faded and her lovely blue eyes filled with tears. "I'm glad I was there, Gemma. No one should die alone. I think—I hope—he knew I was with him, but he didn't say anything to me. I told Ryan that."

If I was right, David Masterson had died of strychnine poisoning. That's a quick, but very unpleasant, death. Unpleasant to be witness to, as Jayne had been. "Why don't I give Andy a call? Ask him to come and pick you up. You should go home and lie down. Ryan won't expect you to stay."

"It's lunchtime on a Saturday, Gemma. Andy's at work."

As the owner and head chef of his own restaurant, Andy was always at work. I knew he'd come if Jayne needed him even if he left his customers lunching on dry bread and warm water.

She pulled her hands out of mine and returned her attention to the fridge and its contents. "I'll stay as long as you're staying.

The people are still here, at least for now. We were hired to feed them. I won't serve the sit-down soup and salad lunch I'd planned, and I'm sure no one will be in the mood for a proper afternoon tea later, but I can throw together some sandwiches and bring out the pastries I've made."

I laid my hand briefly on her arm and went back to the drawing room where everyone was helping themselves to the tea and coffee Annie had brought in. Everyone, that is, except for Jennifer, wrapped in her own world, Kyle who seemed content with his scotch, and Cliff who'd poured himself one. I wandered over to the window and pulled back the drapes. Police cars, marked and unmarked, filled the driveway at the front of the house and uniformed figures moved across the lawn.

I poured myself a cup of tea, grabbed a vacant chair, and dragged it to where Miranda had returned to the couch with her coffee and picked up the magazine.

"Did you know David well?" I asked her.

She looked at me through dry eyes. "We've been friends for many years."

"That's nice. *Good* friends?"

"I don't know what you mean by that. David is . . . I mean he was married."

Which, I thought, had never before stopped two people from becoming *good* friends, but I didn't pursue the matter. More to the point, however, they'd never expressed any degree of fondness toward each other. Not even in an attempt to do so secretly.

"David's late mother was a dear friend of mine," Miranda admitted at last. "After her untimely death, he and I kept in touch. I like to think she would have wanted us to be friends."

"That's nice. It was nice of him to invite you to this weekend, seeing as how you aren't interested in Sherlock Holmes."

Her makeup cracked as she smiled. "I believe in showing an interest in many things. Curiosity keeps a woman young." She returned her attention to her magazine. I can tell when I'm being dismissed.

I don't necessarily do anything about it, but I can tell.

"Do you live in New York City?" I asked.

Slowly, ever so slowly, she raised her head. She stared at me from beneath her thickly mascaraed lashes. "Is that any of your business?"

"Just being friendly," I said.

"I don't know why it matters to you, but yes, I live in Manhattan. I love the energy and vigor of the city."

She was saved from more of my friendliness when Steve and Estrada came in, and Estrada said, "Ms. Ireland, we'll speak to you now."

Miranda stood up. She patted down her skirt, fluffed her hair, and left the room.

Steve headed for the bar cart. He poured himself a shot of bourbon and swallowed it in one gulp. His hands shook slightly. Not quite as casually disinterested as he wanted to appear.

"I need to get out of this horrid dress." Annie tugged at her collar. "I can't believe people actually wore things this uncomfortable."

"I'm sorry," Johnson said, "but the detectives would like you to remain here until they've spoken to you."

Annie pointed to the ceiling. "My room's upstairs. A dark, damp little thing under a sloping celling. I'll be back before they know it."

Johnson shook her head. Annie dropped back into her chair and didn't press the point.

I studied them all. Donald took the seat next to me, recently vacated by Miranda. He leaned toward me and instinctively I leaned toward him.

"How can I help, Gemma?" he whispered.

"Help with what?"

"The case, of course."

"Ryan and Detective Estrada are here. They don't need any help. I'm staying well out of it."

Donald winked at me.

"Really, I am."

He winked again.

"How did you get invited to this weekend anyway?" I asked. "Had you met David before?"

"Not in person, but we have corresponded. They say he has an excellent collection of first editions of the Holmes books and other works by Sir Arthur and several original *Strand* magazines. He corresponded regularly with many of the most prominent Sherlockian scholars around the world, but he didn't normally go to public events such as meetings of the Baker Street Irregulars or attend the BSI weekend."

"Not a joiner then. Do you know why you were invited this weekend, Donald? I mean, you're well known in the field, but . . ."

"But no one would consider me to be one of the most prominent, you mean. That's okay, Gemma. I'm happy with my own small area of study. My invitation came via Arthur. Arthur, as you know, does have a considerable reputation. It was thoughtful of him to mention my name to David."

"Do you know if Uncle Arthur has ever met David?"

"I know he hasn't. He mentioned it when we discussed the invitation. It was Arthur who told David about Suffolk Gardens House being available for rent when David casually said he'd love to put together a small, intimate Sherlock weekend in a suitable environment. Arthur's familiar with this house from previous visits, and he knew it would be perfect for what David had in mind."

"Uncle Arthur's been here? When? I thought no one from the community was ever invited."

"You know Arthur, Gemma," Donald said. "You yourself always say he's been everywhere."

"Yes, but I didn't mean everywhere as in *everywhere*."

Miranda was soon back and Jennifer invited to chat to the detectives in the dining room.

I stood up. "All right if I visit the loo, Officer?" I asked Johnson.

"Okay," she said.

I hoped Stella Johnson hadn't acquainted herself with the layout of the house, as when I walked out of the drawing room, rather than turn left for the downstairs powder room, I turned right, walked down the hall, and exited via the front door.

A uniformed officer stood on the steps, guarding the scene. He whirled around as I opened the door and his hand might have reached for his gun before he remembered where he was and lowered it with a sheepish expression. He was very young, and I'd never seen him before. His badge, his uniform belt buckle, and his boots were so shiny they reflected the sunlight. His trousers were ironed to a knife point, with no sign of wear on the knees or the hem. First week on the job, I guessed.

"Good afternoon," I said in my snootiest British accent. I find it often goes a long way toward intimidating nervous Americans. "I'm in search of a breath of fresh air."

"Who are you?" he asked in a nervous squeak. He coughed and lowered his voice. "I mean, who are you?"

"A house guest. Never mind me. I've spoken to the detectives already. Carry on!"

"Ma'am, I don't know if you're allowed to leave the house."

"Quite all right." I walked away from him at a rapid pace, pretending not to hear his protestations.

Every time the drawing room doors opened, and when I'd been in the kitchen making tea, I could hear voices as officials walked through the house, worked in the library, or crept about outside, crawling through the shrubbery.

The West London police had wasted no time in putting a full investigation in motion. They were good at their jobs, but in case they overlooked something that might prove to be important, I wanted to have another look at the path the killer had taken after throwing a poisoned dart through the ripped screen door of the library. I was interested, very interested, in the dart itself, but I knew I'd be allowed nowhere near it. I'd simply have to wait, like Ryan, for the toxicology report to say what had been on it. Assuming Ryan would tell me, which was by no means guaranteed.

Unlike Sherlock Holmes, I do not have an encyclopedic knowledge of poisons, their origins and effects, but unlike Sherlock Holmes I have access to the internet. When I had a chance, I'd try to find out what I could about what might have been used. Not everyone has ready access to a poison so powerful a mere scratch can fell a grown man in less than a minute, but these days, almost anything's available for those prepared to do a bit of research and with the right mindset.

I was also interested in what the killer had used to propel the dart. Not their own hands, I'd decided, therefore Ryan had probably been right when he guessed a blowgun, although it could have been some sort of bow. Whoever it was must have been extremely confident of their abilities. If they'd missed, David, Jayne, and I would have seen the thing flying through the air and embedding itself in the wall or the carpet. From then on David would have been on his guard, and I would have called the police—aka Ryan Ashburton, the kitchen maid.

Although, depending on what we were doing at the time and the lighting in the room, we might not have noticed the dart whiz past. Was it possible this was not the first attempt? I'd have to warn everyone not to pick up any darts they found lying around.

Or did Ryan want to keep that detail to himself for now? I'd better check before I started talking of things the police were keeping mum about.

I made my way around the house to the pool enclosure and the door to the library. It seemed odd that the patio and pool would be off the library, but perhaps the layout of the rooms in this house had moved over the years.

I placed my feet with care, watching where I went. I put my hands behind my back and studied the screen door. The edges of the largest of the tears were clean and sharp. Meaning they were recent and had been cut, not decayed over time. The library was empty. The police had completed their search for evidence. They wouldn't have found anything in the library, as the killer hadn't needed to step inside.

I followed the path I'd taken earlier, moving slowly this time, studying the ground. Nothing. No footprints marred the stamped concrete or the hard ground. Unfortunately, I found no dropped driver's license or abandoned piece of clothing either. I also didn't find a blowgun or a small bow.

I ducked through the hedge into the kitchen garden, where I found evidence that the police had taken casts of footprints, but as most of us had been in there earlier in the day, those wouldn't help much.

Dust from a soft gray powder was trapped in the crevices of the iron gate I'd admired earlier, meaning it had been finger-printed. Again, any one of us could have touched it. I had.

I retraced my steps, hoping I'd overlooked something. I stopped under a wide window with the curtains pulled across it and thought. What might I have missed? Had I been right to chase the killer where I had? Was it possible they'd taken a different route and not gone into the house by the kitchen? Had I been wrong in assuming this person had been one of the weekend party? I closed my eyes to draw up a picture of the scene as it had happened.

I leapt out of my skin at a bellow in my ear.

"What on earth do you think you're doing listening at the window?" Ryan Ashburton's head stuck out of the window, the white drapes curling around his shoulders.

"Oh. Sorry. Is this the dining room? I didn't realize. I wanted some fresh air."

Estrada's head was next to pop out of a window. "You're supposed to stay in the house with the rest of them."

"I am? Sorry."

"The officer at the door has orders to keep you all inside."

"Sorry," I said again. "Don't be too hard on him. I bullied him."

"Why does that not surprise me?" she said.

"It's his first week on the job," Ryan said. "I should have warned him about you. Please go back inside, Gemma. We can talk later about . . . uh, anything you might have noticed."

"Which is nothing, I'm sorry to say."

Chapter Six

"You're not serious," Jennifer was saying as I reentered the drawing room.

"Totally serious." Steve said. "It's what he would have wanted."

"Seems rather poor taste to me," Donald said.

"I'm with Steve," Kyle said. "It's a great idea. David hated waste."

"He did not," Annie said. "And even if he did, how would you know?"

"What are you talking about?" I asked.

No one answered me, so I glanced at Jayne. "They want to go ahead with the formal dinner tonight, as planned," she said.

"It would be in honor of David," Miranda said. "A fitting tribute."

"As long as we're stuck here anyway, we might as well enjoy ourselves," Billy said. "But, to make things perfectly clear, I'm not waiting on you." He looked down at himself. "And I'm not wearing this blasted suit any longer either."

"Well, I'm not doing it." Annie had undone several of the buttons at the top of her housekeeper's dress and rolled some of the material up into the belt so her knees were clear. "He was my uncle too."

Billy pointed to Jayne and me. "Isn't that why they're here?"

"You can deduct tonight's meal from our fee," Jayne said.

"Not that you're likely to get paid," Miranda said, "now that David's dead. I hope you got a good advance."

Irene said nothing. She'd been warned, very sternly, by Detective Estrada that not a word of this was to appear in the papers. Earlier she'd excused herself and slipped off to the loo. I'd noticed her touching her pocket, as though to confirm that her phone was there, and she'd been gone a long time. Ordering her editor to clear the front page, I assumed. Today was Saturday and the *West London Star* didn't print on Sunday. All she'd be able to do today would be get something onto their Twitter feed.

"We'll all chip in to cover the expense," Cliff said. "Come on, let's do it. For David. One last time." He lifted his glass. It had been refilled while I was out of the house.

"No," Jayne said. "I don't want—"

"Sure," I said.

Jayne threw me a look.

"Why not? We've bought all the food. We've done the prep. Jayne will cook and I'll help serve. Seeing as how we've lost our best kitchen maid, Irene will take that role."

"I will?" Irene said.

"Donald can be the butler. He can serve the wine, as well as enjoying dinner, of course, if you don't mind a little informality."

"I'd be happy to," Donald said. "If you think it appropriate, Gemma. A man did die in this house today."

"As others have said, David would want us to carry on."

"How do you know what he'd want? You only met him yesterday. Didn't you?" Jennifer's eyes narrowed as she studied me.

I had no answer to that so I didn't try. Instead, I began gathering used coffee cups.

"Perhaps we can watch the movie before dinner," Donald said.

"The screen and DVD player are still in the library," I said. "The police have told us not to go in there."

"Can't you ask Detective Ashburton? As a personal favor I mean?"

"I don't think so, Donald," I said.

All eyes turned to Officer Johnson.

"I'll mention it to him," she said. "Won't promise though."

"How about some lunch first?" Steve said. "It's almost three. Dinner won't be for hours yet."

"Isn't afternoon tea on the schedule for four o'clock?" Miranda said. "I was looking forward to that. I had a light breakfast so as to allow myself a teatime scone. I do love a proper afternoon tea. I remember one time in London—"

"No tea," I said. "Jayne doesn't have time to get that ready, but we'll lay out sandwich ingredients and the tea pastries in the kitchen. How's that sound? We'll be ready in ten minutes or so. Come along, Jayne, don't dawdle."

As soon as we arrived in the kitchen, Jayne put her tray on the counter and turned to face me, hands on hips. "I do not want to cater this dinner, Gemma. It's unseemly, and we're not so hard done by we can't afford to cut our losses."

"Of course it is, and yes we can." I touched her arm. "I meant it when I said you should go home. You've had a shock and it's going to hit you later. I can manage the dinner."

"You can't cook."

"How hard can it be? You've done most of the preparation. Irene and I can finish it off."

"Can Irene cook?"

"I've no idea."

"The prep's the easy part, Gemma. Why do you want to do this, anyway?"

"I do have a reason: I want to keep these people together for as long as possible and observe their interactions."

"You're snooping?"

"I prefer to call it using my deductive powers for good. Get them liquored up, feed them a hearty dinner, and see what details they let slip."

"It's not a bad idea," Ryan said as he came into the kitchen. "Unfortunately, I don't think I can pretend to be the waiter."

"They'll be charging in here in a couple of minutes in search of sustenance," I said. "If you've learned anything I need to know you can tell me later. What are you up to now?"

"I love the way you're assuming I'll share with you what I learned."

"Won't you?"

"Not necessarily. But, seeing as how no one has been marched out in handcuffs, I can tell you I'm not arresting anyone at this time."

"David was married," I said, "but his wife didn't come on this weekend."

"Annie gave me her contact information. I called her and she's on her way. Louise is outside checking with the forensics people. It's a Saturday but I managed to persuade the pathologist that due to the possible nature of the poison used this is a rush job, and she's going to do the autopsy at five. The lab's promised to get that dart examined as soon as possible. I have to go."

"Can I get my things out of the library?"

"No. The room's sealed."

"But—"

"No buts. That room is sealed. I have also, perhaps belatedly, had the pool enclosure taped off. I trust you'll respect those boundaries, Gemma."

"Of course," I said innocently.

"I'm staying if Gemma is," Jayne said firmly.

"Are you sure?" I asked her.

"Working is better than brooding," she said.

"There truly is a Holmes quote for all occasions. The Great Detective himself said, 'Work is the best antidote to sorrow.'" In this case it might be for Jayne. Perhaps she would be better off here, busy doing what she loved—cooking—rather than sitting at home remembering what had happened.

"I'm not leaving you two alone," Ryan said. "Not with a possible killer in the house. I'll take Stella with me and Louise will stay."

"We don't—"

"Louise will stay," he repeated. "I don't necessarily agree with you, Gemma, that the killer has to be one of the people in this house. I intend to start checking into Masterson's personal and business affairs. Need I remind you that if you learn anything at this dinner party, you are to share it with me? Immediately. Not go haring off in all directions trying to trick the killer into attacking you so as to prove their guilt or some such foolishness."

"Would I do something like that?"

"Yes. Jayne, I'm putting you in charge of keeping Gemma out of trouble."

"Ha!" Jayne said. "That'll be the day."

"Before I go," he said, "Jayne, have you had any reason to suspect someone's been in your room again? Since you noticed your ring had been moved?"

"No. It must have been my imagination. I probably didn't put the ring away properly."

Ryan and I exchanged a look. Neither of us believed that.

*　*　*

I'm not much of a cook, but I can lay out sandwich ingredients, which I did, as well as arrange the delicate fruit tarts, macarons, and mini-cupcakes Jayne had earlier prepared at Mrs. Hudson's for the intended afternoon tea. If the house guests were nervous at the presence of the police outside—poking around the gardens and checking the property line—and in—Detective Estrada watching everyone—they managed not to show it. I studied them as they lined up to fill their plates. The mood was solemn, no one laughed or chatted, and they left the kitchen as soon as they had their food in hand.

"Dinner will be at eight," I announced. "Drinks in the drawing room at seven thirty."

"Which gives us time for the movie." Donald snatched a pistachio macaron off the serving platter. "How about the library at four thirty?"

"The library's out of bounds," Estrada reminded him as she assembled a chicken salad sandwich. "Detective Ashburton and I did, however, agree that you can have your DVD player and screen back. They're in the dining room."

"Excellent," Donald said. "Why don't we use the music room? The chairs in there can be arranged so everyone can face the screen. Smithers, I mean Billy, can you set it up for us?"

"Sure," Billy said, as I got the DVD of *Murder by Decree* out of the bag I'd used to bring props from the store.

Lunch served, guests departed, Jayne swung into action. She had a leg of lamb marinating in the fridge and she gave it a stir. The first course would be a clear consommé served with Jayne-made dinner rolls; the fish course, smoked salmon crostini; then the lamb with roasted potatoes and root vegetables, followed by a traditional English trifle and shortbread.

Jayne's interpretation of a Victorian meal.

She assigned Donald to peel the potatoes and carrots and me to set the table. Detective Estrada, having finished her sandwich, perched on a stool with her police radio on the counter next to her, munched on a coconut cupcake, and watched us work. Irene had somehow managed to slip away before I could catch her and get her to help.

"You can wash up the lunch dishes," I said to Detective Estrada.

"I'm already working, thanks, Gemma. It's my job to watch you and Jayne."

"Can't you do two things at once?"

"Not those two things."

Donald scraped his potato peeler across a potato, said "ow," and studied the tip of his finger.

"Oh, for heaven's sake," Estrada said. "I don't want to have to do an emergency run to the hospital. Donald, hand me that thing. You can wash the lunch dishes." She took off her leather jacket and draped it across the back of a stool.

Trying not to chuckle too loudly, I went into the dining room to start laying the table. I heard voices in the front hall and stuck my head around the corner.

Irene and Kyle stood together at the bottom of the stairs. "Interesting furniture in my room." Kyle laid a hand on her arm. "How about I come up and see yours? Only because of my intense interest in period furniture, you understand."

She plucked the hand off. "Kyle, I understand exactly what you're saying."

"Everything okay here?" I asked.

Irene turned to me with a relieved smile. "Perfectly okay, thanks, Gemma. I was telling Kyle here to run along and play. By himself."

He touched one finger to his forehead, gave her a wink, threw me a wicked grin, and took the stairs two at a time.

"Problem?" I asked Irene.

"Nah. He's harmless. He's the type who flirts because he thinks it's expected of him. Annoying, but nothing more. I suspect if he ever catches a woman, he doesn't quite know what do to with her."

"I don't know about that, but if you say so . . . What are you up to for the rest of the day?"

"I thought I'd go for a walk. I might wander down to the property line and ask the cops if they're finding anything of interest."

"I'm sure they'll tell you."

"I heard they've closed the front gate and put a guard on it. To keep away the curious members of the public and the fourth estate. Good thing I find myself on the right side of that line."

"I thought you might be taking your leave of us."

"Ha! Anything but. This is a hot story, Gemma. Wealthy New York City philanthropist murdered at Suffolk Gardens House. Your intrepid reporter is not only on the scene, but part of the weekend house party." She rubbed her hands together. "It's the scoop of a lifetime."

"Except for the small matter that the police haven't yet ascertained whether or not it was a murder."

"Sure it was, and you know it. You were a witness. I need to interview you."

I gave her a look.

"Jayne then."

"Don't you dare."

"Can't blame a girl for trying, Gemma."

"Yes, I can. And I will if you badger Jayne." I kept my eyes fixed on her face. Irene was a good friend to Jayne and me, but she was, above all, a newspaper reporter.

She had the grace to flush and look away. "I figured I'd stay another night as long as the others are. Who knows what confessions might come out over dinner? Besides, I never pass up an offer of Jayne's cooking."

"How's your room?" I asked.

"It's great. Spacious, with a big four-poster bed, a writing desk, chaise longue, and adjoining bathroom. I assume Arthur was to be the guest of honor, so I got the best guest room. Lucky me." Her eyes narrowed. "Why are you asking?"

I shrugged nonchalantly. "I overheard someone saying the house has poltergeists. That some of their things had been moved."

"Surely you, of all people, don't believe that rubbish?"

"Just asking."

* * *

I've seen *Murder by Decree* several times. It's one of my favorite Holmes movies: absolutely dripping with atmosphere and an increasing sense of dread as Holmes and Watson participate in the hunt for Jack the Ripper. I joined the others in the music room at four thirty for the viewing, but as much as I like the movie, I didn't pay a great deal of attention to what was happening on screen. Instead I watched the audience in the flickering light.

Miranda had not come down, and I'd gone up to her room under the pretense of checking that she was okay. She yelled at me through the closed door to go away as she was taking a nap. The rest of the party were here.

My initial impression was that no one, with the exception of Annie and Jennifer, was particularly upset at the death of our host. Whether they didn't like him, or didn't know him all that well, I couldn't tell.

The centerpiece of the music room was a grand piano. The walls were painted Wedgwood blue, and the chairs, carpets, and drapes patterned in matching blue and yellow. The art was mass-produced prints of English masters, Gainsborough portraits and Constable landscapes, in ornate, but dusty, gilt frames. When I came in, the drapes had been closed and the round center table pushed up against the wall so the chairs could be lined in rows facing the portable screen. A side table had been pulled in front of the screen, and Billy had set the DVD player on it to project the image. I didn't see any signs of the sound system that had been used to play the music I'd heard earlier, and I assumed it resided in the cabinet on which glasses, a bottle of wine in a cooler, and several beer bottles, both opened and not, now rested. I wasn't sure why we were bothering with a formal time to gather for predinner drinks later as many of the guests, not to mention the former staff, were now happily helping themselves.

Donald had taken a chair next to Steve, and they carried on a steady commentary with each other on their favorite parts, repeating lines along with Christopher Plummer, James Mason, and the other actors. Kyle and Billy watched the movie with one eye, while keeping the other on the screens of their phones. Irene, Annie, and Cliff seemed to be enjoying it, but Jennifer was fidgety: she couldn't settle in her seat. She kept shifting position, and constantly tugged at the hem of the arms of her baggy sweater and twisted the fabric around and around her fingers.

Not wanting to make herself too comfortable in the soft damask-covered chairs, Estrada had carried a straight-backed chair in from the dining room and put it at the back of the room. She turned down the police radio stuffed into her pocket, but the annoying sound of static burst through every now and again. Officers were still outside, poking through the undergrowth, studying the ground, taking fingerprints, shoe prints, and tire treads, guarding the front door. Most of the guests had stood at the windows watching, off and on, but what was going on outside was less exciting than the on-screen exploits.

At last the movie came to a satisfactory conclusion. I switched on the lights, and everyone began to stand up.

"Do you think there's something to that?" Kyle asked. "That the Duke of Whatever was Jack the Ripper and they hushed it up to avoid a scandal?"

"Such has been speculated," Donald said, "but never seriously. Serious Ripper scholars will tell you that—"

"There's such a thing as Ripper scholars?" Estrada said to me.

"It's still a mystery. A sensational mystery at a fascinating time in history."

She shook her head. I suppose for someone who deals in murder and mystery in real time, the details of a case more than a hundred years old aren't worth worrying over.

The guests filed out of the music room and everyone headed for the stairs to get changed or have a rest before dinner. "I'm going to the kitchen to check in with Detective Ashburton," Estrada said. "Try not to get into any trouble while I'm gone, Gemma."

"Dinner's at eight," I said. "Cocktails at seven thirty. Dress was supposed to be formal, but I don't know who's going to make the effort, so you should be okay in that outfit."

She glared at me and stalked out of the room.

I'd only been trying to be helpful.

I crossed the floor of the music room and pulled open the thick drapes we'd earlier closed to darken the room. I was in time to see a nifty little white Mercedes SLK pull to a screeching halt by the front door and a woman leap out. The fresh-faced young officer guarding the door stepped toward her and put up his hand. She yelled something at him, and he glanced around, clearly panic-stricken, searching for help.

Estrada was in the kitchen on her phone, so I decided to do what I could to be of assistance. I opened the front door and stepped outside. It was just past six thirty; the sky to the west was streaked in shades of gray and pink, and the trees lining the driveway formed dark, indistinct shapes.

The new arrival was waving a red-tipped finger in the uniformed officer's face. "I demand, yes, demand, to speak to the person in charge. At once!"

He heard the door open and gave an almost visible sigh of relief at the arrival of a higher authority. Even if it was only me.

"Hi," I said. "Welcome."

The woman peered down her nose, quite a feat considering I was standing on the steps and she was about five foot one. She was in her mid-forties, with streaked blonde hair cut in a razor-sharp line at the level of her pointed chin and small dark eyes, expensively dressed in artfully distressed jeans and a scoop-necked pink silk shirt worn under a waist-length blue leather jacket. Gold and diamonds sparkled in her ears and on the tennis bracelet around her right wrist. Her hands were freshly manicured, the long nails painted a dark red. She might have been pretty, I thought, but for the narrowness of the eyes and the thinness of her lipsticked mouth. Her entire being spoke of money and arrogance. I can tell a lot about a person from their appearance, but I try not to make instant judgments as to their character.

I decided, on the spot, that I did not like this woman.

She studied me and then she said, "I want to speak to the person in charge. Is that you?"

"Uh, no," said the young cop. We both ignored him.

I didn't say yes. I didn't say no. I said, "Can I help you?"

Standing in front of the Mercedes SLK, dressed as she was, she practically screamed money. But all of it new money. She had not grown up rich; there was far too much aggression in her attempts to push her weight around, as if fearing we'd see through her soon enough. "I certainly hope someone can," she sniffed.

"Mrs. Masterson," I said. "I'm Gemma Doyle."

"Good," she snapped. "You know who I am. Are you in charge here?"

"You might say that." I had, after all, earlier set the dining room table, and if all went well I'd be allowed to whip the cream for the trifle later.

The young officer cleared his throat. "Ms. Doyle, I don't think—"

"Oh, all right," I confessed. "Detective Ashburton has gone into town. Detective Estrada is in the house."

"Call them. The detectives. Tell them I'm here." She marched past me into the house. "I've had the worst possible news and a long drive."

I followed her. "Have you come from New York?"

"I was at a friend's place in Bridgeport when I got the call from this Detective Ashburton. I came immediately, of course. The traffic onto the Cape was a nightmare!" She stopped so abruptly I almost crashed into the back of her. She sucked in a breath, and said, "My . . . uh . . . husband? Where is . . . he?"

"He's been taken to West London Hospital."

She let out a relived sigh as she studied her surroundings. "My, this is . . . nice. I didn't quite believe David when he told me he'd found the perfect house for his Holmes weekend."

At that moment Donald, Miranda, and Steve came into the front hall. Miranda stopped dead and her eyes widened. Mrs. Masterson sucked in a breath and her eyes narrowed.

"Oh, hello," Donald said.

"Rebecca. I thought I saw your car drive up." Annie approached from the other direction, and Mrs. Masterson turned.

"Good afternoon, Ann." Her tone was polite but chilly enough to keep the predinner drinks on ice.

"I guess you heard what happened, eh?" Annie said. She'd removed the lacy cap and run her fingers through her hair and kicked off the shoes, but otherwise she hadn't changed out of the drab housekeeper costume. "We're all pretty upset. Are you . . . okay, Rebecca?"

"I will be. I haven't yet fully processed the dreadful news." She dug in her tiny Kate Spade bag and found an unused tissue. She sniffled and dabbed at her eyes, but the tissue came away dry. I'm well aware that everyone handles grief in their own way, and I made no judgment of Rebecca Masterson on that account. Not yet.

"My suitcases are in the car. See to them, will you, Ann. If the house is full, I'll take David's room." She glanced quickly at Miranda and added, "I assume that room's free."

"It is, far as I know," Miranda said.

Annie looked like she was about to say something, but she bit her tongue, and said, "I'll bring your bags up."

"Why don't I show you the way?" I said. "We're having drinks in the drawing room at seven thirty and dinner at eight. The group thought it would be a fitting tribute to David to continue with the formal dinner."

"David was born far past his time. He sure liked to stand on ceremony," Rebecca said. "That's why he loved those old-time English people so much. I think they're nothing but dull."

"Donald," I said. "Would you mind helping Annie with the suitcases?"

"I'd be happy to," my friend said.

The staircase matched the rest of the house: grand and majestic and shabby, with a heavy dark oak banister, worn and bleached red runner on the creaking steps, fading prints of eighteenth-century portraits in frames thick with dust hanging above the landing.

I led the way toward the staircase before I realized I didn't know which was David's—now Rebecca's—room. I turned around to face the people watching us. "Uh?"

"Second on the right," Annie said. "David got the master suite."

Rebecca tossed her hair, grabbed the banister, and ascended.

The upstairs hallway was wide and badly lit, the floor covered by a threadbare red carpet, doors disappearing in the distance. I grabbed the knob on the second door on the right, and opened it. Rebecca walked through, and I followed. For a bedroom, it was a very masculine room. All wood paneling and dark wallpaper, heavy furniture, deep red drapes matching the bedspread and pillows. Framed prints of English hunting scenes circa the eighteenth century hung on the walls, and a brown hobnailed leather chair was pulled up to the dressing table.

"This is rather . . . dark," Rebecca said.

"It is," I replied. This was obviously a man's bedroom. I glanced toward a door that almost certainly led to the adjoining suite. The wife's boudoir in a house in which the married couple slept apart.

Rebecca turned to me and gave me the first smile I'd seen on her. "Thank you. I'm sorry, but I didn't get your name."

I had told her, but I told her again. "I'm Gemma Doyle. I'm here to help organize the weekend."

"Oh, yes." She threw her purse on the bed. "This dratted weekend. I didn't want David to come, you know. Why on earth, I said, would he go all the way to Cape Cod when our house in the Hamptons would be perfectly adequate to host his friends, plus of course there we have the staff at hand. We haven't been to the Hamptons all season and it would be nice to go before winter arrives. Renovations, you know how it is, they simply dragged on and on, far over budget and far over time, but David said the work's almost finished." Her face settled into a deep frown. "No, that would never do, not for David. He wanted to play at being an English country gentleman, and the cost was no object. You're English, I see. I'm sure that impressed him no end."

"Not that I noticed."

She studied my face. What she was looking for I didn't know, and finally she turned away and crossed the room to pull the drapes open. The room faced west, and the dying light of the day flooded in. I stood beside her and looked out. Below us, the lawn and gardens stretched to the line of woods, the trees proudly displaying their colors. In the far distance the azure sea sparkled in the sunlight. "What a lovely view," Rebecca said.

I didn't mention the sight of a group of police officers walking slowly, examining the property line for signs of an intruder, or searching for an abandoned blowgun.

We turned at the sound of heavy grunting and the thud-thud-thud of a solid object being dragged up the stairs, step by laborious step. "Here you go." Donald wrestled a hard-sided pink suitcase into the bedroom, and I helped him hoist it onto the bed. I refrained from saying "What do you have in here, rocks?" Annie followed with a small square case of a matching color and an over-the-shoulder pink leather bag.

"Thank you," Rebecca said to Donald. For a moment I thought she was about to tip him. But she didn't.

"My pleasure," he said. "Please accept my condolences on your loss."

"Thank you."

"Drawing room at seven thirty," I reminded her. "Anyone will show you the way. You wouldn't want to confuse the drawing room with the library or the parlor or the music room or the morning room. I'll let Detective Estrada know you're here. She'll want to speak to you."

She waved her hand in the air, shooing us all out. "Yes, yes. Tell her to call ahead and arrange a time. I need to freshen up before dinner."

"I don't think it works that way," I said.

"Everything works that way, for Rebecca," Annie said in a low voice as she passed me on her way out.

* * *

But this time, it didn't work that way for Rebecca. When I got downstairs Estrada was opening the front door to Ryan. "Louise tells me Mrs. Masterson has shown up here," he said. "When I spoke to her to give her the news, I asked her to go to the police station in West London as soon as she arrived."

"I get the feeling she doesn't take instruction terribly well," I said. "She's upstairs. She plans to stay, at least for tonight. The autopsy can't be finished yet?"

"It's not. Hasn't even started, there's been a delay. I left Officer Johnson cooling her heels at the hospital. I want to talk to the dead man's wife as soon as possible."

"Shall I get Mrs. Masterson for you?"

"No. I don't want you interfering, Gemma. Although it sometimes doesn't seem to matter what I want, this time I mean it."

"That," I said, "often can't be helped." I lowered my voice. "What are you doing with the information about David's cause of death? You've kept us inside today but people will be wanting to go out tomorrow. You can't have someone absentmindedly picking up a discarded dart they see lying on the ground."

"Yeah," Ryan said. "I know. I'd like to keep it under wraps, but that won't be possible. Among other background checks, I'm trying to find out if anyone here might be their local darts champion."

Estrada raised one sculpted eyebrow. "Aren't the English championship darts players?"

"Most amusing," I said.

"I want to keep that detail restricted at least until after the autopsy. Can you do that, Gemma?" Ryan asked.

"Have you ever known me to gossip about police information?"

"Once or twice," he said.

Estrada might have muttered something along the lines of "every single time."

"Rebecca Masterson?" I reminded him.

"I'll get her," Estrada said. "Which room's she in?"

I told her, and Ryan said, "Bring her to the dining room. We'll talk there."

As Estrada headed for the stairs, I said, "You can't use the dining room."

"Why not?" Ryan asked.

"We're having dinner at eight. I've already set the table."

"Your dinner, Gemma, can wait. The dining room, Detective Estrada. Now."

Estrada nodded and ran lightly up the stairs.

"Gemma, please don't listen at the window," Ryan said.

"If you are referring to what happened earlier, I wasn't listening. I was thinking and I just happened to be doing my thinking under that window."

Ryan rolled his eyes. I stepped toward him and lowered my voice. "Do you think you'll be coming back later? I mean, tonight? We can save you some dinner."

He gave me a wicked grin. "As much as I'd like to, probably not. I've got lots of work ahead of me, unless one of these people confesses at your dinner. You'll let me know if that happens?"

"I'll try not to forget to tell you." I gave him a smile and, hard as it was, refrained from running my fingers across the rough stubble on his cheek. I heard voices in the upstairs hallway and stepped back.

"I am, however," he said, "going to suggest Louise stay tonight. I want someone here."

"I'll have you know, I have only just arrived, Detective, and I'm very tired," came an imperious voice from above. Ryan and I looked up to see Rebecca slowly descending the stairs, one hand trailing along the banister, as though she were starring in a Cecil B. DeMille movie. Estrada, usually so strong and confident, scurried along behind her like a movie extra playing the poor relative.

"I appreciate you giving so freely of your time," Ryan said. "Seeing as how I'm trying to determine what happened to cause your husband's death."

Rebecca didn't take offense at his tone. She stopped on the second step from the bottom, still shorter than Ryan but not by too much, and said, "At least they sent me a young and handsome one."

Estrada choked. I bolted for the safety of the kitchen.

* * *

"Mrs. Masterson is what I believe is called a man-eater," I said to Jayne.

"I can think of other words." Annie said. "Not suitable for use in polite company."

The preparation of Jayne's dinner was well underway. The kitchen was fragrant with the scent of lamb, rosemary, and mint. The salad rested in a huge wooden bowl, waiting to be dressed, and delicate curls of smoked salmon were laid out next to capers, thin slices of red onion, and toasted hunks of baguette. The delicate pieces of shortbread had been brought from the tea room, and the trifle was finished and waiting in the fridge. To my intense disappointment, Jayne had already whipped the cream to decorate the top.

"What's the story with her and their marriage?" I asked.

Annie sighed. "I'll be honest and say that anything I have to tell you about her is clouded by the simple fact that I can't stand her."

"I got that impression."

"Uncle David was fifty-two, but he'd never been married before. He and Rebecca had only been married a little over a year. She arrived on the scene after I moved out of his place, so I don't know her all that well. Her background's in theater. She has more than a minor amount of talent, from what I've heard, but she's so short she didn't have much of a chance of making it as an actress, certainly not on stage. She hung around the edges of the Broadway scene for years, always wanting the big break, waiting tables like all the rest of the wannabes. Which, I'm honest enough to say, includes me. She did some commercials and had bit parts in soaps, playing the cute bouncy housewife or the cute bouncy best friend, but that's about it for her career. I've never understood what she and David saw in each other. They're total and complete opposites."

"No accounting for taste," I said.

"Money on her part maybe," Jayne said. "He was rich."

Annie grinned. "I'm sure that had something to do with it. About three years ago, Rebecca's first husband died. They were divorced, but he had no family and was apparently completely friendless. He'd made a fair amount of money since they'd been married, and he left it all to her for lack of anyone else. Not one to carefully invest her inheritance so it would last into her old age, Rebecca immediately went about getting herself a place in the social stratosphere, with all the expense that involves. She quit trying to act, and definitely quit waiting tables, and hit the Manhattan party scene hard. Where she met my Uncle David."

"I wouldn't have thought of him as the party-scene type," I said. "Except for board games around the table in the library with whiskey and cigars."

"And Doritos," Jayne said. "Can't have a game night without Doritos and bowls of peanuts."

"He's not," Annie said. "They were introduced by Miranda at a fundraising function for an orchestra that his mother had been a prominent sponsor of."

My research had shown that David discontinued his family's generous donations to classical music organizations in New York City about a year ago. I wondered if that had anything to do with the interests of his new wife. "Interesting. Miranda didn't have intentions in that regard herself?"

"What?"

Jayne interpreted. "Gemma means did Miranda have her eye on David?"

Annie's grin was not friendly. "She was overheard saying to one of her friends that if she'd known David was, after all these years, on the marriage market, she'd have made a play herself."

That caught my attention: had Miranda come here this weekend in order to "make a play"? "How would you say the marriage has been doing?" I asked.

"I haven't seen Uncle David much since their wedding. I've been busy with the waiting-on-tables gig and trying to get auditions." Annie sighed. "And going to auditions and never being called back. Never mind that, even when I was living with Uncle David he didn't talk about his feelings or stuff like that. But I've picked up a few things here and there. Rebecca's time was just about over, and I don't think she has a whole lot left of her inheritance to go back to."

I was about to ask what that meant when Annie's phone rang. She pulled it out of the pocket of her housedress and checked the display quickly, almost eagerly, as though she'd been waiting for the call. Her eyes lit up and she sucked in a breath. "Oh, my gosh. I have to take this. Hi, Joshua, did I get—" She ran out of the kitchen.

I was prevented from wondering what that had been about by a loud rap on the kitchen door. My assistant Ashleigh waved at me. I let her in, and she staggered in under a load of games and puzzles. I'd called her earlier and asked her to bring some things after the store closed to replace what was trapped behind the police tape in the library. As long as we were pretending to carry on with our weekend, might as well keep the guests entertained.

"Fancy house," she said. "Nice kitchen. Hi, Jayne."

Jayne waved a big wooden spoon at her.

"Is that what you wore to work today?" I said.

Ashleigh looked down at herself. "Sure. Why?"

"You look . . . normal."

And she did, dressed in clean dark jeans, a pink knit sweater and gray over-sweater, small gold earrings, and flat black shoes. Ashleigh's clothes were usually more . . . elaborate.

"There's a cop at the gate," she said. "He called up to Detective Estrada to ask if I could come in. Everyone in town is talking about nothing else, Gemma. I'm surprised the police have let you stay."

"That's because—" Jayne began.

"Did you remember to write in the log that you took these pieces out?" I asked quickly. I didn't know what facts and rumors were spreading through town, and I didn't want to add to anything.

"Of course I did," Ashleigh said. "Come on, Jayne, what's happening?"

Jayne clamped her lips tightly together.

"What are they saying in town?" I asked.

"A lot of nothing," Ashleigh admitted. "Someone died here and the police are investigating. The *Star*'s Twitter feed said they were withholding the name of the deceased pending notification of next of kin. You can tell me, Gemma, was it murder?"

I shook my head.

Her face fell. "You mean it wasn't?"

"I mean I'm not saying. Thanks for bringing these. Don't let us keep you."

"No problem. I've nothing planned for tonight. Jocelyn told me it's an inside job. This house is for sale and the owners are getting desperate because they can't unload it, so they killed one of the renters so as to get the insurance."

"That makes absolutely no sense," Jayne said. "If they wanted the insurance, they'd have to burn the house to the ground."

Ashleigh gasped. "Oh, my gosh. That's it. The would-be-arsonist was caught in the act and killed trying to get away. Was it you, Gemma? Did you save Suffolk Gardens House?"

"It was the resident ghost," I said. "Trying to protect her home. Now, we've a busy night ahead of us. If you've nothing planned, take off your sweater and put on an apron. You'll find one behind that door. Those dishes need to be washed and the garbage taken out, and then—"

"I didn't mean I have nothing planned, Gemma. I meant nothing I can't be late for. But now it's getting late. Bye. Will you be at the store tomorrow?"

"I'll let you know."

"Okay, bye. I wonder if the police will want to search me when I leave. The cop at the gate was kinda cute."

"Bye," I said.

The door slammed behind her.

"You shouldn't have said that, Gemma, about the ghost. It will be all over town by suppertime. Which," Jayne glanced at the clock on the stove, "is about now."

"No one will believe that. Houses built in the 1960s don't have ghosts." I picked up the stack of boxes Ashleigh had brought. "I'll lay these out in the drawing room for after-dinner entertainment. Can your dinner keep if it has to? I don't know how long Ryan's going to use the dining room."

"For a while, yes. If necessary I suppose we can serve in here and they can eat in another room."

"Holmes," I said, "would not approve. On that note, I'm running upstairs to change."

* * *

113

I'd given a lot of thought, and spent a lot of time, on my outfit for tonight. I wanted to be suitably dressed for a dinner party in 1898, but not look as though I was in a theatrical costume. The dress I eventually found (the dress Jayne eventually dragged off the rack at the secondhand shop and made me try on, I should say) was a sleeveless, ankle-length, raspberry chiffon number with ruffles draped across the bodice and running down one side. I topped it with a dark gray fascinator adorned with gray lace and a fountain of raspberry-colored feathers, slipped my feet into soft gray flats, and added the diamond earrings that had been a birthday gift from my parents many years ago.

In a total breach of Victorian etiquette, I would be not only a dinner guest but helping serve as well. Shocking, I know.

I decided I might as well enjoy playing the lady guest, and so I took the main staircase rather than using the dark, enclosed servants' stairs. As I passed, I checked out the "ancestor" portraits on the landing. More mass-produced prints. I can't say I was surprised; the owners wouldn't want to leave valuable art and antiques lying around a rental house, but they still wanted the house to have the air of elegant, refined (read: rich) country living. Before coming here, I'd checked out the cost of renting the house for a week and it was, to say the least, eye-popping. Feeling quite the grand lady in my fancy clothes, I descended the stairs. To make the scene even more perfect, I was accompanied by a recording of a mezzo-soprano singing to the accompaniment of a single piano as the sound drifted through the closed doors of the music room.

Unlike a lady guest, I carried on down the hallway to the kitchen, where I found Jayne and Louise Estrada enjoying a break. A blue china teapot sat in the middle of the island, and the women had proper teacups in front of them. Jayne had brought the pots along with fine china cups and saucers and side plates for the serving of afternoon tea. Which, because of David's death, had not happened.

Jayne clapped her hands together. "You look great! I told you that dress was perfect for you."

"Who are you?" Estrada asked. "And what have you done with Gemma Doyle?"

I decided to take that comment as a compliment and I said, "Thanks. Where's Ryan?"

"We're finished with Mrs. Masterson, for now. He's gone back to town," Estrada said. "A couple of leads to follow up on."

"Oh," I said ever so casually, "what sort of leads?"

She sipped her tea equally casually. "One thing I will say for getting to know you, Gemma, far better than I might otherwise like . . ."

"What might that be?"

"You and Jayne have introduced me to tea. Before now, the only tea I drank was the cold stuff out of a can."

I repressed a shudder. "My work here is done. I can toddle off back to England content."

"Don't I wish," she mumbled around her cup.

"What did Rebecca Masterson have to say for herself?"

"Nothing I'm going to share with you. That dress is pretty impressive. You look like you should be in a movie."

I twirled around to display all of it. "As long as we're carrying on with the dinner, might as well dress the part. It smells great in here," I said to Jayne.

"Everything's so under control, I'm afraid I missed something."

"I feel rather bad about this. I'll be enjoying your lovely meal while you slave away in here all evening." Not bad enough to offer to change places, though.

"Don't worry about it, Gemma. It's not often—like never—I get to put on a formal meal. You know how much I like to cook."

"Which is why you're so good at it."

Estrada put down her cup. "I'm going to check with the folks outside. They should be finishing up about now."

"Fiona called while you were getting dressed," Jayne said once Estrada had left. Fiona was one of Jayne's assistants at the tea room. "She said they were unexpectedly busy today and ran out of almost all of the muffins and other baked goods I'd put in the freezer."

"Not scones, I hope. You can't run a tea room without scones."

"Not yet, but stock's getting low. I have to get back to town tomorrow as soon as possible, Gemma. I need to get muffins made for Monday morning."

"Let's talk about it tomorrow. If we're doing soup and sandwiches for Sunday lunch, I can take care of that and you can leave early. I'll get Irene to help, if she's still here. Otherwise, maybe Annie. Where is she, anyway?"

"She went up to her room." Jayne lowered her voice. "I don't think Annie's going to be any help this evening. I asked her to give me a hand earlier, and she said she was paid to pretend to be the housekeeper, not to work in the kitchen. She's worried she won't even get paid for that, not now that David's . . . gone. She's going to tell Rebecca she won't do the turndowns tonight, or strip the beds and do the laundry in the morning, as is apparently part of the contract for the rental, if she doesn't get paid right now."

"If my bed is not turned down when I retire for the night, I will be so disappointed," I said with a martyred sigh.

Jayne grinned, and I gave her a grin in return and went off to the drawing room. The music I'd heard earlier had stopped.

The bar cart had been set up, but Billy wasn't staffing it. Instead, he was enjoying a glass of whiskey and talking to Kyle, who had a beer. I assumed that, like turning down your own bed, drinks would be self-serve tonight.

"I'm looking forward to my role as butler this evening," Donald said.

"You look the part," I told him. And he did. The suit jacket was buttonless, with satin lapels, cut to the waist in front and draping to the knees in back, worn over a deeply cut waistcoat, a starched white shirt, and white bow tie. "That's quite the getup."

His cheeks turned pink with pleasure. "The Victorians knew how to dress for dinner. May I say, my dear, you have risen to the occasion yourself. May I get you a drink?"

"You may. I'll have a gin and tonic, please." While Donald bustled off, I looked around the room. Most of us had, as Donald said, risen to the occasion. Miranda's dress was modern and elegant, a sleek sliver sheath that showed her thin frame and long arms to perfection. A silver scarf was draped loosely around her neck to cascade down her back, and earrings of thin lines of silver brushed her shoulders. Jennifer was in an elaborate dark blue and gold gown with a deeply cut neckline, full skirt, and tight bodice. An elaborate, multitiered necklace of black pearls was around her throat and chandelier earrings with pearls and sparkling stones in her ears. She carried a lace handkerchief in her gloved hands, and as I watched she lifted it to her eyes. She'd washed her face and applied a light touch of makeup, but her eyes and nose were tinged red. She saw me watching her and gave me an awkward smile.

"I was admiring your necklace and earrings," I said.

She lifted one hand and lightly touched her right ear. "Oh, thank you. Do you like them? I bought them to wear tonight but then I started to worry they'd be too gaudy."

"They're prefect with your dress," I said, and she gave me a smile.

Irene, in contrast, had chosen an outfit of white jacket worn over a tight knee-length black skirt and a black satin blouse. Her black shoes had sky-high heels.

"You look very modern," I said. "The Victorians would be scandalized."

"I wanted to wear something different tonight, that's all."

"Good choice. I wouldn't want you to get that lovely suit you had on yesterday dirty when you help Jayne with the dishes later."

"If I must," she said.

"Oh, yes," I said, "you must."

Steve had put on a tuxedo, and Cliff wore a dark gray business suit. Kyle looked very hipster in beige corduroy trousers, brown jacket, and rumpled pink shirt. Billy, who probably hadn't brought anything else to wear tonight, was still in his butler's uniform.

In contrast to everyone else, Annie, who also wouldn't have brought evening clothes, wore a pair of pale blue jeans, a gray T-shirt, and her Doc Martens. The shirt featured a portrait of Bach.

Donald handed me my G&T and left to join Steve and Cliff. I sipped my drink—which was excellent—and watched. Was one of these gaily dressed people a killer?

Almost certainly.

By quarter to eight, I was beginning to wonder if Rebecca Masterson was going to join us after all when I felt the air move. Conversation died immediately, Billy froze in the middle of pouring himself another drink, and, as one, the party turned toward the door.

Rebecca stood there, her arms spread out, her hands resting on the doorframe. It was a dramatic pose and had the effect of drawing every eye, which she clearly intended. Her scarlet dress clung tightly to her hips before flaring out and cascading to a pool at her feet. Rubies shone around her neck and in her ears. A single red ostrich feather was tucked into the blonde hair.

She'd told Ryan she was visiting a friend when he called her with the news of her husband's death. I found it hard to believe they regularly dressed like that for dinner at her friend's house. Maybe she made sure she was always prepared.

She'd had a bath, judging by the scent of bath products surrounding her, and reapplied her makeup. But even the most skillfully applied makeup can't hide signs of fresh, deep grief, and Rebecca showed none of those signs.

"Good evening," she said. "I hope you're all enjoying yourself. I am, for those you I haven't met yet, Mrs. David Masterson."

Everyone muttered some form of condolences. Jennifer smothered a sob and pressed her handkerchief to her mouth. Miranda swept across the room in a silver river. "Darling! It's been so long. I'm only sorry it took this tragedy to bring us together again." She sounded as though they hadn't met this afternoon in the hallway.

The women exchanged air kisses, managing not to actually touch. The air between them was no warmer than it had been earlier.

When Miranda had stepped away, Rebecca said, "Please, ladies and gentlemen, continue to enjoy yourselves. My husband loved nothing more than Sherlock Holmes. I sometimes thought he loved his idol more than he did me." The attempt at a joke—if it was a joke—fell flat. "He'd consider it an honor that you continue with this weekend in the style he intended."

Donald clapped politely. He was the only one to do so, and the applause dribbled to a halt.

"Billy," Rebecca said. "I'll have a glass of wine." With that, she sailed into the room.

"I don't believe we've met, gentlemen," she said to Cliff and Steve. "How did you know my husband?"

"Always the drama queen," Annie muttered. I followed her to the bar cart, where she poured herself a hefty serving of whiskey. She added a splash of water from the jug provided and lifted her glass to me. "Cheers, as you say in England."

"Cheers." I returned the gesture. "Did you sort out your financial arrangements for the rest of the weekend?"

"After a fashion. Rebecca said I can stay in the house tonight, but people can make their own beds. I think she thinks she's being generous. I'll take what I'm owed out of Uncle David's booze and the dinner your friend's giving us. Before I came in, I set a place for me and one for Billy at the table."

"Fine by me," I said. Annie had seemed shocked and upset earlier at the death of her uncle, but now her face was clear and the redness gone from her eyes. Whether because her grief hadn't been long-lasting, or because sparring with Rebecca had temporarily taken precedence, I couldn't tell.

"I've never been in your store," she said, "but I saw it when Billy and I passed through West London on our way here. I'm not all that interested in Sherlock Holmes, I have to admit, although I pretended I was to keep Uncle David happy. Do you stock other things?"

"We have a good range of historical fiction," I said. While we made light conversation, I wondered if Annie had expectations of inheriting from her uncle. No doubt most of his estate would go to his widow, but he might have made provision for his niece, particularly if what Annie had said was true and he was on the verge of divorcing Rebecca. I glanced at Billy, huddled in the corner with Kyle after delivering the drink to Rebecca. Did he also have expectations?

If so, might one, or both, of the cousins have decided to hurry their inheritance along? Wouldn't have been the first time. Annie spoke as though she'd been fond of David, but how humiliated might she have felt here? To be paid to act as a servant while he lavishly entertained his friends?

"Did David do this sort of thing often?" I asked. "Rent a house for a house party?"

"No. Never. He saw a TV show called *Lords and Ladles*, about re-creating the menu as once served in grand Irish country houses, and that gave him the idea of having a Holmes-themed weekend at such a place. One of his Sherlock friends told him this house was available for rent and it sounded perfect." She held out her arms to indicate the entirety of the house and property. "What do you suppose this place is going for? Ten, twenty million? Perfect place for him to play lord of the manor. David wasn't much of a party guy, like I told you. Rebecca, on the other hand, lives for parties. The more people, the louder the music, the faster the booze flows, the better. She's never rented a place. She doesn't need to. She has David's house in the Hamptons to throw her parties in, that and his apartment in Manhattan. When she was in the Hamptons carousing with her friends, he was in Manhattan poring over his Holmes collection. When she put on a big shindig at the apartment, he was in the Hamptons or maybe hiding in a hotel room somewhere. When she was out clubbing, he was alone in his study with his nose buried in some journal or other."

"Sounds like a strange marriage. A marriage of opposites."

Annie lowered her glass and peered at me. "Take it from me, Gemma, it wasn't going to last much longer. No, the bloom fell off that rose mighty fast. They married hastily, and he came to regret the marriage before the end of the honeymoon. Which, by the way, was in Saint-Tropez, not exactly Uncle David's scene. Uncle David was beyond tired of her lifestyle and her histrionics and the constant whining for money. More and more money."

"I thought you said she had money of her own?"

"Her inheritance, yes, but that's running out, and fast. Her own parents are average middle-class people; they can't support Rebecca in the style to which she's become accustomed, and I got the feeling they wouldn't even if they could. The only time I met her parents was at the wedding, which was a pretty fancy affair, although far less lavish than Rebecca wanted, but never mind that. They seemed to me to be practical, sensible people. Nice people. Totally unlike Rebecca. They were delighted when she married David, and hoped she'd settle down to a quiet married life, maybe even have children if she's not too old yet, but that never happened."

"How do you know all this?"

She shrugged. "Uncle David told me. He also told me that when he got home from this weekend, he was calling his lawyers to get divorce proceedings started."

Annie was very forthcoming all of a sudden. Less than an hour ago, she'd been cagey about her uncle and his marriage, and now she was telling me all. Whatever that phone call had been about, it had been good news. Her face was animated and her eyes sparkled.

Rebecca laughed heartily at something Steve said. He beamed, clearly pleased at the reaction his joke had received.

"Looks like Uncle David's death worked out rather well for Rebecca, doesn't it?" Annie said.

Chapter Seven

Twelve of us gathered for dinner around the big table. Candles glowed, glassware shone, silverware sparkled, and the linens were ironed. The chandelier was turned down low, and the soft light hid the peeling wallpaper, the damp spots on the ceiling, and the dust on the picture frames, mirror, and the chandelier. It was a warm night, and no one had started a fire.

Donald began the evening by offering a toast to David Masterson, and from then on the mood was solemn. Rebecca was either not a good hostess or didn't want to be bothered, and without a host to lead the conversation, everyone retreated into their own heads or spoke mainly to their immediate companion.

The mood might also have had something to do with the presence of Louise Estrada, seated at the table, drinking nothing but water, speaking to no one, listening to everything.

The specter of death hung over the table; the laughter was too loud and voices strained. Jennifer sat wrapped in sadness, said little, ate less, and stared off into space as though imagining something that would never be. I wanted to know more about her relationship with David, and why she seemed to be the person most upset at his death, but I hadn't grabbed my seat at the dinner table fast enough, and instead of being next to her I was stuck between Donald and Steve, across from Miranda. Rebecca had taken the chair at the head of the table, and Annie glared at her from the foot. Irene and Billy had joined us, leaving only Jayne in the kitchen doing the actual work. That meant I wasn't able to follow the table conversation as closely as I might have liked as I was constantly popping up and down, clearing the dishes after each course and bringing in the next round. As the meal began, Donald went around the table pouring a light white wine to accompany the consommé, but he soon wasn't needed as people began helping themselves.

Louise Estrada sat on Rebecca's left. Still in her black leather jacket, she did not look entirely comfortable. In fact, she looked entirely uncomfortable. I hadn't wanted her to join us, and politely tried to suggest she was needed in the kitchen to guard Jayne, but for some reason she didn't take my advice.

I'd feared her presence at our dinner table would inhibit the free flow of conversation, but I needn't have worried. The whole thing was so surreal, the presence of an observant and armed officer of the law soon became unremarkable.

I did notice, however, that Kyle, seated next to her, subtly tried to move his chair a few inches away, and he half turned toward the diner on his other side.

Kyle wasn't fond of police officers. I could only speculate as to why that might be.

"I forgot to mention," Donald was saying as I returned from the kitchen with the platter of smoked salmon crostini, "that I

contacted the Baker Street Irregulars and other Sherlockian societies to tell them about David's death. They all send their condolences, Mrs. Masterson."

"So kind of them," Rebecca said. We were only onto the fish
course, and she was already on her third glass of wine, and that
following the drink she'd had in the drawing room earlier.

I took my seat and turned to Steve. "Are you from New York
City also?"

"Nope." He scooped up a crostini. He then helped himself to
another. "I live in Chatham."

"Chatham? You mean on Cape Cod?"

"Isn't that where Chatham is?"

"Yes, but . . . How did you know David?"

He shifted in his chair and picked up his wine glass. He took
a deep drink, avoiding my face and giving himself time to think.
Interesting. "Online. We met online. Holmes stuff, you know."

"Yes, I know."

"My particular field of expertise is the Afghanistan campaign
in which Doctor John Watson was injured."

Donald leaned toward me. "Steve's a former Marine. Isn't
that right, Steve?"

Steve bit into his crostini.

"After active service," Donald continued, "he taught at several war colleges. The Afghanistan campaigns of the nineteenth
century are critical to understanding irregular warfare in difficult
desert and mountainous terrain, and naturally as a Sherlockian,
Steve was particularly interested in where Doctor Watson might
have served and what adventures he had while he was there."

Steve mumbled something around a mouthful, and Donald
began telling me, as if I didn't know, the various theories as to

why Sir Arthur Conan Doyle first gave Watson a wartime injury in his shoulder and then it moved to his leg.

"What the heck does it matter?" Miranda said. "It's just a couple of silly stories."

Donald gasped in horror. Rebecca laughed and grabbed the wine bottle.

"Please do tell us again why you're here, Miranda," Jennifer said. "Surely not because you have anything *intelligent* to contribute to the conversation this weekend."

Miranda's eyes sparkled and the edges of her mouth lifted. She picked up her glass and held it out in front of her in a toast. "I naturally assumed I was invited to add a touch of glamour and beauty to the gathering. I mean, my dear, someone had to."

Jennifer shoved back her chair and leapt to her feet. She looked around the table, taking in everyone. Her eyes settled on Miranda. "You really are quite horrible, aren't you?"

"I try," Miranda said. "For some reason, dear David liked that in me."

Jennifer ran from the room.

I exchanged a glance with Estrada. Her eyes opened wide.

"This crostini is delicious," Miranda said. "My compliments to the chef."

"You can crawl back into your den, dear," Rebecca said. "I'm here now and if anyone's going to offend David's guests, it's going to be me."

"Have at it, *dear*," Miranda replied.

Estrada's eyes opened even wider. Annie chuckled. "Now now," Cliff said. "We're all friends here, aren't we?"

"Considering I met you for the first time a short while ago, I'd say that's still to be determined," Rebecca said.

"Rebecca doesn't have friends," Annie said. "She makes the acquaintance of people she can use and keeps them as long as that usefulness lasts."

Rebecca stiffened. "That was uncalled for."

"You used Uncle David to give you some respectability, but you soon found out he wasn't interested in being friends with the sort of people whose approval you so desperately want."

"Do tell," Miranda chuckled.

"Can I get anyone more wine?" Donald leapt to his feet.

"Won't say no to that." Kyle shoved his glass across the table.

"I'll forgive you, this time, because you were close to my dear husband," Rebecca said. "Don't let it happen again, Ann. Remember who's paying for your little walkup in the Village. Or was paying, I should say."

Now it was Annie's turn to stiffen.

"I'm glad Rebecca's here tonight," Billy said. "It's only fitting, isn't it, that she's with us as we remember Uncle David."

"You are such a suck-up," Annie said in a low voice.

Billy pretended not to hear. "Who has some nice stories to share about Uncle David?"

"He had a good collection of first editions," Cliff said. "Some of them I sold to him myself. Gemma, you and I haven't had much of a chance to talk, perhaps you don't know that I'm a dealer."

Kyle laughed.

"Antique and rare book dealer," Cliff hurried to clarify.

"Cliff has a good reputation." Donald poured the wine.

"Doyle collectables, first editions of books and magazines, some signed by Sir Arthur," Cliff said. "You might be interested in stocking some things in your store. Why don't we talk after dinner?"

I blinked in surprise. When we'd met Friday evening, when I tried to make polite conversation by telling Cliff I owned the shop, he'd brushed me aside, almost to the point of rudeness, and rapidly made his escape. David had been standing close, I remembered, and it was when Cliff realized David was listening, he'd left me so abruptly. "That doesn't sound like the kind of things I sell," I said. "The Emporium's strictly retail. We don't deal in anything collectible, other than the occasional second edition in not particularly good condition. Nothing valuable."

"For your Uncle Arthur then. He's a collector." Cliff glanced at Donald. "Or so I've been told."

"If you'd like to talk to Uncle Arthur, you can contact him when he gets back from Spain. He knows what he's interested in, and I never act as an intermediary."

"That crostini was great," Rebecca said. "It looks as though we're done. Is someone going to clear the table?"

"Kitchen's that way." Annie pointed. Both Annie and Rebecca were getting through the wine with considerable speed. Not that I was going to encourage them to slow down. Neither of them was driving anywhere tonight, and I was happy to see the wine loosening their tongues.

I stood up. "Irene, can you collect the plates, please."

She began doing so, but to my considerable surprise Louise Estrada got to her feet. "Let me help, Gemma. You've done plenty."

"How's it going out there?" Jayne asked as we came in. She'd sprinkled fresh green herbs on the gorgeous lamb and placed it on a platter surrounded by a colorful array of glistening roasted vegetables.

"The meal's going well," I said. "The conversation even more so."

"Don't think I've heard such cattiness since I was in high school." Estrada dumped her load of dirty dishes onto the counter.

"Tensions are overflowing, to be sure," I said. "In some way that's natural when there's been such a sudden death, but I had the feeling even before David died that these people don't like each other much. And that's if they even knew each other before yesterday. To stir the pot even more, Rebecca's arrived, desperate for attention and causing disruption wherever she goes."

"The husband or wife is usually the prime suspect, or so they say," Jayne said. "Is it possible she did it?"

I cradled a stack of dinner plates in my arms.

"Gemma?" Jayne said.

"Sorry. Just thinking. No, I don't think she did. She wasn't in the house, and my working theory is that it was an inside job. But more to the point, I don't see her throwing a poisoned dart through a window. I doubt she has the skill or the knowledge. But I've been wrong before."

"You have?" Estrada said. "That comes as a surprise to me. Not that you've been wrong, but that you admit it."

"Try not to drop that platter," I said. "It looks heavy."

"As for having working theories, Gemma, I suggest you leave that to the professionals." Detective Estrada picked up the lamb.

* * *

Back in the dining room, Cliff was trying to interest Donald in a first edition of Conan Doyle's book *The Case for Spiritual Photography*. Donald politely pretended to be considering it, but

I knew he didn't have the money that would allow him to collect rare books. Steve was telling Rebecca about his heroic exploits in the United States Marines, and Rebecca couldn't have looked more bored if she tried. Miranda told Irene she'd known David far longer than anyone else at the table—sly glance at Rebecca—and if the *West London Star* wanted to print a tribute to him, she'd be happy to contribute all she could. Rebecca perked up at that and said, "Oh, you're with a newspaper, how interesting." Kyle and Billy periodically checked their phones under the table. Annie scowled alternatively at Miranda and Rebecca and drank steadily.

Jennifer's chair remained glaringly empty.

I put a plate in front of everyone and Estrada arranged the platter in the center of the table. Kyle dug in first.

"Kyle," I said after he'd filled his plate and passed the platter to Miranda. "What brings you here this weekend?"

He shoved lamb into his mouth. "A free meal, what else?"

"Kyle's a dear friend of mine," Rebecca said. "I dared to hope David could help Kyle with his music career. David was interested in helping talented young people and he knows . . . knew . . . many influential people."

Annie snorted and served herself lamb.

Rebecca's eyes flicked toward Annie. "I said talented, dear."

Annie stabbed her knife into the helpless piece of lamb on her plate.

I glanced at Kyle. His hair was too long and in need of a wash, his goatee unkempt, and he hadn't bothered to put on a suit, or even a clean shirt, for this formal dinner. I couldn't see David, with his late mother's influence and his family's donations to the symphony and opera houses, being of any help to Kyle. His fingertips had none of the calluses associated with being a guitar player and he didn't have the muscular arms of a rock drummer. His hands were clean and soft, his nails cut short with no hang-nails or signs of being bitten. He probably played the keyboards or was the lead singer in a down-and-out touring band. David would have been of no help to him, even if he wanted to, which I considered unlikely.

"To make things even better," Rebecca went on, "Kyle's inter-ested in Sherlock Holmes, so I figured this weekend would be the perfect opportunity for them to get to know each other." She smiled at us all.

If Kyle was interested in Sherlock Holmes, he was doing a good job of keeping it secret. I'd be interested in knowing the real reason he was here. My first thought might have been that he and Rebecca were lovers and for some twisted reason she wanted him to meet her husband, but it was obvious that was not the case. They were not lovers and never had been. They didn't exchange what they thought were secret little glances or shy away from looking at each other. He continued to attempt to flirt with Irene, and Rebecca clearly didn't mind. Maybe Kyle was here for the free food, like he said.

I sliced a piece of lamb, added a dab of mint jelly, and put it in my mouth. My goodness, but it was wonderful, the meat as soft and rich as butter, the sauce fragrant with herbs, the mint jelly bright and peppery.

"We're supposed to be going home tomorrow," Kyle said. "Do you think the cops will make us stay?" He looked around the room, taking in the opulence of his surroundings, the table laden with food, the sideboard holding bottles of excellent wine. "Can't say I'd mind if they do."

"Good question," Billy said. "I'm in no hurry to rush away, either. I could get used to living like this." He speared a potato. "Detective Estrada?"

"Regardless of any instructions you get, or don't, from the police," she said, "as this house is rented for the weekend, I can't see the owners allowing you to stay on. Not without paying."

"Which I am most certainly not going to do," Rebecca said. "Not for you lot, anyway."

"David rented it for a week," Billy said. "Thursday until Thursday."

Rebecca beamed. "Is that so? It's such a beautiful house. I can stay on and be close to dear David until"—she dabbed her eyes with her napkin—"the police allow me to take him back to New York City to join his beloved parents in their eternal rest."

"First rule of acting," Miranda said to Steve in voice she didn't bother to lower. "Don't lay it on too thick."

Rebecca ignored her. "I wonder what they're asking for it. Do you know, Ann?"

"What?"

"Do you know how much they want for this house? To buy it, I mean. I've been thinking a place on the Cape would be nice. The house in the Hamptons is pretty small."

"Not if you have to clean it," Annie said. "But whatever they're asking, Rebecca, you can't afford it."

Rebecca smiled over the rim of her wine glass. "I'm sure I can."

"Not once Uncle David's will's been read."

Rebecca's grip on her glass tightened so much I feared it would crack. Her smile did crack, but only for a moment. She took a sip of wine to compose herself. "Mr. Morris, I didn't have a chance to tell you I like your suit. Did you have it custom made?"

Donald blushed at the sudden attention. "I had the honor of attending the BSI weekend dinner last year, and had it tailored for me then." Donald was referring to the major gathering of Sherlockians in New York City, held every January in honor of the birthday of the Great Detective.

"I had to miss that," Steve said. "Came down with a dreadful cold a couple of days before. I was sure disappointed. Some other guys with a specific interest in Doctor Watson's army career were going to be there."

"I would have enjoyed that discussion," Donald said. "I'm sorry I didn't get to meet them. Perhaps you and I can find some time later . . ."

"Sure," Steve said.

And the conversation moved on.

Once everyone's plate was clean and the serving platters decimated, I began gathering up the used dishes. I kicked the back of Irene's chair as I passed, and this time she did get to her feet to give me a hand.

"You've done a marvelous job, Jayne," I said. "Now it's time for you to sit down and relax. Did you get something to eat?"

"I made myself a sandwich. How was the lamb? I was worried it was overdone."

"Superb," I said.

"Best I've ever had," Irene hiccupped. Irene had also made free with the wine.

Jayne smiled and began loading the dishwasher. The huge glass bowl containing the trifle rested on the island, next to the plate of shortbread cut into small squares and sprinkled lightly with sanding sugar. Coffee and tea were made and laid on a tray loaded with cups and saucers, a bowl of sugar, and small jugs of milk and cream.

"Oh, no." I plucked a dirty plate out of Jayne's hand. "You deserve to sit down and have some dessert and coffee. Irene, Donald, and I will do the dishes later."

"I don't mind," Jayne said. "It's what we're being paid for."

"If we ever get paid, which might not happen. You might not mind, but I do. Come along, Jayne." I put the plate on the counter, grabbed her by the shoulders, spun her around, and undid her apron.

She didn't require any more persuading.

"You carry the trifle in," I ordered.

She did so, blushing with pride and pleasure, and Irene brought the biscuits and the dessert plates. Without David at the head of the table to announce that coffee would be served in the library, I made the executive decision to have it in the dining room at the same time as dessert, and I followed them with the tray and arranged things on the sideboard for people to help themselves.

"Thank you for the lovely meal, Jayne," Donald said. "It was excellent."

Everyone applauded and she blushed even more as she took the chair vacated by Jennifer. Which reminded me . . . "Why don't I take some dessert and coffee up to Jennifer, check she's okay?"

"She's okay," Rebecca said. "Never mind her. She seems like a drama queen to me."

If she was a drama queen, as Rebecca said, Jennifer would have come back down, eager to engage in more drama. I'd considered going up to check on her earlier, but so much was happening down here, and even I can't be in two places at once. But Jayne was here now, and between her and Irene I'd get a report on what I missed. I couldn't count on Louise Estrada to share anything with me.

I balanced a bowl of trifle, a small plate of shortbread, and a cup of coffee on a tray and left the dining room. First room on the right, Annie had told me. The one next to David's, which was now Rebecca's.

I climbed the stairs and knocked lightly. "Jennifer. It's Gemma. I hope I'm not bothering you."

"Come in," a voice called, and I edged the door open.

"I brought you some dessert and a coffee. If you'd prefer tea or something stronger, I can get that."

She was sitting on the bed, propped up on pillows, the duvet pulled up to her waist, showing the thin straps and lacy bodice of a delicate peach negligée. A thick hardcover book rested on her knees. The blue and gold dress was tossed over a chair; the necklace had been thrown onto the dresser, but she was still wearing the earrings.

The room was decorated in shades of dusty rose with light gray accents; very feminine, with gray curtains, a white dressing table with a tiny stool covered in fabric matching the curtains pulled up to it, a large antique wardrobe, and paintings of wheat-filled fields or calm seas. Two doors led off the room, apart from the one I'd entered through.

I put the tray on the dresser and carried the individual plates to her night table. She gave me a sad smile and put the book she was reading to one side. *The Life and Times of Sherlock Holmes: Essays on Victorian England* by Liese Sherwood-Fabre. "Thank you. You're very kind."

"You must come and visit my shop one day," I said. "That's exactly the sort of book we carry."

"I'd like that. Although I don't know if I'll ever want to come back to Cape Cod." She chewed her lip and looked away as tears filled her eyes. The light from the night lamp shone on the earrings, and I realized the stones were not glass as I'd first believed.

I glanced quickly at the necklace as I said, "I'm sorry for your loss."

She turned back to me. "How'd . . . ?" She burst into tears, and I awkwardly patted her hand and mumbled useless platitudes. "We thought we were being discreet," she sobbed at last.

She and David had been discreet. While he was alive. His death obviously hit Jennifer hard, harder than anyone else, including the man's wife, but she hadn't sought solace from the others in the group. She'd kept the depth of her grief to herself. Now that I was looking, the evidence was everywhere. The grief, the peach negligée, the his/hers bedrooms with connecting doors. She'd mentioned earlier that she'd toured the garden "first thing Friday morning." Meaning she'd arrived on Thursday, a day before the guests were due. As had David. They'd had pizza and wine and put the garbage into the kitchen bin.

"Had you and David been . . . together for long?" I asked.

She shook her head. I handed her the box of tissues resting on the night table beside the book, and she blew her nose with gusto. "We met a few months ago in a Sherlock Holmes online discussion forum. He was so interesting, he knew so much, Gemma! He was interested in all the things I'm interested in. We soon broke off from the rest of the forum. We were online for hours, night after night! Just talking, exchanging information and discussing theories. It was . . . it was . . . the best time of my life." More sobs. More blowing noses. More hand patting and platitudes.

"I . . . I live in Los Angeles, where I grew up. I lead a fairly quiet life, and it suits me. I'm a copy editor at a company that publishes history textbooks. I don't travel very much. I don't like airplanes, you see. David said if I took the train to Boston, he'd meet me there. I wasn't sure, at first, but the idea was so exciting. Traveling across the country by train, staying at a big country house. Like Sherlock Homes and Dr. Watson on their way to the Copper Beeches or the Abbey Grange! David was there, at the station in Boston, waiting to meet me when I got off the train. He was . . . everything I'd ever dreamed of."

"That was this week?"

"Thursday. We came straight to West London from Boston. We had the house to ourselves on Thursday, so romantic!" She colored slightly and let out a small giggle. "Not at all like Sherlock Holmes and Dr. Watson! We stopped in town to pick up pizza and wine and we ate by the fireplace in the library. We talked for hours and then we . . . came upstairs." Her sigh was full of loss and of sorrow.

"I hate to ask you this," I lied, "but did you know he was married?"

"Oh, yes. David and I kept no secrets from each other. He and Rebecca hadn't been married for long. He realized almost immediately that marrying her had been a dreadful mistake, and he was planning a quick and easy divorce. I'm not at all surprised, now that I've met her. What a horrid woman! What could he have been thinking! He was going to tell her he was leaving her as soon as he got home. We were . . . going to stay here for a few more days after the rest of the group left tomorrow."

"If you don't have a ride," I said, "Jayne or I can help you make arrangements to get to Boston to catch your train when you're ready to go home."

She lifted her head and looked at me. "Oh, no. I'm not going back to LA. I quit my job and sublet my apartment. Don't worry about me, Gemma. I'll be okay. David will continue to take care of me. He changed his will once he and I got to know each other. We knew, before we'd even met in person, that we were soul mates."

Chapter Eight

"You need to have a look at David Masterson's will," I said into the phone. "As soon as possible."

"I thought you'd decided the wife couldn't have done it as she wasn't in the house at the time?" Ryan said.

"The wife, the lover, the feuding cousins. The whole situation here is extremely odd."

"It's Saturday night now. I doubt anyone'll be wanting to talk to me on Sunday, but Monday morning first thing, I'll have a peek into Masterson's bank accounts and talk to his lawyer about his will. I can tell you that your theory's right, at least where Rebecca Masterson's concerned. She didn't kill her husband. She was clocked going a hundred miles an hour on the outskirts of Bridgeport, Connecticut, at ten o'clock this morning and pulled over and given a ticket."

"David was attacked at eleven, and there's absolutely no doubt about that. How long's the drive from here to Bridgeport?"

"Three to three and a half hours at an absolute minimum."

"I don't suppose the police could have made a mistake?"

"No, Gemma. They didn't. Can't ask for a better alibi than a traffic cop and a ticket with a time stamp."

"That's true. Which of course leads me to wonder if she was deliberately setting up an alibi for herself. Did she pay someone to do the deed while she could prove she was far away?"

"Don't speculate, Gemma. Doesn't Sherlock Holmes advise against that?"

"'It is a capital mistake to theorize before one has data.'"

"And you have not one piece of data pointing to Rebecca as the killer."

I was in the kitchen, whispering into my phone. Ryan was at the police station, following up on leads (such as the whereabouts of Mrs. Masterson around the time of her husband's death). The autopsy, unfortunately, had not happened. The pathologist's five-year-old son had broken his leg on the soccer field and been rushed to the hospital. She, inconveniently, wanted to be with him.

"Have you found whatever was used to fire the dart that killed David?" I asked.

"Yes," he said.

"And?"

"Have a good night, Gemma."

When I came downstairs from consoling Jennifer, I'd found the dining room empty, save for all the dirty dishes and glasses and piles of used linens, and the company gathered in the drawing room with the plate of shortbread biscuits and their coffee and liquors. I'd excused myself and sought privacy in the kitchen for my phone call.

I went back to the drawing room after talking to Ryan. I stood in the doorway for a moment, watching them all. Steve was bent over a jigsaw puzzle, Donald and Miranda were playing games out of the brain teaser book, Cliff was examining the collection of attractive porcelain vases displayed on a side table. Jayne, Annie, and Irene were chatting in a corner, and Billy was flipping through *Sherlock Chronicles*, about the making of the Benedict Cumberbatch series. Kyle and Rebecca sat together, not talking. Estrada leaned against the wall, watching.

"These pieces." Cliff put down the vase he'd been examining with a thump and turned away, his face a picture of disgust. "Aren't worth anything. Bunch of old junk you'd find in any cheap antique store along with the cutesy stuff Grandma collected her whole life and no one wants."

"What of it?" Kyle said. "Were you planning to steal something? You didn't expect them to leave their valuables lying around, did you?"

"No, I am not planning to steal anything. I'm simply commenting, that's all."

"You better make a note of everything in this room, Officer," Kyle said to Estrada. "In case something goes missing."

"I'll get right on that," she said dryly.

"I'm not a thief," Cliff snapped.

"Glad to hear it," Kyle said.

Cliff dropped into a chair with a grunt.

In the distance, thunder rumbled.

Donald stood up. He cleared his throat. "This evening, Mr. Masterson was scheduled to read his essay for the enjoyment and education of us all. I believe this would have been the first time the work was presented to the public."

"That might be because no one wanted to read it," Rebecca said.

"Did he show it to you?" Donald asked.

"He might have suggested I have a look over it." She yawned. "As if I have nothing better to do with my time."

Donald, Sherlockian to the core, looked momentarily taken aback. "Uh, uh. I'd like to hear it. I'm sure David wouldn't mind. I don't suppose anyone knows where it is?"

Heads shook. When Jayne and I had been in the library this morning for the meeting with David, he'd not been working on anything. Not that I'd noticed. And I would have.

"It's probably on his iPad," Estrada said. "We've taken that, and his phone, as evidence."

"I don't suppose—" Donald began.

"No," she said.

"As it happens, one person has had the honor of reading it. That person would be me. I have it." Jennifer stood in the doorway. She'd washed her face and made an attempt to tidy her hair and put her evening dress back on. She held up a sheaf of papers. "David was kind enough to ask for my opinion. My opinion is that it's brilliant. Absolutely brilliant." Her voice broke. "It's such a tragedy that he'll never again produce anything of this quality. An enormous loss to the community."

"Would you care to read it to us?" Donald asked.

"I'd like to hear it," Steve said.

"I've nothing better to do tonight," Miranda drawled.

Jennifer glanced at me, as though asking my permission.

"He wanted us to hear it," I said. Jennifer's timing was excellent, appearing at the very moment we were wondering what had happened to David's paper. Coincidence, or had she been lurking behind the door waiting for an opportune moment? I quickly surveyed the mental blueprint I'd made of this house. Jennifer's room was directly overhead. As I'd noticed more than once, this house wasn't as solidly built as it might have wanted to appear. A light layer of dust was trapped in the folds of the fabric of Jennifer's dress, and the skirt was badly rumpled across the front. As though the wearer had risen from her bed of sorrow, got dressed, and then lay down on the floor next to an air vent, ear pressed to the thin carpet. Listening and waiting for the right time to make her appearance.

Jennifer caught me looking and brushed nervously at her skirts.

Donald bowed deeply. He swept his hand in front of him, indicating that Jennifer could take his seat. Miranda closed her book and shifted over.

"I'd like to hear it," Jayne said. "Although I might not understand all the references."

"If we must," Rebecca said. "But first, I need fortification. Kyle, I'll have another brandy." She held out her glass, and he hurried to refill it.

"While you're at it . . ." Steve said.

"I'm getting myself another beer." Billy stood up and headed for the bar cart.

Jennifer stepped into the room. She stopped, took a deep breath, and said, "I don't . . . I don't . . . I won't be able to get through it without breaking down." Shaking hands shoved the papers at me. "You read it."

I took them. "If you want me to."

"Exactly what I thought," Rebecca said to no one in particular. "Drama queen." She accepted her drink from Kyle without so much as a smile of thanks. The brandy was Courvoisier, and expensive. Rebecca threw it back as though it were water. "Do come and sit by me, dear," Rebecca said to Jennifer, patting the cushions next to her. "I'm sure we can make room for that dress. I've often wondered about fashion in older days. Did they deliberately use all that fabric to make . . . already large women look more . . . substantial? Miranda, what do you think?"

"I think you should know about compensating for size, Rebecca."

Jennifer sat down and settled her skirts around her. She glanced at Rebecca through narrowed eyes, but she said nothing.

Another rumble of thunder sounded, and in the east the sky lit up.

"Big storm coming," Cliff said. "I checked the weather report earlier. Going to be a bad one."

"Good thing none of us are going anywhere then," Irene said. "This is just like a high school sleepover. Including the not very nice people. The watching cop makes a change, though." She lifted her glass in a toast to Estrada.

Irene, I thought, was making rather free with the contents of the bottle of Drambuie. She'd had a substantial amount of wine at dinner, and had enjoyed a generously poured G&T before dinner.

Donald clapped his hands. "Is everyone ready? Yes? Gemma, please begin."

Drinks refreshed, everyone settled down with varying degrees of anticipation or boredom on their faces. I didn't take a seat. The papers were folded in half, and I opened them. Ten sheets, double spaced, large margins. This should take me about ten minutes.

"A Scholarly Analysis," I began to read, "of the Character of Charles Augustus Milverton by David Masterson."

"Who's that?" Rebecca said.

"Shush," Jennifer said.

"This should be interesting," Donald said. "Milverton is one of the best villains in the Canon."

"Agreed," Steve said. "I've often thought that many other Canonical villains have been overshadowed by the not-at-all-impressive Professor James Moriarty."

"Wait until you hear what David thought about that," Jennifer said. "You'll be so impressed."

"Unlikely," Rebecca muttered.

I cleared my throat. "Uh . . ."

"Sorry, Gemma," Donald said. "Please continue."

As I read, I had trouble keeping myself awake, never mind my audience. David's writing style can only be described as drone-on. Never mind his writing style, what he had to say wasn't at all interesting. Charles Augustus Milverton appears in the short story named for him, and he is, as the others had said, a villain. A blackmailer of innocent young women at a time when upper-class women could be totally ruined, permanently, by the slightest indiscretion. David's point, if I understood him correctly, and that was not entirely clear, was that if these women didn't want to be blackmailed they shouldn't have written blackmail-able letters. So there!

I lifted my eyes from the paper and glanced around the room. Jennifer was listening to me with rapt attention, her hands clasped, her eyes glistening with tears, while next to her Rebecca studied her fingernails. Rebecca, I decided, had no idea Jennifer had been having an affair with her husband, much less that he was, or so he said, planning to leave her.

Estrada's thumbs were moving rapidly across her phone, as were those of Billy and Annie. Jayne was trying to pay attention to my reading, but she couldn't smother an enormous yawn. Irene's eyes were closed, her head lolling back. She'd fallen asleep.

The rest of the Sherlockians, Cliff, Steve, and Donald, struggled to pay attention. Donald kept shaking his head, and a couple of times he leaned over and whispered into Steve's ear.

Finally, I droned to a halt.

Jennifer broke into rapturous applause.

"Goodness," Donald said.

"What a load of tripe," Steve said.

"An . . . unusual interpretation," Cliff said.

"Thank goodness that's over," Kyle said. "Anyone for another drink?"

"Don't mind if I do," Rebecca replied.

Irene woke with a jolt. "What! What!"

Jayne stood up. "I've had a long day. Good night, everyone."

"Don't you dare touch those dishes," I said. "Donald, Irene, and I will take care of it."

"Wha—?" Irene said.

"Donald and I'll take care of it," I said.

Kyle jumped to his feet and held his hand out to Irene. "Why don't I help you upstairs? You look absolutely bushed."

"Please don't put yourself out," Jayne said. "I'll go up with Irene."

Kyle threw Jayne a nasty look. Jayne smiled at him sweetly, as she put her hand on Irene's arm. "Come along now. Time for beddie-bye." Irene struggled to stand.

Jennifer had risen to her feet and crossed the room to stand in front of Steve, hands on hips, face set into serious lines, all ready for a knock-down-drag-out battle of words. "I don't understand what you meant by tripe, Steve. Surely you'll agree that . . ."

"Breakfast will be at eight tomorrow," I announced. "And then Jayne and I are leaving. You can manage on your own for lunch."

"I thought lunch on Sunday was part of the schedule?" Kyle said.

"So was us being paid." I looked at Rebecca. "Someone's being cagey about that."

"Sue me," she said.

"That can be arranged," I replied.

She had the grace to look away. "Don't worry. You'll get your money. Eventually. Obviously, David's and my finances are up in the air at the moment. I'm confident it'll all be settled soon."

"Give it up, Rebecca," Annie said. "Admit you've run though all your own money, and you've no idea how long it'll be before you can dive headfirst into David's bank account. If you can."

I left them scowling at each other and began gathering glasses. I'd clean the kitchen out of courtesy to the homeowners, who didn't deserve to come back to their house and find the tenants had left a mess.

"Anything?" I nodded to Estrada's phone as I passed her.

"Not that I'm going to tell you," she said. "Except that Detective Ashburton has asked . . . not told, asked . . . me to stay tonight. I said I would."

"Thank you," I said.

Chapter Nine

The other half of my bed was unoccupied as Ryan had returned to town, but the idea of Estrada taking his place wasn't something either one of us were prepared to consider. So Jayne moved in with me, and Estrada settled in Jayne's room.

"Have you figured out who did it?" Jayne said as she crawled into bed fresh and sweet smelling from the shower.

I'd arranged a pile of pillows behind my head and had my iPad propped on my knees. "I won't pretend that I haven't been thinking about it, but I haven't come to any conclusions. Rebecca would be my instant first pick . . ."

"She's a nasty piece of work, all right," Jayne said.

"She's terrified."

"Her? Terrified of what?"

"Of not having any money. Of being cut adrift by her late husband. Most of all terrified of the scorn of people like Miranda. I won't say she doesn't deserve it, if it comes to that, but a life of keeping up appearances can't be fun, not for long. Unfortunately for any theories I might consider, Rebecca has a virtually unbreakable alibi." I told Jayne what I'd learned from Ryan.

"She could have paid someone to kill David."

"I considered that, but the mode of death is hardly that of a contract killer." I tapped the screen in front of me. "In my nonexistent spare time today, I've been learning what I can about deadly poisons and delivery methods thereof. There are various reptile venoms that can result in death almost instantly. Difficult to get hold of, though."

"Thank heavens for that."

"But never impossible. I'm fairly confident strychnine was used, as we initially suspected. The results of the autopsy and the tox reports will tell us for sure." Outside, rain drummed against the window, the trees nearest the house groaned in the wind, and thunder roared above our heads. "Ryan said they found the instrument used to deliver the dart, but he neglected to tell me what it was."

"How hard is it to get and use strychnine?" Jayne asked.

"Not as hard as people might think. A great many deadly poisons are readily available to anyone who bothers to do some research."

"As I learned the hard way in the Anna Wentworth case."

"Exactly. Strychnine is an extract of a plant, which is not found naturally growing in North America, but it's still used sometimes in common rodent poisons and by farmers as wild animal control, although that habit is highly frowned upon and increasingly restricted."

"Why not just shoot David through the window? With a gun, I mean. Why go to so much trouble?"

"I've been thinking about that. In *The Sign of Four*, the murder is committed in such a fashion."

"So the killer's a Sherlockian?"

"Or someone wanting to make it look that way. Plenty of people who aren't keen followers of the Great Detective know that story, it's one of the best known. As it happens, I brought a copy of that book from the shop and put it on the desk in the library."

"You think that's significant?"

"It might be, if I'd killed him. But I didn't, so . . . No, I can't see that it's anything but a coincidence. There are four novels in the Canon, and I brought the three I happened to have at hand in the shop. As far as I can determine, David was never in the British Army, never traveled to India where he took part in a conspiracy to steal valuable jewels, and never spent time breaking rocks on a prison island from which he escaped by stealing a boat. So no, just a coincidence, even assuming the method of death was chosen deliberately."

"Have you found out anything incriminating about the guests here?" Jayne asked.

"I haven't had a lot of time to look into them." I was finding it difficult to be a detective and run a catering/entertainment operation at the same time. "So far, nothing. Ryan will have learned more, but from what I can tell, these people appear to be what they claim to be. Steve doesn't have much of a social media profile, but a great many people in the world don't."

"Sometimes that's a good thing."

"So it is." I would have preferred not to have any social media presence myself, but that was impossible if I wanted publicity for the bookshop. Authors came to visit and do book signings; they often had their picture taken with me or snapped me in the background and posted the pictures on their own pages.

"Cliff does," I said, "through his antiques and collectables business. He sometimes sells to the rich and famous and wants to make sure everyone knows it."

"Reasonable enough," Jayne said.

"I found some photos of Miranda, from her days of model-ing, but she hasn't done much recently, although she was in a commercial for floor cleaner about a year ago. That has to be quite a comedown. I haven't been able to find anything out about Annie's acting career, so I suspect she uses a stage name. I can find it, if I have to, but I haven't had the time to do that yet, or to look into Kyle. Jennifer's still listed on the company web page for the publishers she told me she recently quit, and she's highly active in online Sherlock groups, but . . ."

I was speaking to myself. Jayne had fallen asleep.

*   *   *

"Dump it all on the table and tell them to have at it," I said.

Jayne lifted the red pepper frittata she'd prepared a few days earlier out of the oven, pulled off one oven mitt, and poked the frittata with her finger. Satisfied, she put the dish on the island. "We can't do that, Gemma. We've already told them we aren't doing lunch. They'll be wanting a nice breakfast."

"It can still be a nice breakfast if they have to serve themselves."

Jayne shrugged. "It's not that much more work. Besides, it's advertising for the tea room. I'm hoping some of these people will start frequenting Mrs. Hudson's or tell their friends about us."

I gave in and loaded dishes, cutlery, and glassware onto a tray and carried the lot into the morning room.

As well as the frittata, Jayne was cooking bacon and grilled tomatoes. She'd brought muffins from Mrs. Hudson's as well as yogurt and homemade granola and would lay out the scones that had been intended for Saturday's afternoon tea. Coffee bubbled in the pot and the tea (for me) steeped in a plain brown teapot. Freshly squeezed orange juice filled an attractive glass jug.

I'd woken to find the pale autumn sun touching the edges of the drapes and the space next to me empty. Jayne had risen, showered, dressed, and headed for the kitchen without making a sound. I yawned, stretched, and reluctantly climbed out of bed. I pulled the drapes back and peeked outside. The night's storm had passed and the cheerful ball of the sun was rising in the east, throwing its soft light through the line of trees, turning the colors of the few remaining leaves into fire. Below, a single police car was parked in the driveway. I squinted against the light of the sun and saw the dark outline of a person in the driver's seat. All the officers who'd been searching the property yesterday appeared to have left.

I was about to step back when a figure emerged from the portico over the front door. Louise Estrada was dressed in the same clothes she'd had on yesterday, natural enough as she hadn't arrived here with any intention of spending the night. Carrying a mug in her right hand, she walked to the patrol car and tapped on the window.

The window lowered, and she handed the mug through. Then she bent over and talked briefly with the person inside. Clearly, neither had much to say to each other as she straightened up almost immediately and returned to the house, dodging puddles that had formed overnight.

I hurried through my morning preparations and went down to find the cooking of breakfast well under way. "You should have woken me," I said to Jayne.

"I can manage, Gemma."

"You can, but you shouldn't always be the one managing. I wonder how Irene's feeling this morning?"

Jayne chuckled. "None too steady, I suspect. Louise has been in already. She took a coffee to the cop guarding the house. Another was stationed at the front gate yesterday, but he's left and the gate's been locked."

"Good morning!" boomed a cheerful voice as Donald came in. "Looks like it's going to be another beautiful day."

"You're up early," I said. "You've already been for a walk."

He grinned at me. "That's my Gemma. Holmes himself couldn't have done better."

"Jayne Wilson could," Jayne said. "Anyone can see that you've got fresh mud stuck to the tip of your walking stick and some on your shoes. You're tracking mud across the floor. You should have taken your shoes off at the door."

"You're beginning to learn Gemma's methods," Donald said. "Well done, Jayne."

I went into the utility room that runs off the kitchen and found a mop. I handed it to Donald. "As the scullery maid is busy, you can mop up after yourself."

He studied the unfamiliar object in his hands. "Somehow I imagined an English country house weekend would entail less . . . work."

Jayne and I laughed. "Be glad you don't have to get down on your knees to scrub the steps with hot water or blacken the fireplace grate," I said.

"As Jayne so astutely noticed, I have been for a walk. The storm has passed, leaving everything fresh and dewy. I fear it won't last though. More bad weather is moving in, or so the forecast says."

"What of the police presence?" I asked. "Anyone still around? Other than the car parked outside."

"Not that I saw. I might have woken him up when I tapped on the window to say good morning. I pretended I hadn't noticed." Donald hoisted his mop and left the kitchen. That cop was darned lucky it was Donald who found him napping and not Estrada.

"When that's done," I called after him, "come back and help with the food." I pulled out my phone. "I'll give Irene a call. She can help too."

"Let her sleep it off, Gemma. We're fine," Jayne said.

I put my phone away. "My good deed for the day."

*   *   *

I insisted that Jayne join us at the table for breakfast. To my surprise, everyone, including a bleary-eyed, pale-faced Irene, had come down. Donald and Jennifer were again in costume—walking suit for him, floor-length shirtwaist dress with rows of buttons up the sleeves for her—but the rest of us wore our street clothes.

We'd laid the platters of food out on the sideboard, next to the coffee and juice, and people helped themselves.

"Next time we do this," Steve said, "it would be nice to have a couple of footmen standing stiffly to attention, waiting to attend to our every need, don't you agree?"

Annie snorted. "Dream on, buddy. There will be no next time. Unless you're prepared to fund it. Are you?"

He didn't take offense. "Out of my price range, I'm afraid. Cliff, what about you? You do a nice little trade, I hear."

"Oh yes," Miranda snapped. "Cliff's antiques. It's all about business for him. Isn't that right, Cliff?"

"Gotta take advantage of every opportunity in my line of work. It's not personal, Miranda."

She didn't reply.

"I can't say this hasn't been fun," Cliff said.

"Well, I can!" Jennifer protested. "A man died. Our host died, need I remind you?"

Cliff lifted his hands. "I haven't forgotten. Other than that, it's been fun, I mean."

"And," Jennifer looked from one person to the next, "someone in this room murdered him."

No one said anything. This was the first time that word had been said aloud, but everyone had to have been thinking it. Before switching off the light and putting my iPad away, I'd checked the West London news. As Ashleigh told me, the police were reporting that someone had died at Suffolk Gardens House. They'd updated their statement last night to provide David's name, and said he was renting the house for the weekend with a "group of friends." The death was described as "under investigation." The cause of death had not been released. I studied the faces around the table.

"Don't be ridiculous, Jennifer," Miranda said. "No one murdered David. He had a heart attack or something. The police are overreacting." She turned to face Estrada. "Small-town cops have nothing better to do. They need to create something out of nothing. Helps justify their budget."

Estrada calmly ate her frittata.

"Jayne and Gemma, you were there when he died. That was it, right? His heart?" Miranda said.

"His heart certainly gave out." I spread butter and jam on a scone. Jayne made scones the traditional English way, small and light and buttery, which she served with afternoon tea at Mrs. Hudson's. I loved them.

"David was over fifty at least," Cliff said. "Goes to show, doesn't it?"

What it went to show, he didn't say.

"I suppose," Jennifer admitted. "Even the strongest of men's hearts can give out no matter their age."

Miranda threw her a quick glance. The edges of her mouth turned up and she looked at Rebecca. Her smile grew even wider. At last Miranda realized what had been going on between David and Jennifer. I was only surprised it had taken her this long. Miranda, I thought, was a woman who lived for gossip. The murkier the better. Jennifer was plain, plump, quiet, and, in Miranda's eyes at least, dull. Blinded by her own prejudices about what made a woman desirable, it hadn't occurred to her that David and Jennifer might have something in common, and that something had been sufficient to spark an attraction between them.

Rebecca tapped the side of her coffee cup with a spoon. All she'd served herself from the buffet was a small bowl of fruit. "I have news," she announced when she had everyone's attention. She paused, enjoying the dramatic effect. "I've decided to stay in the house for the rest of the rental period. Until Thursday."

"Why would you want to do that?" Annie said.

"Because I don't feel like rushing home," Rebecca said. "I'm here now and I'm comfortable." She let out a long dramatic sigh. "And, as long as my dear, dear David remains in West London, I want to be near him. The police told me yesterday they can't say when they'll be releasing his body."

Jennifer burst into tears and pulled a lace handkerchief out of the pocket of her dress. Miranda threw her a malicious smirk.

"Might as well," Annie said. "I don't have to be in New York until Thursday."

"Did I invite you to stay, Ann?" Rebecca asked.

"Nope. But seeing as how Uncle David did, and unless you've signed another rental agreement he's the one footing the bill, you can't throw me out. What about you, Billy?"

"Sure," Billy said. "I'm temporarily between jobs at the moment."

"Kyle," Rebecca said. "You're welcome to stay."

He shrugged and helped himself to more bacon. "Might as well. You got any plans, Irene?"

"Sadly," Irene said, "I have a job to get back to."

"What an excellent idea," Miranda said. "This is such a lovely house. So nice to have the enjoyment of clean country air, isn't it?"

Rebecca sputtered.

"Even better," Miranda said, "I'll be close by to give you what moral support you need in your time of grief."

More sputtering.

Miranda turned to Jennifer. "I hope you'll agree to stay on with us, dear. I'm sure you and Rebecca, now the Widow Masterson, will soon make fast friends."

Jennifer's face turned puce. She sucked in a breath. Fresh tears filled her eyes. She picked her napkin off her lap, folded it neatly, and placed it on the table in front of her. She'd loaded her plate, probably out of habit, but hadn't taken a bite. She pushed her chair back. "I think not. I have a headache all of a sudden. I'm going up to my room." She headed for the door and paused as she passed my chair. "If you're still offering, Gemma, I'll take that ride into town."

"Sure," I said. "Jayne and I are planning to leave as soon as everyone's finished breakfast and we've cleaned the kitchen. I'll come up and get you."

"Thank you. I'll be ready." Jennifer walked out of the dining room, her back straight, her steps firm, her dress swishing around her legs.

"Not me," Steve said. "I'm off home. Enough's enough."

"I'll give you my number," Cliff said to Rebecca. "If you need anything, feel free to give me a call. And . . . uh . . . when you get around to going through David's things, I'd like to have first refusal."

You can't get much more blunt than that, but Rebecca didn't take offense. "So kind," she said.

I helped myself to another scone.

*   *   *

"Friday night," I said to Louise Estrada, "I overheard someone telling David they wouldn't have come if they'd known someone was going to be here. I've been wondering about that."

"You heard someone talking about someone? May I remind you, Gemma, that *someone* didn't die. David Masterson did."

"May I remind you, Louise, that it is the small details that are infinitely the most important."

"I don't know what that's supposed to mean, but in the West London PD we look for the big details. Details like who killed Masterson. What's this?"

"It's a bowl. Our bowl. Jayne brought it from the tea room. You can put it in that box, please." Reluctantly, Estrada took the bowl out of my hands and did as I'd asked. Jayne and I were cleaning the kitchen, while Donald carried in the used breakfast dishes. Irene had avoided kitchen drudgery by asking Rebecca if she'd mind giving her a short interview about David that she could write up for the paper. The two women then adjourned to the drawing room. As they left, I heard Rebecca ask if the paper would be sending a photographer and where did Irene think the light would be best.

Estrada had avoided kitchen drudgery by simply refusing to do anything to help.

"Did you hear from Ryan this morning?" I asked.

"Yes," she said.

"And—?" I said.

She said nothing. I didn't push it. These walls had ears. If the police wanted to keep details back from the suspects, so be it.

Although I saw no reason they'd keep details back from *me*.

With Donald's help, we got everything cleaned up and our things loaded into the bakery van and were ready to leave not long after ten. As we didn't have Ryan to drive the van, Jayne would take it to Baker Street, and I'd follow in my car. Estrada had sat on a stool at the kitchen island and watched us carry the boxes and coolers outside. Fortunately, they were a good deal lighter leaving than they had been arriving. We'd left cold meats and a selection of cheeses in the fridge and rolls in the bread box so the party could make their own lunches.

A patrol car pulled up to the back door, summoned to take Estrada to the police station. She got into it and they drove away. She did not wave us a cheerful goodbye.

"I promised Jennifer a lift into town," I said to Jayne. "I won't be long."

"What's she planning to do?" Jayne asked.

"She doesn't want to go back to California, and she intends to stick around to hear the contents of David's will. She has, as they say in the classic novels, expectations in that regard."

"That'll come as a shock to the man's wife," Jayne said.

"If that's what happens. It might not. David was in his fifties and apparently in good health; he had no intention of dying anytime soon. Rewriting his will would not have been a priority for him. After I've dropped Jennifer off, I'm going into the store for the day. As I didn't know what time we'd be finished here, Ashleigh agreed to work today, although she usually doesn't on Sundays."

"You were in such a rush yesterday to hurry her out the door, I didn't get a chance to ask how things had gone Friday and Saturday."

"I wasn't in a rush to get her out the door, as you put it. She was more than welcome to stay and pitch in. If she wasn't going to do that, I didn't want her continuing to ask questions about what had gone on here and making up her own wild stories when information was not forthcoming."

"Whatever," Jayne said. "The effect was the same. She left."

"When I called to ask her to bring more games and such, she told me business had been quiet on Friday night, but busy on Saturday. Someone brought in a dog and, to the surprise of everyone, Moriarty didn't attempt to engage it in a battle to the death. The lack of my presence has calmed him down."

Jayne shook her head. "You give that cat far too much credit, Gemma. Give him another name and you'll soon forget he's supposed to be some sort of criminal mastermind."

"How about Milverton?" I said. "Has a certain ring to it."

"After the guy in that paper you read us last night? How's that supposed to be an improvement? Although honesty forces me to confess I couldn't follow David's argument all that well."

"No one could. Even those few who remained awake. Which barely included me." I stepped back and Jayne climbed into the van. She tooted the horn and drove away.

I took a deep breath. Donald had been right: the storm had blown away all the dust and stale air, leaving the morning clean and fresh. A few puddles lingered in depressions in the asphalt of the driveway or between cracks in the cement walkway, but they were rapidly drying in the sun. Instead of going inside, I walked slowly down the path. The police tape had been removed from the kitchen garden gate.

I rounded the house and approached the library windows. Last night's heavy rain had soaked deeply into the earth. If there'd been any footprints, they were gone now, but I'd checked for prints yesterday, as had the police. I didn't expect to find anything I hadn't noticed yesterday, but it never hurts to have another look. In the shrubbery a couple of small branches were bent, some snapped completely off. The evidence meant little in the absence of a scrap of torn fabric or drop of blood that might contain DNA. That someone had stood in these bushes yesterday, looking through the window, calmly and patiently waiting for the chance to throw a poisoned dart into the room, was not in doubt. I studied the distance between where I was standing and the far side of the room, where David had been. The library was the biggest room in the house. It had to be at least twenty-five feet, maybe more, from here to where David had stood as he rounded the desk at the far side of the room. As Estrada had pointed out, the English are keen dart players, but our national pastime excludes me. I've never thrown a dart in my life, but I have observed the game being played. Even in championship tournaments, the player stands about seven feet from the dart board. Any further and the dart's going to lose momentum, fall out of the air, and tumble uselessly to the ground before reaching its target.

Unless something's used to provide it with extra range and power, such as a blowgun or perhaps a bow. Ryan hadn't told me what they'd found.

I'd wondered why the killer chose to do the deed when two other people were in the library. Obviously, we would have called immediately for help, and it was possible someone would then give chase. As had happened. Wouldn't it have been better to wait until David was alone? It might have been a considerable time until someone thought to go looking for him.

Standing outside, I could see the problem. The desk chair itself was tucked into a small alcove, next to a solid bookshelf. An enormous and dusty fake philodendron stood between the bookshelf and the sliding door. The killer simply would not have been able to get a successful hit on someone seated at the desk from outside the room. They couldn't stand there all morning, waiting for David to get up and cross the room. Too many people were around, and the door to the library was visible from the walking paths and the lawn. If they'd overheard David planning to meet with Jayne at eleven o'clock, then they had reason to expect he'd stand up and come around the desk at eleven o'clock. David was a man of old-fashioned manners. He would not have remained seated when two women came into the room.

I continued walking. The patrol car was gone from the courtyard. The front door of the house was unlocked and I went inside.

Piano music drifted from the music room accompanying what sounded like the same singer I'd heard yesterday.

Footsteps sounded overhead, followed by the clunk-clunk-clunk of a suitcase being dragged down the stairs. Donald had changed into a crisply ironed pair of jeans and a ragged cardigan worn over a T-shirt that proclaimed "You know my methods."

"Off home?" I asked as though it wasn't completely obvious.

"Despite how it turned out," he said, "it was an interesting gathering. Arthur will be sorry to have missed it. Although . . ."

"Although?"

He lowered his voice. "I expected this to be a far more enthusiastic and, dare I say, knowledgeable group, Gemma. David was well known for his love of and commitment to the community. What he was thinking inviting some of these . . . less informed people, I don't know."

"I guess we'll never know," I said.

"Have you seen Cliff recently?"

"No. Why?"

"I've invited him to stay at my house for a few days."

"Why?" I hadn't noticed Donald and Cliff being particularly friendly.

"It's more like he suggested it and I couldn't say no. He's never been to Cape Cod before and is in no hurry to return to New York City."

"Don't let him talk you into buying any of his rare books or other things you can't afford."

"You're probably right, Gemma. As usual. I suspect he has reasons for staying other than wanting to enjoy a few more days of vacation." He snapped to attention and threw me a sharp salute. "Like Doctor Watson, I shall stand resolute, regardless of the temptation. I'll pop by the store in the next few days to see if the copy of *Castle Shade* by Laurie R. King that I ordered has arrived."

My phone buzzed to tell me I had a text from Ryan. "Hold on a minute," I said to Donald.

Ryan: *Still at SGH?*
Me: *Yes. About to leave.*
Ryan: *On my way. Need to speak to everyone again.*
Me: *I'll wait.*

I put my phone away. "Ryan wants to meet with everyone. I doubt that means you, if you want to be going. Cliff can find his own way to your house later. Did he drive here?"

"He flew down and caught a cab to the house. I'll stay. I'd like to be of be of help if I can. I might have observed something critically important I'm not aware of." He looked absolutely delighted at the very idea. "I'll put my luggage in the car and be right back."

He dragged his suitcase out the door, and I shut it behind him before wandering through the house. The police tape had been taken down from the library, and I slipped inside.

There would, I knew, be no evidence to be found in here. The killer had stood outside. If he or she had come in earlier to check out the room, what of it? All the guests had been free to wander through the house, and this was an interesting room.

I've never wanted to be a police officer, either back in England or in my new home of West London. When I'd last been in London, my sister Pippa had offered me a position of some importance (undefined, as is Pippa's own role) with the British government, but I declined. The quiet life suits me. I love owning my quirky little bookstore and being part owner of the tea room.

But when the quiet life fails me, as it seems to be doing increasingly often, I wish I had police resources.

My three books were still on the desk, lightly covered by fingerprint powder. I reached out my hand and was about to pick up the topmost when the bell rang, and I heard footsteps on the stairs and voices in the hall. I hurried out to find Ryan and Estrada coming into the house, trailed by Donald and Stella Johnson. Ryan was freshly shaven and his hair washed, and he'd changed into a pair of beige trousers and a blue sweater worn over a blue button-down shirt and matching tie. Estrada had barely had enough time to get to the police station before turning around, and she was still in yesterday's, and this morning's, clothes. Ryan gave me a nod and I gave him my private smile in return.

Rebecca had opened the door. Steve and Cliff gathered in the front hall, and Miranda peered down from the landing. The music stopped abruptly and a moment later Kyle and Annie emerged from the music room.

Ryan studied the watching faces. "I have further information I'd like to share with you. Where are Mr. Belray and Ms. Griffith?"

Shrugs all around.

"Jennifer should be in her room," I said. "She's waiting for me to give her a lift into town."

"I'm here." Billy appeared above us next to Miranda. "I'll get Jennifer."

"Ms. Talbot?" Ryan asked.

"I think she left," Rebecca said. "She interviewed me for her newspaper—she's promised to do a tribute to David—and said she had to be on her way."

I peeked outside. Irene's car was gone.

Billy ran down the stairs, followed by Jennifer. Ryan pushed his way through the crowd of onlookers. Estrada and Stella Johnson hung back until everyone had followed him into the drawing room.

We all took seats. Donald lifted one eyebrow at me in a question, and I shook my head. Otherwise, notably, no one looked at anyone else. These people were not friends, able to rely on one another for comfort.

Johnson stood on one side of the door and Estrada on the other. They both had their legs apart and their hands clasped behind their backs. They watched everyone, and no one returned their icy stares.

"Thank you," Ryan said when he had everyone's attention. Which hadn't been hard to get. "I need to inform you that I am investigating the death of Mr. David Masterson as a murder."

Gasps, moans, tears, shouts of "You've got to be kidding."

Ryan lifted one hand. "That is not in doubt. I have a warrant to search the rooms and suitcases of everyone in this house."

Protestations, arguments, agreements, and cries of "That's an insult."

Ryan shrugged. "Detective Estrada will wait here while Officer Johnson and I go upstairs. Before we do so, does anyone have anything to tell me? We can talk in confidence if you'd like."

"You won't need to go through my things, Detective," Rebecca said. "I wasn't here at the time of my husband's death."

"The warrant doesn't exclude you, Mrs. Masterson."

"That's preposterous. I don't—"

"Any reason you don't want us searching your room?" Estrada asked.

"I have some valuable pieces of jewelry."

"We're not going to steal them," the detective replied.

Rebecca sputtered. Ryan nodded to Johnson and they slipped out of the room.

I studied everyone. Ryan had to go through the motions, but I could have told him he was wasting his time. No one here had a set of darts, a vial of poison, or incriminating letters in their luggage. Even Kyle, who didn't care for the attentions of the police, showed no sign of being concerned at what they might find.

Cliff stood up. "I'm getting myself a drink. If you have no objections, Detective?"

Estrada shook her head.

"I'll have a beer," Billy said.

"None here." Cliff opened the drawers of the bar cart. "Nothing cold. Scotch, Steve?"

Steve glanced at Estrada. "Thanks, but no. I'm driving home as soon as this nonsense is over with."

"What makes you think David was murdered?" Jennifer clutched a pile of tissues in her hands. "I thought it was a heart attack."

"Has the autopsy been done?" Steve asked.

"Not yet," Estrada said. "But the evidence is conclusive."

"Then you should be out there tracking down the killer, not wasting time on us." Miranda pointed at me. "What about her friend?"

I blinked. "What friend?"

"The little blonde. She was in the library with David. We heard shouting from the library. When I got there to see what was going on, David was on the floor and the cop who'd been working in the kitchen was there and so was the cook."

"Ms. Wilson," Estrada said, "has been eliminated from our inquiries."

"What about her, then?"

"Me?" I said.

"Where were you when all that was going on?" Miranda asked.

I waited for Estrada to assure Miranda of my innocence. When such was not forthcoming, I said, "Detective?"

Reluctantly, I thought, Estrada said, "Ms. Doyle is not a suspect." Then she added ominously, "at this time."

"But you're saying I am!" Annie said. "Preposterous. If I'd wanted to kill Uncle David I had plenty of opportunities to do it at his place. I could use a beer myself." She headed for the door. Estrada stepped in front of it. "Why don't we wait here?"

"Because I don't want to wait here without a drink. I'll be right back. I'm not going to make a run for it."

"Glad to hear it," Estrada said, but she didn't move out of the way.

Annie stared at her for a moment, and then her shoulders collapsed and she turned around. "Whatever."

"I hope you and your colleague have considered motive, Detective," Jennifer said. "Cliff, Steve, Kyle, Donald, Miranda, that newspaperwoman, and I were invited for a weekend of comradery. We had a pleasant evening on Friday and an enjoyable time Saturday morning. Nothing at all happened that would cause someone to want to kill someone else. Nothing I noticed." She looked around the room. "Anyone?"

People shrugged or muttered "No."

I remembered that snatch of overheard conversation between David and an unknown person. *If I'd known he was coming I would not have.* If the unknown speaker or the equally unknown "he" had been killed, I might have a line of investigation. But David had died.

"Therefore," Jennifer continued, "the killer wasn't part of our group." Jennifer stood up and slowly crossed the room to stand in front of Rebecca. "You were quick to arrive on the scene, Rebecca. What do they say? The husband, or the wife, is usually the killer."

Rebecca leapt to her feet. The two women stood nose to nose. Everyone stopped what they were doing to stare. Steve stood up, ready to intervene.

Rebecca blinked first. "Get me a scotch, Kyle," she said. "It's early, but I'm not accused of murder every day. It's none of your business, but I'll tell you anyway. I was nowhere near West London when David died and I can prove it." She turned to Estrada. "I assume that's been checked?"

Estrada said nothing.

Rebecca gave Jennifer an ugly smile. "Don't try to play Sherlock Holmes. It doesn't suit you."

Donald glanced at me, and I gave him a slight nod. He crossed the room and touched Jennifer's arm. "I'm having a lot of trouble with one of those brain puzzles. Come see what you think of it."

She allowed him to lead her away. Rebecca sat down with a smirk.

All the while, we'd been conscious of sounds coming from overhead. Doors opening, floorboards creaking, luggage being moved.

Slowly, everyone settled down. Steve returned his attention to the jigsaw puzzle. Miranda picked up *Sherlock Chronicles*, and Donald and Jennifer worked at the brain puzzle. Cliff flicked through *Canadian Holmes*, not reading a word. Kyle stood at the window, drinking his scotch and looking out, and Billy leaned back in his chair, stretched out his legs, and closed his eyes. Annie paced up and down, but I didn't read too much into that. She was a high-energy person.

No, the police would find nothing in this house that would point to the killer. Whoever that person was, they were confident they'd destroyed their traces and were not going to give themselves away by an unconsidered remark or gesture.

More noticeable than what people were saying was what they were not saying. No one talked about David. I would have expected them to fill the conversation with humorous anecdotes about him and recollections, particularly by the Sherlockians, of his knowledge and exploits. But, other than the toast Donald led at dinner last night and Jennifer's outburst, there'd been barely a word said about the man.

It was like being at a visitation or funeral reception where no one knew the deceased.

Footsteps on the stairs, crossing the front hall, coming down the corridor. Ryan and Stella walked into the room.

"Thank you," Ryan said. "We're finished here, for now, and you can be going about your business."

"We're no longer to be treated like common criminals," Miranda said. "Thank heavens for that."

"Feel free to leave anytime," Rebecca said to her.

"What a charming invitation," Miranda said. "I'll stay a few more days, thank you. Love this country air."

Annie, Kyle, and Billy pushed their way past the police without another word.

"I'm outta here," Cliff said. "Donald, I'll grab my bags and be right with you."

I walked outside with the police. "You didn't find anything," I said to Ryan.

"I note that was not a question," he said. "And no, nothing at all."

"I expected you to ask them if anyone played darts."

"I considered it, but that question would be so out of the blue, it would be obvious the man's death had something to do with a dart, and for now I'm keeping that to myself. None of them were likely to put up their hand and say yes in any event."

"We've got people searching membership records of blowgun and dart clubs all over the East Coast," Estrada said.

"There are dart clubs in America?" I asked.

"Far more than I would have expected," she said. "Okay, Gemma. I hate to ask it, but I have to. Did anyone give themselves away in there? Like lift their eyebrow at an inopportune moment, revealing all to you. Did you remember that the seven fifteen bus from Boston was half an hour late last week, and thus our killer had to be on it?"

"No."

"No?"

"Which is why I didn't have to ask if you'd found anything in their possessions. Whoever our killer is, and I'm convinced that person had been in that room, they're supremely confident. And clever enough to know not to appear too arrogant about it. If you need anything from me, I'm going to the shop now and I'll be there until closing at five."

Estrada and Stella headed for the car. Ryan gave me his private smile and followed them.

I let myself into the house and went upstairs. I knocked on Jennifer's door. "Jennifer. It's Gemma. I'm ready to go."

The door opened and Jennifer peered out. "Would you mind giving me a hand?" She'd changed into twenty-first-century clothes of a loose brown pantsuit with a yellow blouse and thick-soled black shoes.

"Not at all." I stepped into the room. "Oh, you do have a lot." She needed more than a hand. As well as the hard-sided suitcase I'd seen when I was last in here, Jennifer had another one of the same size, a garment bag for the heavy period dresses, two carry-ons, a backpack, a shoulder bag, and a large purse.

A lot for a weekend.

Then again, she thought she was coming here permanently to start a new life with David. Every piece of luggage, except for the well-worn purse, showed almost no signs of wear. It was all brand new and of good quality. The suitcases still had Amtrak tags fastened to the handles.

I found it incredibly sad. I looked into her eyes, and she gave me a small smile. "Thank you for this."

I shrugged into the straps of the backpack and grabbed the handles of a large suitcase with one hand and a smaller one with the other. "My car's at the back. Have you said your good-byes to the others?"

"Why would I do that? The only one of them I liked was Donald, and he stopped in to say goodbye before he left. Him, and you and Jayne, that is. As for Rebecca and Miranda, I hope never to see either of them ever again. Cliff tried to talk me into buying a first edition from him, but when I told him I don't collect, he lost interest in talking to me. At first, I thought Steve was okay, but then he was so rude about David's essay. That wasn't very nice."

"It's okay to have a difference of opinion. Isn't that what Holmes societies are for? Reasoned debate?" I dragged the two suitcases after me. They got stuck in the door, meaning I got stuck in the door. I backed up and pushed the larger one into the hallway. I clattered and clunked my way down the stairs and then alternately shoved and dragged the luggage down the hallway.

"A difference of opinion, yes," Jennifer said as she followed me closely, too closely, down the stairs. I could only hope she was holding on tightly to her cases. "But Steve was out and out rude."

No one came to investigate what was making such a racket. The others didn't seem to care any more for Jennifer than she did for them.

"David was a genius," Jennifer said. "People often don't appreciate genius in their own time."

We went through the kitchen, spick and span, and left the house via the back door. Jennifer came to a sudden halt when she saw my sporty little convertible. "Oh, dear. Will all this fit?"

"We can make it fit," I said optimistically as I eyed the two-seater Miata not at all optimistically. But make it fit we did once I'd put the top down and tied the tower of suitcases with a length of rope I'd found in the trunk, last used to bring home our Christmas tree. I eyed the precarious stack and hoped the police wouldn't stop us on the way into town.

"Where to?" I asked.

"I don't know," Jennifer said from beneath her garment bag, backpack, shoulder bag, and handbag.

"How can you not know? Didn't you find a hotel?"

"I hoped you'd recommend something."

I put the car into gear and we pulled away. I drove slowly, taking care to avoid any bumps for fear of the suitcases tumbling off.

The gates at the bottom of the driveway were closed. I pulled up to a panel mounted on a post and pushed a big green button, hoping for the best. The gates swung open and we drove through.

"At this time of year you're probably in luck," I said. "In the summer, you can't get a room in West London at the last minute for love nor money. What's your price range? Motel? Mid-price hotel? B&B? The Ritz? Not that there's one of those."

"Something nice," she said. "I have my savings to tide me over until David's will's read and his funds released."

"My favorite's the Harbor Inn. It's a small, privately owned boutique hotel in what was once a private home, but it is pricey, no matter the time of year."

"That'll do."

I drove through West London toward the Harbor Inn. At midday on a Sunday in fall, tourists poked around the shops, or relaxed on restaurant patios, but it was nowhere near as busy as it would be in July and August.

"This is Baker Street," Jennifer said in a voice full of delight. "Oh look, that dress store's number 305. Is there a 221?"

"There is, but it's a cheap souvenir shop. If you look on the other side of the street, just up ahead, the Sherlock Holmes Bookshop and Emporium is at number 222, and Mrs. Hudson's Tea Room's at 220."

Jennifer clapped her hands. "I see them. Oh, your store looks so amazing. I love the silhouette of Holmes with his pipe hanging over the door, and look at all those books in the windows! I'm going to check it out as soon as I can. Is it walking distance to the hotel?"

"Yes." I took a quick glance at the store as we passed. Moriarty basked in the sun streaming through the front windows, his head resting on a copy of *Villains, Victims, and Violets*. Next door at Mrs. Hudson's an older man, going in, held the door for two young women coming out gripping takeaway cups. One of them thanked him and he dipped his head. In the short time I'd been away, the company hired to maintain the beauty of the Baker Street business district had dug up the purple and white petunias in the flower boxes under the windows and the pots on the sidewalk and replaced them with yellow and gold chrysanthemums.

At the end of Baker Street, I turned left onto Harbor Road and drove parallel to the boardwalk. To our right, the open Atlantic Ocean stretched into the distance. Jennifer settled back in her seat and admired the scenery. "I've lived near the ocean my entire life, being from LA. But this is so different, isn't it? The sky's different, the water looks different. The trees sure are. I've never seen trees that color before, although I've seen it in books. You're from England, is the sea different there too?"

"It can be. But this is the Atlantic, we're just on the other side of it. England's right over there." I pointed. "To the north east."

"I've always wanted to go to England. To London. I've never gone, as I'm terrified of flying, and to take a ship both ways would take more than my job's vacation time. But . . . David said he'd take care of me and it would all be okay. We were planning to go there for our honeymoon. We'd see 221B Baker Street and the Sherlock Holmes Museum and the British Library, and then go to Edinburgh, where . . ." Her voice trailed off. "Now, I'll have to do all those things without him."

"Perhaps you can go on a guided tour. There are plenty like that. You'd travel with like-minded people and see the things you're all interested in."

"That would be marvelous," she said.

I pulled into the half-full parking lot of the Harbor Inn. Jennifer struggled to throw off the garment bag, backpack, and shoulder bag, and I ran around to help her. I then untied the rope holding the suitcases in place and we dragged, shoved, and carried the lot into the inn.

A handful of people were scattered about the lobby, enjoying coffee in the lounge bar, or lingering over a late breakfast on the restaurant veranda, but at midmorning on a Sunday it was fairly quiet.

Andrea Morrison, owner of the inn, stood behind the reception desk. She spotted me and gave me a wave. I waved back. "I'll watch the cases while you check in," I said to Jennifer.

She looked around her, wide-eyed. "Oh, this place is absolutely beautiful."

It was nice, it was very nice, but I've never thought the Harbor Inn was all that exceptional.

"It's been a long time since I stayed in a nice hotel," Jennifer said to me.

"Really?"

"When I was a child we usually went camping on our holidays. The weather had to be pretty bad for my father to move us to a hotel." She chuckled fondly at the memory. "My parents still love to travel in their RV. When I was in college, I had a couple of fun vacations with my sorority sisters, but that's about it. My company has a big sales conference every year at a hotel in LA. Because I lived locally, they never paid for me to have a room."

"Go to the desk and tell her you want to check in. Andrea will take care of you. I'll wait here with your things. Uh . . . you do have a credit card?"

"Yes." Jennifer approached the reception desk, did what was necessary, and then rejoined me, gripping the plastic key card tightly in her hand. Andrea's husband, Brian, came out of the door next to the reception desk. He might have briefly started when he saw the pile of luggage, but he fixed his professional smile into place. "Allow me to help you," he said to Jennifer.

"Thanks, Brian," I said. "I'll be off now. The shop's open until five on Sundays, Jennifer, so pop in and say hi if you're out for a stroll."

Chapter Ten

Ashleigh was delighted to see me walk through the doors of the Sherlock Holmes Bookshop and Emporium, although Moriarty was not.

He hissed at me, displayed his backside, and stalked off to his bed under the center table.

I did a quick mental inventory of the shop, and was pleased to see that a healthy amount of our stock had been sold during my absence.

"Did you have a good weekend?" Ashleigh asked when the customer she'd been helping had left, lugging a cloth bag heavy with books. "I suppose when that guy died it spoiled the mood."

"It managed to put a damper on the festivities, yes. Not that most of the guests noticed, or cared."

"What does that mean?"

"I'm not entirely sure."

"How was the dinner last night? Everything Jayne was making looked fabulous."

"It was fabulous. The food anyway. Send me the details of the things you brought to the house yesterday. I'll try to get someone . . . anyone . . . to pay me for them, but I don't have much hope. Aren't you slightly overdressed today?" Ashleigh's clothes closet would put a repertory theatrical company to shame. She dressed according to her mood and the role she felt like playing on any given day. Today, she obviously felt like being a boss. Not that I, who am the boss, ever come to work in a dark gray business suit, pink shirt with gigantic floppy bow, stockings, and beige pumps.

"Overdressed? I don't think so. One should dress professionally at all times, wouldn't you agree, Gemma? You're back early."

"We decided to cut our losses and skip Sunday lunch. Have you heard anything more about what happened there?" The shop was momentarily empty and we could talk freely.

"It was reported in the *Star*'s Twitter feed last night, and a story went up on their website a short while ago. It'll probably be in the paper tomorrow. Irene wrote the story and filed it directly from the scene this morning. So exciting!"

"What did she have to say?"

"Just that the host of a Sherlock Holmes weekend, being held at historic Suffolk Gardens House in West London, had died and the police were on the scene. Nothing specific. She interviewed the dead man's wife and some of the guests but they had nothing to say except it came as a complete shock. I didn't see mention of your name. Or Jayne's."

"Irene knows better. She didn't say anything about cause of death?"

"No. She said the police are not commenting at this time. The man was in his fifties and in good health. That kinda implies he was murdered, doesn't it?"

"Not necessarily. Accidents happen. Health problems can go undetected no matter what one's age."

"Yeah," Ashleigh said. "I thought so. He was murdered."

The chimes over the door tinkled, Ashleigh put on a welcoming smile, and we both went to work.

Moriarty continued to sulk.

*   *   *

At four o'clock, Fiona closed the sliding door joining the Emporium and Mrs. Hudson's, and she and Jocelyn began stacking chairs on tables prior to sweeping the floor. Jayne didn't appear, but she'd told me she had a lot of work to do tonight to replenish the fridge and the baking tins to be ready for opening on Monday. I'd popped into her kitchen in the middle of the afternoon to check on her, still concerned that she might have a delayed reaction to witnessing David's death. She'd seemed perky enough and I hadn't pressed the point.

I had, however, texted Andy to tell him to look after her.

Andy: *Need you ask?*
Me: *Makes me feel better*
Andy: ☺

Business in the shop was quiet over the hour before closing. At four thirty, Ashleigh began to prepare to leave. Moriarty had eventually come out of his self-imposed quarantine to greet customers. Moriarty was generally an excellent shop's cat. He didn't care much for dogs, but otherwise he greeted our customers, particularly children, warmly and with guarded affection.

It was only me he didn't like. I try not to take it too personally. Other animals seem to like me okay. I have two dogs, who like me a great deal.

At least they pretend to like me. Maybe they don't, but they know who fills their food bowls. I'd never looked at it that way before. I'd only been away two nights, but I found myself looking forward to seeing to Violet and Peony. Had they missed me and were eager to go home or had they regarded the time at Leslie's as we would a vacation at a luxury hotel? Would I have to drag them, kicking and screaming, all the way home?

"I loved your story for the online news," Ashleigh said, and I turned to see Irene coming through the door.

"Thanks," Irene said.

"Have you learned anything new?" Ashleigh asked. "Can I get a sneak peek at tomorrow's paper?"

"No," Irene said.

"Okay," Ashleigh said cheerfully. "Night, Gemma. See you tomorrow."

"Why's she dressed like that?" Irene said to me once Ashleigh was skipping happily down Baker Street. "Is she going to a funeral?"

"Don't ask. What's up? Any breaking developments in the story?"

"You'd know better than me. My sources called to say the police arrived right after I'd left and searched everyone's room, but they didn't say what they were looking for. Are you going to tell me what they learned that caused them to do that?"

"Is Sherlock Holmes a Russian spy? No."

Moriarty leapt onto the counter and rubbed his body against Irene's arm. "Hello there, big boy," she cooed. "You're looking particularly handsome today, you lovely fellow." She stroked him and he purred. "My bad luck. I left earlier than I should have because I was beginning to fear I'd grow old listening to Rebecca prattle on about herself, except for the odd moment when she remembered we were supposed to be talking about David."

"Did you get the sense she was genuinely grieving, and hiding her feelings under her chatter?"

"That's a good question." Irene thought for a few moments. "A couple of times, she did have to stop and collect herself, and I might have seen a trace of sadness in her eyes. Thing is, Gemma, my take on Rebecca is she's so self-absorbed that she hasn't got the mental capacity to care for anyone else, even someone she might love."

"That's a good insight." To me, the fact that Rebecca moved into David's room and happily stayed in the house where he died indicated his death had little emotional impact on her. But, as I've observed before, we all grieve in our own way.

"I went straight home and filed a preliminary story for the online news. I called Ryan, but he had nothing to share with the press."

"No surprise there."

"He did say the police continue to investigate, which means he thinks it's a suspicious death. My inside source at the house, who's Miranda in case you're wondering, said Ryan told them they were treating David's death as a murder."

I nodded.

"You don't want to tell me what the police are thinking, but you can tell me what you're thinking."

"I can't help you, Irene. I don't have any insights into this case at all."

"You were there, Gemma, in the library when David died. I know you saw something. You bolted out of the house leaving Jayne to call for help."

"Irene, you can ask all you want. You can keep asking. But I'm not going to tell you anything."

"Can't blame a girl for trying. Can you, Moriarty?" she asked the cat. "I do have something to tell you."

"Are you talking to Moriarty or to me?" I asked.

"Sometimes I think I'll get more information out of him. I won't even ask for an exchange of information. I got a strange, very strange, phone call about twenty minutes ago. A gentleman by the name of Daniel Steiner, who . . ."

"Is the owner of Suffolk Gardens House."

"The very one. He asked me to keep his house's name and location out of the papers. I said it was too late, the story was out there. All the neighbors saw the police activity, and West London's a small town. Word gets around, and Suffolk House has always been a place of interest. He didn't like hearing that."

"That's understandable. He's trying to sell the house. News that a murder might have been committed there won't help."

"So it is murder!"

"I said might. That's what he's thinking anyway."

"Thing is, Gemma, he implied, strongly, that things can go wrong for me if I mention the property again."

My ears pricked up. "What sort of things?"

"He knows people. People who know people—"

"Sounds like lyrics to a song."

"I'm not joking. And neither was he. Influential people in the world of print media."

"Did he say that?"

"Yes, that and more. The *West London Star*, like community papers everywhere, is barely breaking even these days. It would be too bad, Steiner said, if the owner found himself unable to continue funding the paper due to an abrupt drop in advertising revenue."

Moriarty hissed, and I leaned back against the counter. "Nasty. What are you going to do?"

"Tomorrow morning, I'll take it to my editor. He can decide. I might be a firm believer in the independence of the press, but this is above my pay grade."

"You'd censor a story because of a threat?"

"Not censor. We can say prominent West London estate, rather than Suffolk Gardens House."

"Sounds like censoring to me."

"Yeah. It does. If he'd threatened me alone, then it would be my decision, Gemma. But he threatened the existence of the paper itself."

"Do you know anything about this person? Does he have the sort of contacts he's implying he does?"

Irene's face twisted. "Some reporter I am. I didn't even check, I came straight here to talk to you."

"It wouldn't hurt to see what you can find. Maybe he's bluffing. Maybe you can counterattack with a headline in the size of font papers are saving to announce an alien invasion. Something like 'Did ghosts in haunted Suffolk Gardens House,' the name all in caps, 'kill a paying guest?'"

Irene gave me a weak smile. "I like the way you think, Gemma Doyle. I'll let you know what I find." She glanced around the store.

"Are you looking for something?"

"I'm thinking a deerstalker cap would be appropriate to wear when I'm investigating Daniel Steiner."

"We have plenty in stock."

"Then again, I don't need a hat when I have a computer. Bye, Gemma. Bye, Moriarty."

Chapter Eleven

Once Irene had left, without buying a hat, I closed up the shop and ran through the usual end of day routine, which included filling Moriarty's food and water dishes and emptying the litter box. I texted Jayne and asked if she needed anything.

Thx but no. Under control. Late date with Andy. Enjoy. See you tomorrow.

As I swept the floor, tidied the puzzle and games table, surveyed the day's sales record, and shut down the computer, I thought about Irene and Daniel Steiner. I briefly wondered if he might have had something to do with the death of David Masterson, but I dismissed that idea almost immediately. I need to avoid the natural tendency to assume that because someone is nasty in one circumstance, they're responsible for other nasty things. Although, once I got home, it wouldn't hurt to check to see if Mr. Steiner has any involvement in Sherlockian societies. Or if he'd been in West London at the time of the murder.

"Now, remember," I said to Moriarty as I let myself out the back door, "be on guard. I'm leaving my livelihood in your capable paws."

He yawned.

I locked the door behind me, got my car, and drove straight to Leslie's house to collect my dogs.

I found Leslie in the yard watching Violet and Peony romp with her dog Rufus. The dogs and I greeted each other with much enthusiasm, and I was privately thrilled at how excited they were to see me. Leslie handed me the bag containing their things. "I was distressed to hear about a death at Suffolk Gardens House. You and Jayne weren't involved, I hope. You weren't mentioned in the papers."

"Nope. Nothing to do with us."

She gave me The Look, the exact expression Jayne uses when she doesn't believe me. "Did you hear anything else, other than what the paper put online?" I asked her.

Leslie Wilson had lived in West London her entire life. She was involved in half the charities and social clubs in town, and the half she wasn't actively involved in, her friends were. She shook her head. "Nothing worthwhile. Lots of gossip, of course, including the possible involvement of the resident ghost."

"The house has a resident ghost?"

"Not that anyone heard of until today," Leslie said. "There's always been gossip about that house. Locals never being allowed inside gets the rumor mill working overtime. The Steiner family kept strictly to themselves when they were at the house, and had almost no interaction with the townspeople at all. They didn't even shop at the supermarket but brought all their groceries with them. Which didn't do much to endear them to West London merchants, as you can understand. The garden club tried several times to get them to allow the house to be part of the spring tour, and they were always politely, but firmly, shown the door. The door in this case being an expression, as they weren't invited to come around and discuss it in person. It's been a long time since the club even bothered, although they're hoping the new owner, if there ever is one, will be friendlier. How did the man die? Natural causes?"

"They're not sure yet," I said. Ryan told the people at the house David had been murdered. With the exception of Donald, who loved keeping secrets, the guests at Suffolk House this morning were not members of this community, so word might not get around as quickly as it would otherwise. Irene had been told by Miranda that the police were regarding David's death as a murder, but until the word was officially out, the paper wouldn't say it.

I thanked Leslie for looking after my dogs and she gave me a hug. "Any time. They're a joy to have. Rufus seems to like having them, although he'll be ready for a long nap as soon as you leave."

Violet and Peony leapt eagerly into the car. I fastened them into their harnesses, and we drove home.

West London faces east so we don't get the sun setting over the ocean, but when I turned into Harbor Road the dying light behind me threw shades of purple and dark pink into the clouds. I passed families carrying dripping ice cream cones, groups of rowdy teenagers, and couples with their arms around each other, oblivious to everything going on around them.

Andy's restaurant, the Blue Water Café, sits on the edge of the pier, leaning out over the water. Lights were switched on and portable heaters glowed. The deck overflowed with conversation, laughter, and the tinkle of glasses and clink of cutlery. Soon it would be time to fold up the umbrellas, bring in the cushions, and stack the tables and chairs in preparation for the long quiet winter to come.

Maybe then Andy and Jayne could get on with planning their wedding.

My phone rang, and I used Bluetooth to answer. Ryan.

"Good evening," I said.

"What are you up to this fine evening?"

"I'm on my way home. I just picked up the dogs. I'm passing the café. It's busy tonight."

"Gotta get that last dockside meal in before winter arrives."

"Great minds do think alike. That's exactly what I was thinking."

I heard his smile come down the line. "As you're on your way home, any chance of a meal for a hungry cop?"

It didn't take long for me to mentally inventory the contents of my fridge when I'd last seen it. "If that hungry cop doesn't mind a tuna sandwich and a bowl of canned tomato soup."

"I'll order us a pizza. Be there in ten."

He was there in eight. His car pulled into my driveway as I was watching Violet and Peony cavort across the lawn, checking to see who'd been on their property while they'd been away.

Overjoyed to see him, they ran to greet him, and he bent over to give them both hearty pats and scratches. They ran off once again, now overjoyed at the chance to bark at a squirrel taunting them from high in the branches of an ancient oak. Violet's a cocker spaniel, all flying ears, and has been with us since she was a puppy. She's Uncle Arthur's dog; he named her after the four Violets of the Sherlock Holmes Canon. Peony's a bichon frise, little more than a ball of curly white fur, and he's lived at my house for only a few months. I adopted him on the death of his owner, who was a keen gardener, thus his name.

Dogs suitably greeted, Ryan gave me a light kiss.

"Dare I hope you've solved the case and can spend the night?" I asked.

"No such luck. I need a break, and then I have to get back at it."

We walked into the house with our arms around each other. The back yard's enclosed and I left the dogs outside so they could run around for a while longer. After Ryan left, I'd take them for a long walk.

Ryan dropped into a chair at the kitchen table. The dark stubble was thick on his jaw, the delicate skin under his eyes purple, and those eyes were red and tired. "No sleep last night?" I said.

"Not much. I have to confess I'm here for more than dinner. Anything happen after I left yesterday I need to know about?"

"Didn't you ask Louise?"

"Louise, as you well know, is a highly competent detective. She is," he cleared his throat, "not Gemma Doyle."

"Whatever that means." Outside Violet barked, and a second later Peony joined in. A second after that, I heard the sound of a car engine slowing and then a door slam. "Hold that thought. Dinner's here."

I met the deliveryman at the door and accepted a heavy cardboard box emitting marvelous smells. Violet and Peony danced eagerly around my feet as I opened the box, put it on the table, and got out two plates and the roll of paper towels. Plus one knife and fork. Ryan eats pizza like an American, with his hands. I do not, although I've often thought it looks more fun that way. Particularly the licking the fingers part.

"They're a strange bunch." I filled Ryan in on the group's activities Saturday night and this morning. "Are you aware that Rebecca Masterson and some of the others are staying on at the house for a few more days?"

"I am. I have no comment as to whether or not I find that inappropriate. It's her business, and I get the feeling she and her husband weren't particularly close, despite them not having been married for long."

"That's my impression also." Ryan knows how I like my pizza, and he'd ordered this one to suit my taste: topped with mushrooms, onions, and peppers. He likes his with the more pepperoni and sausage the better.

I helped myself to a generous slice, trailing a long ribbon of melted cheese after it. "What's your take on Jennifer Griffith?"

Ryan took two slices. "She came all the way from California for this weekend. She doesn't fly, so she took the train, and she was planning to stay in the east for a while. She's a keen Sherlockian, and she and Donald seemed to have hit it off."

"Nothing more?"

He peered over the top of his pizza. "According to Louise, Jennifer's upset at the death of David. At dinner last night, Jennifer was the only one who appeared genuinely distressed, and that includes the wife and the niece and nephew." He took a big bite of pizza.

"In Annie's defense, she was originally upset, as you put it, but otherwise . . . Jennifer and David were having an affair and he'd told her he was divorcing his wife to marry her."

The pizza went down the wrong way. When Ryan recovered, he said, "You know this and Louise and I do not?"

"They were being discreet, in her words. In fairness, I did have my suspicious that something was up, but it was only when I was in Jennifer's room that I put together all the signs. That's what she told me they were planning at any rate. Whether David was intending to do anything of the sort, I can't say. Now, I've been wrong before—"

Ryan muttered something and took another bite.

"—but I believe Rebecca knows nothing about the situation, although the penny finally dropped for Miranda. Rebecca could barely be bothered to insult Jennifer, much less accuse her of stealing her husband."

"What's your take on the others?"

"Annie and Billy were treated as the poor relatives, dependent on Uncle David for his largesse. Annie grieved, genuinely I believe, but more than one killer has come to regret what they did immediately after doing it. Some don't regret doing the deed, but they do regret being forced into it, as they see it. Steve and Cliff weren't grieving, but I never thought they were friends of David's in the first place, more like casual acquaintances with a common interest. I don't know why Miranda was there, other than that she and David were friends of a sort, and had been for some years, I believe. She has not the slightest interest in Sherlock Holmes. As for Kyle, also not a Sherlockian in any way. He was invited to this weekend by Rebecca, not by David, as Rebecca hoped David could help his musical career. Which seems highly unlikely to me."

"You think Kyle and Rebecca had something going?"

"No, I do not. He was wary, very wary, of Louise. I'd check into his record if I were you."

The edges of Ryan's mouth turned up. "I'm doing that, Gemma, for all of them. Kyle has, shall we say, come to police attention before."

"As I suspected. I assume you're not going to tell me under what circumstances he earned this attention, so I won't ask. My overall impression, even before David died, was that most of these people didn't know each other, and if they did, they didn't like each other much." I told Ryan what I'd overheard on Friday evening, someone complaining they wouldn't have come if they'd known someone else would be there. Ryan didn't dismiss my observation as quickly as his partner had.

"You think it's possible David was not the intended victim?" he asked.

I leaned back in my chair, steepled my fingers, closed my eyes, and pulled up a mental picture of the scene in the library Saturday morning. David behind the desk, Jayne and I in front of it facing him. Him standing up, rounding the desk, coming toward us. The low murmur of conversation in the rest of the house, the creak of floorboards overhead, the drapes moving in the soft wind. "No. Unless they were aiming at me or at Jayne and missed, which isn't worth considering. Not Jayne anyway. Once David came around the desk, the view from the window was unobstructed. The killer had to have clearly seen what he, or she, was aiming at in order to make the hit." I then told Ryan my theory as to why the killer had made his or her move when other people were in the room.

I opened my eyes to see Ryan smiling at me. "What?"

"It's incredible watching you think."

"I have not the slightest idea what that means." I picked up my half-eaten slice of pizza. "Everyone thinks, Ryan. Speaking of poisoned darts . . ."

"This is confidential . . ."

"Understood."

"Only because you've helped us so much in the past am I telling you."

"Also understood. Does Louise know I know? Or rather that I am about to know?"

"She does, as does the chief. First, we easily found the probable weapon. No attempt had been made to hide it: it had been tossed into the bushes, close to but not in the kitchen garden."

"They must have tossed it as I chased them."

"There were no fingerprints on it, meaning this person had worn gloves. No prints at all, meaning the weapon had been wiped clean before being used. When we searched the guests' rooms we found exceptionally long gloves in Miranda's and Jennifer's."

I nodded. "Part of the costume. I wore gloves the first night."

"That's what I thought. Considering the time of year, anything else would have been suspicious. Several pairs of cleaning gloves were under the sink in the kitchen and in the storage closet. Some of them had been used, but it's impossible to tell how long ago. On the other hand, our killer might have simply wrapped a scarf or even the edges of a sweater or other piece of cloth around their hands."

"Miranda likes to accessorize her clothes with a scarf, and these nights are cool enough that anyone would have brought a sweater. I did."

Ryan licked pizza sauce off his fingers.

I had a brief moment of wishing I'd been the one to clean them off, before I focused on what he'd pulled out of his jacket pocket. It was a photograph of a long, thin metal instrument resembling a tube. The ruler laid beside it showed it was eighteen inches in length and about an inch in circumference.

"Goodness," I said.

"Good word for it."

"I assume that's a blowgun."

"It is."

"Excellent. All you have to do is find out who recently purchased, or had made for them, such a rare instrument."

"And therein lies the problem, Gemma. This isn't rare at all. You can buy one on Amazon for fourteen dollars and ninety-five cents."

"You can? Why would anyone want such a thing?"

"They come in all sizes and all prices. Ones this size are used for shooting birds—"

"Why would anyone want to shoot a bird?"

"Irrelevant, Gemma. They can, and are, used as kid's toys also. A set of darts comes as part of the set. We've contacted Amazon and other suppliers to get their sales records. It's possible our killer was kind enough to leave a trace of the purchase, but I'm not counting on it. Of interest, these blowguns are illegal in New York City and in California."

"Sensible of them," I said.

"Which means little, as the purchaser could have used a temporary address for the delivery or visited a store outside of those areas."

I studied the picture for a long time. "I've never seen anything quite like this before. If I had, certainly if I had this weekend, I would have remembered. The traditional English country house weekend, which David was trying to re-create in West London, Massachusetts, included a shooting party for the gentlemen, while the ladies wrote letters and then gathered for afternoon tea and vicious backbiting gossip. Sometimes the ladies ventured out of the house to meet the men in the fields for a picnic. All terribly civilized. No shooting party was planned for this weekend, which was just as well as the property's no larger than five acres and they'd have been shooting at the windows of the house or each other."

"Your point is?"

"I don't know if I even have a point. Did someone drop their blowgun into their suitcase expecting a round of shooting, and was this person so disappointed at there not being something like that organized that they took revenge on their host? Unlikely."

"Meaning malice aforethought."

"Yes. It had to have been brought with the express purpose of using it. And not to shoot birds out of trees." I picked up the photograph again. "This would fit easily into a suitcase, and could have been carried into the house without anyone noticing. Annie's job this weekend was as housekeeper and maid. She made up the rooms. You need to ask her if she saw something like this. I know you're trying to keep the cause of death to yourselves, but you'll have to ask them all."

"Louise has a copy of this photo, and she's paying a call on Donald now, then she'll go to the house. Unfortunately, we have to ask Irene also."

"And then the cat will indeed be out of the bag."

"It hasn't escaped my notice that firing a poisoned dart from a blowgun is a mighty complicated way of killing someone," Ryan said. "Why not just shoot the man or climb in the window and knife him?"

"The advantage of the blowgun, of course, is that it's completely silent. I was standing no more than a few feet away and I didn't hear anything. A knife attack can be messy, leaves traces on the attacker, and is not always reliable if the victim has time to react. David, we must remember, wasn't in particularly good shape, but he wasn't old or frail."

"Is there the possibility of a Sherlock Holmes tie-in?"

"Sherlockians can tie their hero to just about anything, but in this case the answer is obvious. In *The Sign of Four* the murder's committed by a poisoned dart fired from a blowgun."

"You think the killer was sending a message?"

"If so, the message completely escapes me. I can see no similarities of any sort between David and his circle and the events and characters in the book, and David didn't behave in any way like a man in fear for his life. Then again, the message, if there was one, was not directed at me." I closed my eyes again. "It was eleven o'clock in the morning, and everyone was up and about. The house was full, and we'd all returned from a walk only a short time before. It was a lovely day, so anyone might have gone outside again for some air. Maybe even the scullery maid, also known as you."

"And wasn't it embarrassing to have to put on the incident report why I was on the scene so quickly."

I smiled but didn't open my eyes. "Our killer carried this strange-looking weapon, the sort of thing that would have anyone asking 'What's that then?' out of the house and across the property. Don't feed your pizza crusts to Violet and Peony."

"How'd you know—?"

"I detect an abrupt change in Violet's breathing and the scratching of Peony's claws as he hastens to your side. The blowgun, therefore, must have been concealed. Carrying a suitcase or a backpack around the property would attract attention. It was, therefore, hidden in something that would not attract attention, but from which it could be extracted instantly and silently when needed." I opened my eyes. "A walking stick."

"A what?"

"A walking stick." I tapped the photograph. "This device is thin enough to slide inside a gentleman's walking stick."

"They're hollow?"

"Not normally, but they can be made so. As can the handles of ladies' parasols. Don't you ever watch historical adventure movies?"

"Obviously not enough. Okay, so who had a walking stick or parasol?"

"David himself, plus Donald and Steve had walking sticks. Miranda carried a parasol. We can't forget modern umbrellas either. It's the rainy season in New England. It rained later in the day on Saturday, so having an umbrella wouldn't have been entirely out of place. Come to think of it, Jayne keeps an umbrella in the van, although I doubt hers has been custom-made to fit a sword or even a blowgun."

"I'll send someone around to the house to look at these parasols and sticks," Ryan said.

"You might get lucky." I pointed to the picture. "But that thing is small enough to slip in the waistband of a pair of trousers or a skirt and be concealed under a loose jacket. It was not a hot day, and no one would have glanced twice at someone who'd pulled on a jacket or sweater before venturing outside. We've ascertained that the blowgun was the instrument of delivery. What have you learned about what was on that dart? We originally suspected strychnine. Was that it?"

"Yes, strychnine. Traces were found on the dart, and the autopsy results confirm it. He died, as you know, within minutes of being hit."

I took a breath. Not a nice way to go.

"You okay?" Ryan asked.

"I will be." I pointed to the photograph on the table. "How difficult, do you think, is it to use one of these things with any degree of accuracy?"

"From the quick reading I've done, not difficult at all. They're capable of hitting birds in trees, but I'd think that to hit the target spot on with one shot from that distance would require practice."

"You're looking for a man, or for a woman who has had a great deal of practice."

"Why do you say that?"

I puckered my lips and blew out a stream of air. "It would be a matter of lung capacity. Sufficient air needs to be stored in the lungs and then expelled in one great breath. No huffing and puffing. Men have larger chests and weigh more, on average, than women, so they have greater lung capacity. None of the women at the house this weekend are at all stout. Rebecca's positively tiny, Miranda unnaturally thin. Annie and Jennifer, in particular, are what's considered overweight in modern society, but that has nothing to do with the size of their frame. Did you learn anything else?"

"David was in reasonably good health, despite being substantially overweight. He was at risk of developing heart disease and diabetes, but not for some years yet, the pathologist says. And that's about it. No sign of drug use or excessive alcohol consumption. Do you want the last slice of pizza?"

"Help yourself. Have you had contact yet with a man by the name of Daniel Steiner?"

Ryan chewed and shook his head. "That's the name of the owner of Suffolk House. No, I haven't met the man. Should I?"

"I suspect you soon will." I filled him in on what Irene told me about threats to her and the newspaper.

"More complications."

I got to my feet and gathered up the dishes and the cardboard box, empty but for chunks of broken crust.

Ryan stood also. "I have to be going."

"One more quick question, If I may."

"Shoot."

"Bad choice of words. Any sign of an intruder onto the grounds of Suffolk House?"

"Nothing. The property's gated and fully fenced, but most of it's a plain wire fence, and in some places it's showing signs of wear and not being repaired. The gate was open when the first responders arrived, and Billy Belray, who met them at the house, told the officers it hadn't been closed at any time, to his knowledge."

I nodded. The gate had been wide open when we first arrived.

"If someone didn't want to chance being seen coming in by the main entrance, the fence wouldn't have kept them out, but scrambling over a fence usually leaves some signs and we didn't find anything."

"It leaves signs, yes. Signs can be erased."

"So they can, Gemma. So they can." He pulled me to him and kissed my forehead. "You take care."

"Don't I always?"

He left, still chuckling.

Chapter Twelve

"Have a nice time last night?" I asked Jayne.

"We did. Andy came around with leftovers from the restaurant. Yummy." She sighed happily. Jayne has always been a happy person, happy and beautiful. But since her engagement to Andy a glow had settled around her. At times, I felt something close to envy.

I was also feeling rather proud of myself. I'd always known Andy was the one for Jayne, and I stood patiently by while she went through one unsuitable boyfriend after another.

Maybe not entirely patiently, I had to admit. But they'd eventually found their way to each other and that made me happy too. "You sure you're okay? I wasn't with David when he died, Jayne, but you were. You toughed it out for the rest of the weekend, but these things can catch you by surprise at unexpected moments."

She leaned over the table and put her hand on top of mine. Her blue eyes looked into mine. "Thanks for caring, Gemma. Yeah, I had a few hard moments when I told Andy about it. But he was there for me, and I know you're here for me, and so I'm okay."

It was four o'clock, and Jayne and I were having our daily partners' meeting at the table in the light-filled window alcove of Mrs. Hudson's over a pot of tea and whatever remained from afternoon tea. Today Jayne had produced open-faced roast beef crostini, cucumber sandwiches, and raspberry tarts and buttery squares of shortbread.

Jayne poured the tea and offered me a cup. "Louise Estrada was in earlier."

"On police business?"

"Yes. I bribed her with tea and a scone."

"Excellent plan. What did she want?"

"She showed me a picture of a blowgun, of all things, and asked if I'd seen one like it recently."

"Had you?"

"No. I shouldn't have been surprised, but I was. I guess I assumed whoever it was had thrown the dart at David."

"The blowgun gives more strength and accuracy, if you know how to use it. I called Ryan last night and suggested he check out everyone's homes and property for signs of blowgun practice."

"What did he say to that?"

"That the police don't have unlimited resources."

"Well, they should have when a man's been murdered," Jayne said. "I was surprised you were in the store all day today. I'd have thought you'd have gone around to Suffolk Gardens and be crawling through the bushes, examining the ground with a magnifying glass, interrogating the suspects. Why weren't you?"

"Because I don't own a magnifying glass, and because the police are handling the case, Jayne, not me, and I don't think Rebecca or Miranda would be happy with me interrogating them, as you call it. We were at the scene when David was attacked, and that makes us witnesses. I'll admit to a certain amount of curiosity, and as long as I was on the property anyway, I poked around to see if the police missed anything of importance. Otherwise the police in general, and Ryan in particular, are more than capable of doing all that poking and investigating and interrogating stuff, and they have resources I do not."

"But you've involved yourself in their cases before. What's different this time?"

"In the incidents to which you're referring, I didn't like the direction in which their investigation was heading or someone close to me was under suspicion."

"Like that time they thought it was my mom, of all people."

"Or the time they, Louise anyway, thought it was me. No, this time I will advise the police if they want my advice. Nothing more."

Jayne might have muttered, "That won't last long," but I pretended not to hear and said, "Jennifer came into the Emporium earlier."

"Did she? I don't suppose she said anything about David's death?"

"We were busy at the time so didn't have a chance to talk. She bought a lot. Stacks of books, brain games and puzzles, some of the I-Am-Sherlocked mugs, and other trinkets."

"Why's she hanging around West London?" Jayne asked.

"Other than a couple of the books, she asked me to have her purchases delivered to her parents' house in Los Angeles. She walked away from her entire life in California and moved here to be with David. It might not have been a wise thing to do, and I suspect her parents told her so, not for a man she'd never met in person, but here she is. Lost and alone and lonely. I invited her to drop in here for tea after her shopping trip, but she said she'd save that treat for another time. I wanted to suggest she go back to California and try to get her job back, but I didn't think she'd welcome my advice."

Jayne grinned at me. "You're learning!"

"What am I learning?"

She was prevented from answering by the sound of tapping on the door. The tea room was closed, the last of the satisfied customers had left, and Fiona and Jocelyn were cleaning up. Irene waved at us through the door.

"Might as well let her in," I said to Fiona.

Irene dropped onto the bench seat next to Jayne. "No tea for me, thanks, but I'll have a coffee if you haven't emptied the pot, Fee."

"I'll see what I can find," Fiona said.

"Great. And a couple of those sandwiches wouldn't go amiss." She took a cucumber one off the plate in the center of the table. "Didn't have time for lunch. A blowgun. Who would have thought it?"

The cucumber sandwiches are my favorite. I love the way Jayne makes them with a touch of mayonnaise and chopped fresh herbs. I snatched the last one before Irene could get it. I said nothing.

"It's not a secret anymore," Irene said. "Ryan came around to my place last night and showed me a picture of something they found in the bushes at Suffolk Gardens. He asked me if I saw anything like it when I was there."

"Did you?" Jayne asked.

"No, and I told him so. Obviously, the police are now acting on the assumption this thing was used to kill David

Masterson. Meaning he was murdered, and somehow a blowgun was involved." She smiled at me.

I took a bite of my sandwich.

"It might not be a secret from you any longer," Jayne said, "but I'll take a wild guess Ryan told you that information is not to appear in the paper."

"Not yet, but in order to be ready when I can use it, I've been looking into those things. They're readily available and the smaller ones are sold as kids' toys. Like for shooting darts at targets." She eyed me. "What sort of a hit would you get from a toy dart that would prove fatal to a grown man?"

I leaned back to allow Fiona to put a cup of coffee in front of Irene and another plate on the table. I was highly disappointed not to see any more cucumber sandwiches.

"I know you know, Gemma," Irene said.

I said nothing.

"And if you know, then Jayne knows."

Jayne clamped her lips tightly together.

"And if Jayne knows," Irene said, "I can get it out of her."

"You can not!" Jayne said.

"So you do know."

Jayne threw me a panicked look.

"What brings you here, Irene?" I asked. "Aside from wanting a free lunch, that is."

"Would you be able to go to Suffolk Gardens this afternoon in my place?"

"Me? Why would you want me to do that? I can't. I'm busy. I have a business to run."

"So I see," she said, eyeing my teacup.

"Even small business owners are allowed a tea break once a day. What's happening at the house, and why don't you go?"

"I called Rebecca about an hour ago, just to check in. To be friendly."

"Right."

"I can be friendly, Gemma. She told me Daniel Steiner's coming around at five today to meet her and invited me to join them."

"Is that so?"

"Who's Daniel Steiner?" Jayne asked.

"The owner of Suffolk Gardens House," Irene said. "He's hoping she'll buy the place."

"She's thinking of making a major investment two days after the death of her husband?" Jayne said. "I can't see that that's a good idea."

"It's not," I said. "And he knows it, thus he needs to move fast before she comes to her senses. I'm assuming you've decided not to go, Irene, because of the threats he made against you and the paper."

"He made threats against Irene? What sort of threats?" Jayne asked.

"I'll tell you later," I said.

"I'd love nothing more than to have a good old-fashioned face-to-face confrontation with the manipulating jerk," Irene admitted. "But such might not be wise."

"I assume your editor told you to stay away from him?"

"You assume correctly." Irene bit into a tart as though wishing it was Daniel Steiner's head. Or maybe her editor's.

"Tell me about the laws of inheritance in America," I asked Jayne.

"I don't know anything about that. When my dad died, my mom naturally got everything. She didn't even get it, she kept it, because it was hers, too. I guess when she dies, my brother and I'll get it. Not that she has much to leave us, other than the house."

"It varies by state," Irene said. "I know a little about how it works in Massachusetts but not New York. What do you want to know?"

"Can a person disinherit their spouse?"

"I covered a case like that several years ago when I worked in Boston. The answer is yes, but. A married person can attempt to cut their spouse out of the will, but a wife, or a husband, has rights of inheritance. They can petition the court to have the will overturned and themselves granted an appropriate share of the estate. It's up to the courts to determine what the appropriate share might be, and that can be a complicated, not to mention potentially expensive and acrimonious, legal procedure. I assume you're asking because you're wondering where Rebecca stands."

"I am." I pulled my phone out of my pocket. "One way to find out." I called up the ever-helpful Mr. Google and searched quickly. "Seems to be much the same in New York. A spouse has rights to at least one-third of the deceased's estate regardless of the provisions of the will. However, there are always exceptions and complications and it seems as though a prenup might be able to invalidate that provision. I have no way of knowing, drat, if Rebecca and David signed such a prenup." I drained my teacup. "I will have to act on the assumption that she expects to inherit something, if not all of it. If you insist, I'll drop around to the house."

"I thought you weren't investigating," Jayne said.

"I'm not. I'm doing my friend Irene a favor and at the same time paying a friendly condolence call on the grieving widow."

"Yeah, right."

"Want to come?"

"Oh, yes."

"Thanks, Gemma," Irene said. "Let me know your take on this Steiner guy."

"I'll tell Ashleigh I'm going out for a while and meet you in the kitchen, Jayne."

Irene and I reached for the last piece of shortbread at the same time. She was fractionally faster and snatched it up, giving me an evil grin.

I pretended I didn't mind and slipped through the sliding door that joins the two businesses. "Ashleigh, I—"

"Okay. Got it. You're going out. Back before closing, but if you're not I can lock up myself." She stroked Moriarty, who'd leapt onto the sales counter in order to be party to the conversation.

"How did you know that's what I was going to say?"

"A man died a couple of days ago, and the police haven't solved it yet. Irene came into Mrs. Hudson's and you huddled together over your tea and sandwiches. I can tell when you're plotting. Can't I, Moriarty? Yes, I can."

"Uh, okay," I said. "Carry on."

Chapter Thirteen

I usually walk to work, and I had done so this morning, so we took Jayne's car. At Suffolk Gardens House, the iron gates guarding the driveway were firmly shut when we drove up.

Jayne rolled down her window, leaned out and pressed the button on the communications box mounted next to the gate. "Jayne Wilson and Gemma Doyle to see Rebecca Masterson."

Nothing happened. "Hello?" Jayne pushed harder this time. Still no response. Not even a burst of static.

"Maybe it's not working," Jayne said. "Or no one's answering."

"Irene's expected, if not us," I said. "Do you have Rebecca's phone number? Or Annie's maybe?"

"I dealt directly with David," Jayne said. "No one else."

"No point in calling that. The police have his phone." I got out of the car. I grabbed the gates and shook them. They squeaked and wobbled, but they didn't collapse into rusty dust and they didn't swing soundlessly open. I randomly pushed buttons on the control console but didn't get any more of a reaction than Jayne had. Neither 0-0-0-0 or 1-2-3-4 worked. I didn't have all day to stand here and try to figure out the combination.

"Rebecca's expecting Irene at five," Jayne said out her window. "It's almost five now. Maybe she'll come down and check."

"She might not know the gates have been locked. It's possible the property manager or realtor came around after the police left and locked them to keep unwanted visitors out."

"It's working," Jayne said.

I peered through the gates, and rubbed my hands together. "Nothing for it."

These gates had once been very attractive, made by the same metal artist who'd designed the gates to the kitchen garden. Ornate swirls and curlicues sculpted to look like vines stretched between iron posts carved to resemble tree trunks. A scattering of real vines wound around the lower supports, nature reclaiming its territory.

I reached up and gave one of the iron bars a good shake. It held.

Behind me I heard a car door open. "Gemma, what are you doing?" Jayne asked.

"Seeking ingress, obviously." I began to climb.

"Okay for you," Jayne said, "dressed in jeans, but I'm in a skirt."

"I won't look."

"This skirt's new. Cost me a lot. I don't like the look of those . . . sticky-outie things."

I reached the top. Slowly and carefully, I threw one jean-clad leg over, trying to avoid impaling myself on the sticky-outie things. Fortunately, there were no iron spikes, shards of broken glass, or electric wires running along the top of the gates, just a solid, smooth, slightly rusty surface. I lay across the top and pulled my other leg up. Then I descended in much the same way I'd ascended, and finally dropped to the ground.

I straightened up and grinned at my companion through the bars. "Nothing to it. Come on, Jayne, you're next. I'll catch you if you fall."

She took a hesitant step toward the gates. "I'm afraid of heights."

"That's hardly a height. Not much taller than Ryan. Never mind, I'm kidding. Even if no one's inside answering the doorbell, people have to be able to get out." On this side of the gate, a control panel was mounted on a plate attached to a pole, placed within reach of a car window. The steel casing shone in the light of the early evening sun. I pushed the green button and, with an ominous creak, the gates slowly swung open.

"Ta da." I skipped across the driveway as Jayne hurried back to the car and drove onto the property. I hopped into the passenger seat and we continued on our way.

Behind us, the gates swung closed as we drove up the long curving driveway.

It was later in the day than when Jayne and I had arrived on Friday, and the setting sun bathed the stone house in a soft rose-gold glow. To the east, clouds the color of lead were rolling in across the sea and the last of the leaves still clinging to the trees shuddered in the wind. The trees threw long shadows across the lawn and the chimneys were highlighted against the deep gray of the sky. A wisp of fragrant smoke drifted out of the drawing room chimney, and a flock of birds flew over the west wing, heading for nighttime shelter.

"It truly is a magnificent house," Jayne said.

"If you don't look too closely."

"Nothing a lot of money can't fix."

"That's true."

Jayne parked in the cluster of cars in front of the garages and we climbed the steps. I rang the bell and listened as the sound echoed throughout the house. A minute passed and I tried again. Eventually the door opened, and Annie's head popped out. "Oh, it's you. Hi."

"Hi. Rebecca invited Irene Talbot to drop by but Irene has been unavoidably detained, so Jayne and I came in her place."

"Whatever." Annie stepped back and we entered the house. No longer playing the role of housekeeper, she wore black leggings under a long, loose, gray tunic with short sleeves that showed the dragon tattoo. Her feet were bare, her toenails painted a bright red, and the light from the chandelier in the front hall bounced off the rings lining her ears.

"How's everyone doing?" I asked.

"About as well as can be expected. Meaning, I don't know as I haven't come out of my room since yesterday. I'm well fortified up there with wine, chips, and candy bars, practicing for my audition, but I'm on my way to the kitchen to raid the fridge. If I can't find anything suitable in there, I'm going to order a pizza."

Rebecca came down the corridor. "I was expecting Irene. Is she coming?"

I brushed dirt off my jeans and explained. "Has Daniel Steiner arrived?"

"Not yet, but he should be here any minute." Rebecca turned to Annie. "Ann, I'm glad you've come down. We have guests. They won't be staying for supper, but they'd probably like a drink."

"We're having supper?" Annie asked.

"Kyle and Billy went into town earlier and did some shopping."

"That's good. As for drinks, you know where the bar cart is, don't you, Rebecca?"

Rebecca's face tightened.

"Never mind. I'll do it," Annie said. "Wouldn't want to put you out too much. Can I get you ladies a drink?"

"Nothing for me, thanks." Deep in my pocket, my phone rang. I pulled it out and checked it. Ryan. "Pardon me. I need to take this." I stepped away from the three women.

"Looks like more rain on the way," Jayne said.

"Gemma." Ryan's deep voice came over the phone. "I have news about David Masterson's financial affairs, and I'm going to Suffolk House at six to talk to Rebecca. That won't take too long, so how about we grab a quick dinner after?"

"What a coincidence," I said. "I happen to be at Suffolk House at this very moment."

His voice dropped into the suspicious range. "You are? Why?"

"Daniel Steiner, the homeowner, is coming to talk to Rebecca, and Irene asked me to find out what he's up to."

"What does that have to do with you?"

"Absolutely nothing. I told you he made threats against the paper, so Irene's boss ordered her to stay away from Steiner. She asked me to get the measure of the man for her. Plus, honesty forces me to admit, curiosity got the better of me."

"You know what happened to the cat?"

"Moriarty? Has something happened to Moriarty? He was fine half an hour ago. Although with Moriarty, it can be hard to tell sometimes."

"Not Moriarty. I mean the expression."

"What expression?"

"Curiosity killed the cat."

"It did?"

"You don't know—? Enough. I'll be there soon."

"If you can't get in, ring me." A security box, which presumably controlled the alarms in the house and opened the front gates, was mounted next to the door. Blinking lights indicated it was activated.

"Why won't I be able to get in?" he said as I hung up.

"If you're expecting visitors, Rebecca," I said, "you need to get the intercom at the gate ringing through somewhere."

"Doesn't it?"

"No one answered us."

"When Billy and Kyle got back from their shopping expedition, they phoned me and I opened the gate for them." She nodded to the box. "Mr. Steiner called me last night, and suggested we lock the gates. He doesn't want crime scene groupies poking around now that the police have left."

"Very wise," I said.

"Someone's pulling up outside now." Jayne was standing next to the window, and she peered out. "Fancy wheels. A Cadillac Escalade."

"Someone who knows the code to the gates," I said.

"That must be Daniel," Rebecca said. "Ann, those drinks? No, better you answer the door, show him into the drawing room. Come along, everyone. Gemma, you're here now. You can serve the drinks."

"I can, can I?" I muttered to myself.

Miranda floated down the stairs, a green and pink silk scarf around her neck, her ankle-length green dress swirling around her. "Did someone say drinks? I'm just in time. Looks like the gang's all here."

In the drawing room, the gang was all here. Kyle and Billy had helped themselves and they sprawled in armchairs with bottles of beer, each occupied with his own phone. Miranda dropped onto the couch in a spray of silk. "I'll have a martini, please."

"Shaken or stirred? One olive or two?" I asked, poking around the bar cart. "Never mind. Moot point, as we appear to have no gin left and I don't know how to make a martini in any event. A bottle of white wine's in here, but it's not cold."

"There's wine in the fridge," Rebecca said. "We finished what was here, and Kyle and Billy picked some up when they were in town earlier."

"That's where it would be. In the fridge." Miranda settled against the cushions and made herself comfortable.

Rebecca glanced at Jayne.

Jayne had started to sit, but she straightened up. "I'll get it."

"Bring a couple more cold beers while you're at it," Kyle said. "I stocked up on those, too."

"Wine for me," Rebecca said.

"Gemma?" Jayne said.

"Nothing, thanks."

Jayne headed off down the hall, and I remained standing by the open door, listening to the activity at the entrance.

Annie had waited until the bell rang, tapped her feet for a few minutes, and then opened the door. Murmured voices as the new arrival introduced himself, and Annie invited him in.

"My condolences on your loss," the man said.

"Thanks."

"I believe Mrs. Masterson is expecting me?"

"Yeah, I think so. She's around here somewhere," Annie said. "Shouldn't be hard to find her, I hear the sound of drinks being poured. This way, please."

I stepped back as Annie and the man came into the drawing room. If he was shocked to see so many faces staring at him, he hid it well. He was in his late fifties, with slicked-back silver hair, a pale face, and small dark eyes. The jacket of his blue and gray suit was open to show a crisp white shirt and black leather belt. His blue silk tie was shot with pink threads, and his shoes were handmade Italian loafers. The suit cost in the two-thousand-dollar range, I guessed, but that money had been spent some time ago. The belt strained under his belly and the trousers were too tight around his plump rear end. A few threads were loose in the cuffs of the shirt, the tie showed traces of a grease stain he'd not been able to get fully out, and a thread of the hand-applied stitching on the right shoe was coming loose. The hair at the back of his head was sloppily cut, and he was relying on an excessive amount of hair product, rather than expert styling, to keep it frozen in place. Mr. Daniel Steiner had fallen upon hard times indeed, and he was desperately trying to keep up appearances.

He needed to sell this house. And fast.

Rebecca floated across the room, her hand outstretched. "Mr. Steiner. Welcome." She laughed prettily. "Although I shouldn't be welcoming you to your own home."

He dipped his head as he took her hand lightly in his. "My house, Mrs. Masterson. Not my home. My condolences on your loss."

"Thank you," Rebecca said. "It still hasn't sunk in fully that he's . . . gone."

"I understand. My brother, of whom I was very fond, died in tragic circumstances and it was a long time before I stopped turning around to tell him a joke."

Rebecca pretended to swallow a sob and then turned to the others. "Mr. Steiner's come around to see that we're settling in okay and to offer his condolences on David's death. Isn't that nice of him?"

Everyone murmured some version of "very nice."

"Please, call me Daniel. I hope my house has been able to offer you some degree of comfort."

"It's such a beautiful home. Thank you, Daniel. I'm Rebecca."

"This house has been in my family for many long years," he said.

Suffolk Gardens House had been built in 1965. In England we didn't say a house had been in our family for a long time unless it was built before 1765, but never mind that.

"Can I offer you a drink?" Rebecca said.

"A whiskey, if you have?"

"Ann? See to that, will you dear?"

Annie shrugged and went to the bar cart. Rebecca didn't bother to introduce Mr. Steiner to anyone; she simply waved her hand around the room and said, "My family and dear friends."

I noticed Miranda checking out the new arrival and his suit and shoes. She smiled at him and patted the couch next to her in invitation. She'd recognized the cost of his clothes, but hadn't noticed the signs of imminent penury. Over the years, I've come to realize that not many people bother to look beneath the surface. They accept things at face value, which is why they seem to think I'm some sort of mind reader when I tell them the truth that lies beneath.

Daniel sat next to Miranda and gave her a polite, but vacant, smile. Annie passed him his drink and then poured one for herself. Rebecca perched on the edge of an armchair. Kyle and Billy had finally torn their attention away from their phones. Jayne returned, carrying an imitation-silver bucket clanging with ice, a bottle of white wine, and several glasses. She put her load on a side table, opened the bottle, and poured.

"Why are you selling this marvelous house?" Rebecca asked Daniel as she accepted a glass from Jayne.

"My parents loved the Cape," he said, "and they spent most of their summers here until about five years ago when my mother's health declined to the extent it was difficult for her to travel. My mother died last year, and my father . . . recently. As much as I love this place and have such happy memories of our summers here . . . I live in Boston and the pressure of business means my wife and I simply don't get down as much as I'd like."

I edged into a corner and stood quietly, just watching.

"I hope you've had a chance to enjoy the gardens here at Suffolk Gardens House." Daniel began his sales pitch. "They're not at their best at this time of year, but in the spring and summer the grounds are magnificent. Are you a gardener, Rebecca?"

Miranda snorted into her wine glass.

Rebecca glared at her before turning back to Daniel. "I've never had the time, but I admire people who can make beautiful things grow."

The drinks flowed freely, and the conversation moved into banalities. Daniel sang the praises of the house, the garden, the proximity to the ocean, even West London itself. He didn't strictly confine the sales pitch to Rebecca either, realizing that anyone here, if they were related to David Masterson, might have the means to buy it.

Jayne kept throwing me questioning looks, clearly asking me why we were staying. Jayne had poured herself a small glass of wine, but she put it on the table next to her and forgot about it. Kyle switched from beer to wine and he, Miranda, and Rebecca made short work of the bottle.

When her glass was again empty, Miranda took the bottle out of the cooler and held it up to the light. "Oh dear. It seems to be finished. Jayne, get us another, will you, dear."

Jayne started to stand, but I waved her down and stepped away from the wall. "Jayne's comfortable there, I'll get it. Miranda, I don't know what you like. Why don't you come with me and help me choose a nice bottle?"

"Anything will do," she said.

"I don't know much about wines. I wouldn't want to make a mistake." I smiled at her and made no further move to walk away.

What could she do but get up and follow me?

"See what you can find to eat in there," Kyle called after us. "I'm starving."

Jayne and I had tidied the kitchen when we left yesterday after breakfast, but we needn't have bothered. The sink was piled high with pots and pans, and the countertops were covered with plastic wrapping torn off the containers of food we'd left, used bottles, dirty glasses, and the residue of chopped vegetables. Cardboard pizza boxes stuck out of the trash container. A plate had fallen to the floor and someone had merely kicked the pieces of shattered china into a corner.

"Bit of a mess," I said as Miranda opened the fridge door.

"Annie'll get around to cleaning it up."

"I suspect Annie's done with playacting the housekeeper."

"I'm not cleaning up after them. Kyle and Billy are pigs." She selected a bottle and slammed the fridge door behind her. "There's only one kind of wine in here. I don't know why you couldn't get it."

"I wanted to take the opportunity to talk to you," I said.

She studied my face. "What about?"

"Do you think Rebecca's serious about buying this house?"

"What's it to you?"

"It might be good for my business if she does. I could put on more Sherlock Holmes parties, like the one David did."

Miranda snickered. "You're outta luck there, honey. Rebecca has no interest in Sherlock Holmes."

I let my face fall. "Oh, that's too bad." I brightened up. "Maybe she'll organize tea parties. Afternoon tea in the garden. Jayne's restaurant does a wonderful afternoon tea, and she's catered many events. She can pull out all the stops, truly impress Rebecca's friends."

"That's the sort of thing that would appeal to Rebecca. She loves nothing more than to show off what great taste she thinks she has. Here's a tip for nothing: if you want Rebecca to send business you and your friend's way, you need to suck up more." She twisted the cap off the bottle and then opened a cupboard, searching for a clean glass. The cupboard was empty. I grabbed a used glass off the counter, rinsed it out, and handed it to her. She grinned at me. "Yes, like that. Thanks. Don't waste your time talking to me. Rebecca and I aren't exactly friends, and she won't take any advice from me. She's more likely to do the opposite." She poured a generous amount of wine into her glass.

"You're the one who introduced her to David."

"My mistake." Miranda took a long drink. "Then again, maybe not. They deserved each other."

"I got the feeling you didn't want to come here this weekend. Why did you?"

She didn't answer, so I took a guess. Although, as I've said many times in the past, I never guess. If I extrapolate from the little I do know, people simply assume I know far more than I do. And so they tell me what I don't know. And then I know it. "He enjoyed manipulating people, didn't he? He liked making them sing to his tune."

Miranda sighed. "I didn't want to come to his stupid Sherlock Holmes party, but he needed another woman, or so he said. He didn't want Jennifer to feel uncomfortable, and Annie was coming to work. Why he cared what Jennifer thought, I have no idea. She's quite the little mouse, isn't she? David implied that he and I could take the opportunity this weekend to talk over our differences." She shrugged. "That didn't happen, did it?"

"Your differences? You mean the money you owe him." Another educated guess on my part.

"I didn't owe him anything."

I'd guessed wrong, but I was convinced I was on the right track. There had to be some reason Miranda came on this weekend. More, that is, than free access to David's hospitality.

"I didn't owe him anything," she repeated. "But he said I did. I paid what we agreed, but then he decided that wasn't enough, and he wanted more." Her lips tightened, and anger flared in her eyes. She finished her drink in one gulp and poured another. "He could have found another woman to come easily enough. Plenty of women are interested in Sherlock Holmes, aren't they?"

I nodded.

"His mother was a good friend to me, despite the fact that she was a good bit older than me." Miranda smiled softly at the memory. "After her death, I maintained contact with David for her sake. I thought he returned the sentiment—he gave me a letter of hers, an actual letter written by Emily Dickinson herself—as a memento. But it didn't take long for the real David to reassert itself. His mother spoiled him rotten, and look how he turned out. You're right that David got a kick out of manipulating people. He pretended he was doing me a big favor letting me come to his stupid house party. He said if I didn't like the favor he was doing me then I'd have to give him more money. I told him I didn't have any more, but he didn't really care. It was all a game to him."

"You played his game, though."

Anger flashed in her eyes. "Tell me what else I could have done? Maybe he wouldn't have gone through with it, but I couldn't take that chance, could I?"

She talked as though I knew what she was talking about. I murmured words of agreement.

"Everyone says that sort of thing doesn't matter these days, but to some people it does. It could completely ruin Mark's life; destroy his career at the least."

I hesitated. I hadn't heard mention of anyone named Mark this weekend, and I didn't want Miranda to realize I didn't have a clue what she was going on about.

The anger disappeared as quickly as it had appeared, and a slow smile took its place. "Doesn't matter now, does it? David Masterson can't do any harm to me or Mark or anyone ever again. I could have gone home yesterday, like I was supposed to, but I like the idea of enjoying the place at David's expense, without having to dance to his tune. Even if it means putting up with Rebecca and all the rest of the miserable bunch." She lifted the wine bottle. "I intend to squeeze every last drop out of David Masterson that I can. He owes me."

She left the kitchen, scarf flowing, skirt swirling, heels tapping on the floor, bottle swinging in her hand.

I let out a long breath. That had been interesting, very interesting. I'd learned far more than I'd expected to. If David was blackmailing Miranda over something to do with someone named Mark, and it certainly sounded like it, then Miranda had a good reason to want to see the man dead.

I needed to get back to the drawing room. I needed to ask the other guests, the non-Sherlockian ones at any rate, what had really brought them here. I glanced at the clock on the stove. Almost six o'clock. Ryan had said he'd be here at six.

Before I could ask any more questions of anyone, I needed to hear what Ryan was coming to Suffolk Gardens House to say.

Chapter Fourteen

Detectives Ashburton and Estrada did not take seats and they did not accept Rebecca's offer of a drink.

"This isn't a social call," Estrada growled.

"Where's Kyle Fraser?" Ryan asked.

"When you phoned me to say you were at the front gates," Rebecca said, "he fell all over himself in a rush to volunteer to press the buttons to open the gate. He didn't come back."

"I wonder why," Annie muttered.

I'd taken the opportunity to follow Kyle into the front hall, hoping to get a chance to speak to him privately, but he'd pounded the buttons on the security panel with panicked haste and then fled up the stairs without appearing to even hear my cry of "If you have a moment, Kyle." I went back to the drawing room, also wondering why. Like Annie, I assumed he didn't want to be in the presence of the police. Whether that indicated guilt over something specific, or simply general wariness of legal attention, I didn't know.

"A most upsetting business," Daniel Steiner said. "It has nothing to do with me or this house, of course. You will, I trust, be keeping mention of the house out of the papers, Detective."

"I'll tell the media what I consider relevant. Nothing more," Ryan said. "Are you the owner?"

"I am. The house is for sale, and I don't need nasty rumors circulating about it. Buyers tend not to like police attention."

"The West London police," Estrada said, "do not deal in rumor."

"I only meant—"

"I'm here to speak to Mr. David Masterson's family," Ryan said. "As well as the people who were in the house when he died. Does that include you, sir?"

"Nothing to do with me." Daniel drained his glass and hurried to get to his feet. "None of my business. I'll be on my way. You have my number, Rebecca?"

"I do," she said.

He stood in front of her chair and peered down at her. "I understand perfectly what an emotionally difficult time this is for you. It can be hard to make important decisions. I was that way after my father died. In all fairness, I must let you know that I have an interested buyer, a very interested buyer. He's driving a hard bargain, and I'd be prepared to reconsider the listed price in memory of your husband's passing."

"That's so kind of you." Rebecca fluttered her eyelashes. "I'll be in touch."

Daniel turned and left the room. As he passed me, I could see the beads of sweat that had broken out on his forehead. He wiped his hands on his trouser legs. Mr. Daniel Steiner was a heck of a poor liar. He didn't have another buyer. He was so anxious to sell as quickly as possible, he was prepared to drop the price.

"You're considering buying this house, Mrs. Masterson?" Ryan asked when Steiner had left.

"I'm thinking about it. It would be nice to have a place on the Lower Cape, but I'm afraid Mr. Steiner's being premature. Obviously, my husband's estate has to be settled first."

For a police detective, Louise Estrada has a highly expressive face. I read that face now, and it told me what the police had come here to tell David's relatives. He had no money to leave them.

Ryan glanced at Billy and Annie. He looked at Miranda, and then at Rebecca. He pointedly avoided Jayne and me. There was obviously no reason we should be here, so I was trying to blend in with the wallpaper before anyone thought to ask us to leave. Jayne sat quietly in a corner. "I've been in contact with Mr. Masterson's lawyers and his bank," Ryan said at last.

"Why'd you do that?" Billy asked. "What about privacy laws?"

"In cases such as this, where the deceased has died under circumstances requiring police investigation, the financial affairs of all the people concerned can be important. Vitally important. Let me assure you that no one gave me any specific details, but they did inform us that Mr. Masterson's debts are considerable."

Miranda waved her hand in the air. "Rich people often have loads of debt. I wouldn't expect a police officer, such as yourself, to know that. People of means borrow money, which they invest at a higher rate of return than the interest payable on the debt. Money, Detective Ashburton, makes money. If that's all you've come to tell us, pour me another glass, Billy dear."

Estrada bit her tongue.

"I have had that explained to me, thank you," Ryan said. "Perhaps I wasn't fully clear. Mr. Masterson had liabilities far in excess of assets. When I do my budget on the kitchen table, and I come up short for the month, I write the balance in red ink. Mr.

Masterson's accounts are swimming in red ink." Ryan, I knew, was speaking metaphorically. He handled his money with care. No red ink there.

Miranda's mouth dropped open.

"That's preposterous!" Rebecca said. "My husband is . . . was . . . a wealthy man." She waved her arms around. "Look at this house. He rented this entire house for a week. He paid staff. He hired caterers." She pointed to Jayne. "And . . . and . . . an entertainer." She pointed to me.

"If by staff, you mean me," Annie said. "I haven't seen a red cent yet."

"I had to pay for my suit rental myself," Billy said. "Then again, Uncle David always was a cheapskate."

Rebecca jumped to her feet. Her face was twisted almost beyond recognition and she sprayed spittle everywhere. "This is absolutely preposterous. You two are saying my husband had no money because he expected his greedy relatives to pay their own way. He'd had enough of the both of you, always with your hands out. Always wanting more, more."

"Hands out?" Annie said. "Greedy? More like he made us beg for what we deserved. We're family and he treated us like beggars."

"Like servants," Billy said.

Rebecca's eyes flashed. "You ungrateful—"

"That's enough," Ryan said. "You can sort out your family issues after we've finished here. I'm sorry, Mrs. Masterson, but that appears to be the case. We can't find anything in the way of legitimate assets owned by Mr. Masterson."

"Do you have any idea what an apartment in Gramercy Park is worth?" Rebecca snapped.

"Mortgaged to the hilt," Estrada said. "I believe the phrase is underwater." She tried, and failed, to hide a smile. "Not that I have any personal experience of that."

Annie sucked in a breath. Her face had gone very pale. Billy snickered. A smile slowly spread across Miranda's face.

"The house in the Hamptons?" Rebecca said weakly.

"You thought he still owned that?" Estrada said. "He sold it six months ago."

Rebecca dropped into a chair. "He . . . he told me he was renovating it, and the work was taking so much longer than planned we weren't able to use the house this past summer."

"He told me the same," Annie said.

"It's definitely time for another drink." Miranda got up and served herself. "Annie?"

"Don't mind if I do."

"David kept his head above water, barely, for the last several months off the proceeds of the Hampton house," Ryan said. "He used the last of those funds to pay for the rental of this place."

"I don't know anything about high finance," Miranda said, "but plenty of people bounce back from bankruptcy."

"Bankrupt," Rebecca groaned.

"At the time he died," Estrada said, "he was using what remained of the proceeds from the Hampton house and some other investments to renegotiate his debts, and he was in discussions with various banks and . . . other lenders to refinance him."

"You spoke to the wrong people!" Rebecca shouted. "He told me he fired that lawyer. David said he wasn't doing a good job."

"He fired his lawyer, that's right," Ryan said. "Although it's more a case of the lawyer quit because he wasn't getting paid. I'm sorry to have to tell you this, particularly under these circumstances, but it would appear as though your husband has never had the sort of income that would enable him to live in the style he maintained. He burned through his inheritance and then began borrowing against future investments, and those investments didn't give the return he needed. It was bound to happen one day that he couldn't borrow any more. Your husband might have other accounts we're not aware of. Yet."

"The details of his and your finances are not our concern," Estrada said. "Only the big picture. We're telling you the big picture now. He squandered his inheritance and made some bad, very bad, investments over the past several years trying to get it back. He sold what remained of his share of the stock in his family's company more than a year ago, at rock bottom I might add, and since then he appears to have had no source of income, other than some small sporadic deposits into his bank account made over the previous few months. We're trying to trace the origins of those deposits."

Miranda laughed.

Ryan's intense blue eyes flicked toward her. "Do you know anything about that, Ms. Ireland?"

"Nope." Miranda's face was a picture of innocence.

"Mrs. Masterson," Estrada asked. "Were you giving your husband money? Do you have income of your own that he might have been tapping into?"

"I . . . I . . . no. David never told me . . . I need to lie down. If you'll excuse me." Rebecca wobbled slightly as she headed for the door.

Seeing that no one intended to offer her support, Jayne stood up. She glanced at me, and I gave her a nod. Jayne slipped past Ryan and Estrada and took Rebecca's arm.

When they'd left, everyone began shouting at once. Billy, I thought, couldn't decide between triumphant glee or despair. He'd resented his uncle for holding money over him, but that source of funds had now been cut off. Annie leaned back in her chair and allowed a small smile to creep over her face. Miranda looked absolutely chuffed, and she didn't bother to hide her pleasure.

"Have you considered, Detectives," she asked, "that David killed himself? You told us yesterday he was murdered, but perhaps you were incorrect? Maybe he planted that blowgun thing to make it like murder."

"Why do you ask?" Ryan said.

Her dress rustled as she indicated her surroundings. "Look around you. Look at this house. Look at the attempt to re-create an English country house weekend, complete with staff and caterers. Look at the apartment in Gramercy Park, the house in the Hamptons. David was not a flamboyant man in himself, and he didn't throw parties at the best restaurants or move in the highest of social circles, which I'll assure you was his choice, not Rebecca's. But he did like to live well, and he certainly enjoyed the . . ."—she fought to find the right words—". . . respect of those he didn't consider his peers. It seems to me that he might have left this earth under his own terms when, if what you say is true, the entire house of cards was about to come tumbling down around him."

"That's a good question, Ms. Ireland," Ryan said. "But the answer is no. That's not a possibility we're considering."

"What are you considering?" Billy asked. "You don't seriously think it had anything to do with that blowgun you were asking us about. The last bunch of renters must have left it behind. I told you that."

Ryan's eyes flicked to Estrada, telling her to answer.

"At present we have not located any previous renters who admit to playing with blowguns or anything similar. Mr. David Masterson was murdered. We have no doubt about that whatsoever."

"Before this goes any further, you need to know that I didn't do it!" Kyle marched into the room.

"Did I say you did?" Estrada asked.

He bristled. "I know the way you people work, well enough. Find a suitable patsy down on his luck, and then build a case. The patsy's tried and convicted and the rich, well-connected people can get on with their lives."

"Is that what happened to you in Virginia?" Ryan asked.

"Yeah. It is."

"Perhaps it did, perhaps not," Ryan said. "But it won't happen here."

Kyle's arrival had been well timed. He'd been listening at keyholes until the moment arrived when he had to say something. I didn't blame him for eavesdropping—I would have done the same had I not been allowed to stand quietly in my corner.

"What happened in Virginia?" Annie asked. No one answered her.

"What's got Rebecca so upset?" Kyle said. "She charged out of here carrying on as though it's the end of the world."

"Pretty much is," Annie said. "For her."

Jayne slipped back into the room.

"Do any of you have anything you'd like to talk to me about?" Ryan looked at Miranda, Annie, Kyle, and Billy in turn. Miranda studied her nails. Annie said, "No." Kyle attempted, unsuccessfully, to stare him down. Billy said, "Any of that cheese left?"

"In that case," Ryan said, "we'll be on our way. Please let Detective Estrada or me know when you make plans to go home."

"House is paid for a few more days," Miranda said. "I for one have no reason to hurry away."

The police left. I followed them and Jayne followed me.

"That was interesting," I said once we were outside.

"As always, you just happened to be hanging around at the right time, did you?" Estrada said.

"Yup," I replied. "That's about it."

"Did Rebecca say anything to you when you went upstairs with her?" Ryan asked Jayne.

"She was crying, quite a lot. I went with her to the door of her room, and she said she'd be okay, so I left her. She was polite about asking me to leave. Should I have stayed with her?"

"No," I said. "You couldn't have gone into her bedroom if she didn't want you to." Perhaps I should have been the one to take Rebecca upstairs. Unlike Jayne, I don't care if people want my company or not. But I can't be in two places at once, and I thought it more important to keep my eye on the others.

"Did she say anything about her plans?" Estrada asked.

Jayne shook her head.

"Did you learn anything in there, Gemma?" Ryan asked.

Estrada made a show of checking her watch, but she couldn't quite pull off the totally disinterested look. She wanted to hear my observations. Although she'd die before admitting it.

"I need to think things through," I said. "It was obvious from the time we first arrived that none of these people were particularly fond of David Masterson, and that includes his wife."

"No brainer there," Estrada said. "Anyone can see they can't stand each other."

"They did try to keep up appearances at first," Jayne said. "I thought it was going to be a lovely weekend."

I smiled at her. Jayne hadn't noticed all the undercurrents swirling around these people. She always thinks the best of everyone and every situation.

"Let's go," Estrada said. "We don't have all day to stand around chatting." She marched across the courtyard to the cruiser and climbed behind the wheel.

I glanced at the house to see a cluster of faces peering through various windows. I refrained from waving.

"What are you up to now?" I asked Ryan.

"I've sent feelers out to New York for more info about Masterson and his affairs. I know you're convinced this was done by someone in the house party, Gemma, and I'm inclined to agree, but I can't forget the man had a lot of debts. And debts unpaid means enemies."

"That was no professional hit, Ryan."

"Not unless the mob has started writing obscure literary references into their contracts. People can have debts to non-organized crime figures."

"Rebecca seemed to be genuinely shocked at what you had to say."

The cruiser's horn beeped.

"I have to go, or Louise will drive off without me."

I didn't ask if that would be so bad. Jayne had also left us and started the engine of her car.

"It's possible Rebecca was aware David was in trouble, but not the extent of it," Ryan said.

"Her shock was genuine. Annie was also initially shocked, but that turned quickly to amusement. Miranda seemed delighted to know David was on the verge of ruin, and Kyle and Billy are more interested in where their next beer's coming from."

"On the surface it looks as though Rebecca didn't kill him, but I have some feelers out to Bridgeport, where she got that ticket on Saturday. Her alibi's good, but it never hurts to follow up." Not only was there a line of faces at the windows, but Estrada was watching us in her rearview mirror, so Ryan didn't kiss me goodbye. Instead he simply gave me a private smile before walking away.

I hopped into Jayne's car. She put her phone away and turned to me with a pout.

"What's wrong?" I asked.

"A message from Andy. He has to cancel our dinner date. One of his sous-chefs cut his hand, badly enough that's he's gone to the hospital, so Andy has to stay through dinner service."

"Isn't that too bad?" I said cheerfully. "Let's go to the Harbor Inn."

"I'm tired, Gemma. If Andy can't make it, I'd just as soon not have dinner out."

"Who mentioned anything about dinner? I have a call to make, and you might as well take me as we're in your car."

Jayne gave me The Look, but she put the car into gear and we drove away.

Chapter Fifteen

I'd never admit it to anyone but myself, but I'd been wrong about David Masterson. I'd liked him when we met. I'd taken it at face value that he was what he appeared to be: a keen Sherlockian happy to use his ample financial resources to treat similar-minded people to a weekend of fine dining, good wines, country walks, movies and games, and above all stimulating conversation about the Great Detective.

Instead he humiliated his relatives by making them play at being servants, blackmailed a family friend, deceived his wife about his financial situation, and extended a shy, lonely woman a proposal he knew he couldn't keep.

If I'd been wrong about David, who else had I been wrong about?

At the moment Ryan seemed to be concentrating on David's family as the potential killers, in light of the revelations of his financial situation, but I knew he hadn't forgotten that other people had been in the house at the time.

I hadn't forgotten the rest of them either.

I took a chance that Jennifer Griffith would be at the inn. I never like to phone ahead to tell people I'm coming, not if I don't have to. If they're trying to hide something from me, better not to give them time to prepare.

We arrived at the Harbor Inn a few minutes before seven. A good time to find someone at dinner. "Let's have a peek into the restaurant first," I said to Jayne as we walked into the hotel. "If she's not there, we can call up to her room."

"If who's not there?" Jayne said. "I hate it when you don't tell me what's going on, Gemma."

"Do I do that?"

"All the time."

"Oh. Sorry."

"We're looking for Jennifer, I assume."

"See. I don't have to tell you things. You figure them out for yourself."

"I knew you couldn't stop yourself from investigating," she said.

I had to admit, if only to myself, that she was right. I waved to Andrea behind the desk as I crossed the lobby, Jayne muttering under her breath beside me.

The approaching storm had brought a decided chill with it, but a good number of guests were determined to enjoy one of the last chances for al fresco dining. Heaters had been set up on the veranda in an attempt to extend the season by a few more weeks, and a pile of blankets rested on the table next to the hostess stand for those needing more warmth. The iron urns and terra-cotta planters bursting with ivy and colorful annuals had been dug up and crimson and golden chrysanthemums planted in their place.

The restaurant was about half full and I spotted my quarry immediately. Jennifer had taken a table for two adjacent to the low stone wall, with a view down the steep hill to the lights lining Harbor Road and the night-wrapped ocean beyond. She wore a thick beige sweater, her nose was buried in a book, and a half-full glass of wine was next to her. One place had been set.

She didn't hear us approach and started when I said, "Good evening."

"Oh. Hello." She blinked rapidly underneath her glasses.

"Enjoying the book?" I asked. She was reading *Arthur and Sherlock: Conan Doyle and the Creation of Holmes*, which she'd bought at the Emporium earlier.

"Fascinating. I learn something different about Sir Arthur all the time." She smiled at me.

I smiled back.

Jayne shifted from one foot to the other.

A waiter placed a bowl of soup in front of Jennifer. It was thick and creamy, overflowing with small potatoes and plump clams. He arranged a breadbasket and a dish containing curls of butter, and then glanced at me. I gave my head a slight shake, and he slipped away.

Jennifer unfurled her napkin, arranged it on her lap, and picked up her spoon.

Clearly an invitation to join her was not forthcoming. I didn't take it personally. I hate being interrupted and expected to engage in friendly conversation when I'm indulging in a rare treat of a nice meal alone in a good restaurant. Although, come to think of it, that treat has been so rare of late, I can't remember the last time I dined in a restaurant alone, good one or otherwise.

As I wasn't going to be invited to sit, I simply pulled out the unoccupied chair and dropped into it. Jayne hissed, "Gemma!"

"The clam chowder's particularly good here," I said.

"Uh . . ." Jennifer said. "Won't you join me?"

"That would be lovely, thank you. Jayne, grab yourself a seat. We won't be able to stay long."

Jennifer didn't say "thank goodness," but her face did. I waved to the waiter. "I'll have a cup of tea, please. Black tea, with milk. Jayne?"

"What? Oh, a glass of water, please." She perched uncomfortably on the edge of the chair she'd dragged over from an adjacent unoccupied table.

"Have you spoken to the police today?" I asked Jennifer.

"An officer came around this morning to go over my statement again, but I didn't remember anything new. I bet his wife did it, but . . . well that's only a guess on my part. She wasn't even there, at the house, but she could have snuck onto the grounds, killed him, and then snuck away again, right?"

I said nothing.

"She had motive. David was going to leave her and take all his money with him. I called Detective Ashburton a while ago and told him that, but he just thanked me for my time. Although, if he's building a case against her, he wouldn't tell me, would he?" She scooped up another spoonful of the soup. It looked and smelled delicious.

Ryan wouldn't share information about David's financial situation with Jennifer. Jennifer had no legal status in David's life, no matter what promises he'd made to her.

"Jayne and I have been at Suffolk Gardens."

Jennifer put her spoon down. "Oh, yes. Visiting the grieving widow. If you're here because you think I want to hear how she's doing . . . I don't care one little bit. Even if she didn't kill him, she didn't love him and he didn't love her, and that's all that matters to me." Her eyes filled with tears and she dabbed angrily at them with her napkin. "I asked Detective Ashburton how I could get in contact with David's lawyers, but he said I had to ask *her*. She's not going to tell me, is she? Do you know the name of the lawyer?"

"I don't," I said truthfully.

She grabbed a roll out of the basket and began tearing it into shreds. "How will I get what's mine? What David wanted me to have."

"If you're mentioned in the will," Jayne said, "the executor will get in touch with you. If you're unwilling to wait, wills are a matter of public record. Once his has been released, you can go to the records office in the town in which David lived and ask to see it. The lawyer's name will be on it, and you can contact them."

"Do you know when the will's going to be released?" Jennifer asked me.

"No, I don't. Jennifer, I hope you understand that David might not have changed his will in your favor. He was a middle-aged man in good health. He would have expected to live for many years yet, plenty of time to take care of that."

"He told me he had," she said firmly.

"Men say a lot of things they don't always mean," Jayne said.

"David wasn't like that. I changed my will before I left California. If I died suddenly, I wanted him to have everything." Tears fell again. "He did the same for me."

I stood up. "We've kept you from your dinner and your book. Please drop into the Emporium any time."

We left Jennifer ripping her bread into crumbs and staring out over the ocean, thinking of what might have been.

"You didn't tell her about David's financial situation," Jayne said. "I expected you to."

"That had been my original intent. I wanted to see her reaction to the news. I changed my mind. It's irrelevant."

"How can her reaction be irrelevant?"

"I believe she genuinely loved him. Whether that would have lasted upon getting to know each other doesn't matter. Whether he returned her feelings or however much money he had, or didn't have, doesn't matter either."

"You're scratching her off the suspect list?"

"Not at all. She's grieving, genuinely, but many a killer has regretted what they've done as soon as they did it. She came a long way to be with him. She left her home and her job, she even changed her own will. Is it possible he told her on Saturday morning, once they'd risen from their comfy little love nest, that he wasn't planning on marrying her? No. Even if that was what he had in mind, he wouldn't tell her until the end of the weekend. He probably wouldn't have told her at all. Just driven away, leaving her standing in the dust. She's a smart enough woman. Maybe she overheard him on the phone making plans with Rebecca. Any one of a number of things might have alerted her to his real feelings and intentions. If so, she would have been humiliated. Humiliation, I've found, is one of the most powerful motives for murder there is. More powerful than money. Now, where shall we go for dinner?"

"Like I said earlier, I'm tired, Gemma."

"Let's pay a call on Donald."

"Donald! That's about the last place I'd want to go to eat. Donald's a horrible cook. He burns canned soup."

"True, but he can provide an evening of scintillating conversation."

Jayne gave me The Look.

"You can drop me at home first if you like, and I can take my own car."

"Oh, no. You're on the trail, and I'm coming with you."

* * *

"Gemma. Jayne. What brings you two here? Not that it's not always a pleasure, of course."

"We were in the neighborhood," I said. "I wanted to check up on you. I hope you've recovered from the weekend."

"Perfectly, thank you," Donald said. "Not that there was anything to recover from. It was quite delightful. Except for . . . the unpleasantness regarding our host."

Which was an unusual way to refer to murder most foul, but I reminded myself that Donald had never met David prior to Friday evening.

"Is Cliff still here?" I asked. "You said you'd invited him to stay with you for a few days."

"He is. We've been having some marvelous conversations, although," Donald's voice dropped, "as I realized earlier, he's not as knowledgeable about Sir Arthur or the Canon as I might have expected, but he is interested in learning more. He's trying to interest me in some first editions, and I will admit, Gemma, I'm sorely tempted." Donald smiled ruefully and lowered his voice. "I fear my budget doesn't match my tastes. Oh well, such is life. I'm embarrassed to say I haven't been entirely honest with Cliff. I haven't told him that I'm . . . temporarily short of funds."

Donald was nothing of the sort: he was permanently short of funds. "You have nothing to be embarrassed about, Donald. Your financial situation is no one's business but your own. I can't invest in first editions either."

"I wish Arthur was in town. He would have enjoyed discussing book collecting with Cliff. Oh, would you like to come in?"

"What an excellent idea. Thank you."

"We've finished eating and are having a postprandial libation in the living room. We're getting ready to watch the Jeremy Brett version of *The Hound of the Baskervilles*. Cliff says he hasn't seen it for years. Marvelous story, of course, and Brett's interpretation of Holmes is, as always, spot on. Would you care to join us?"

"Not to watch TV, thanks. We won't stay that long. Morning comes early for Jayne, as you know. A cup of tea would be nice, though."

"Come in, come in," he urged, and Jayne and I stepped into Donald's small, untidy, 1960s-era, never-updated bungalow.

We found Cliff in the living room, all ready to settle down for an evening's viewing, glass of whiskey at hand. He leapt to his feet when we came in. "Hello, uh . . ."

"Gemma and Jayne," I said. "We were passing and Jayne said, 'why don't we drop in on Donald.' Didn't you, Jayne?"

"I did? I mean, yes, that's exactly what I said."

"You sure you don't want something stronger than tea?" Donald asked.

"Thanks, but no. I haven't had dinner yet, and mustn't drink on an empty stomach."

"No tea for me," Jayne said. "Or I won't be able to sleep. I'll never understand how you can drink that stuff so late, Gemma, and not be up all night."

"I have a clear conscience," I said. "Take your time, Donald. No need to hurry." I gave my head a quick jerk to one side. I wasn't sure if he understood that I was saying "take a *long* time, Donald." He bustled off to tend to the tea making, and Jayne and I attempted to make ourselves comfortable. I assumed the one empty chair, next to the side table holding a glass of whiskey, was for Donald, so I lifted a stack of yellowing copies of the *West London Star* off a ragged armchair and dropped them on the floor while Jayne did likewise with a jumble of books, many of which came from my own shop. She held the books in her arms, looking around the room for a place to put them. Let's say Donald's housekeeping leaves something to be desired. I took the books from Jayne, and as I did so I stared into her eyes. Her own opened in a question, and then she nodded, handed me the books, and sat down. I put the books on top of another bunch and flicked idly through them.

"How are you enjoying West London?" Jayne asked Cliff.

"Pleasant little town," he said. "I haven't dropped into your store yet. Donald's been singing its praises, so we're hoping to get there tomorrow."

"It's not my store," Jayne said. "Gemma and her Uncle Arthur own it."

"I've heard of Arthur Doyle. Never had the pleasure."

"Suffolk House was fun, wasn't it?" Jayne said. "Like being in England."

"If I wanted to play at being in England, I'd have gone to England," Cliff said.

So there was that copy of *Jeremy Brett: Playing a Part.* I'd wondered where it had gone. Donald never actually stole anything, but sometimes his enthusiasm got the better of him, and if Ashleigh was alone in the store and busy, he simply left with what he needed. He usually got around to remembering to come back and pay. Eventually.

"Terrible what happened to David," Jayne said.

"Terrible," Cliff agreed. I glanced up from my book. I wasn't entirely sure what I heard in his voice, or what I saw on his face, but it wasn't grief. He stroked his beard.

"Were you two good friends?" Jayne asked.

"Not friends as much as people with mutual interests."

"You mean in Sherlock Holmes?" she said.

"Sherlock Holmes, yes, but also in collecting rare books and papers. I'm an antique dealer. Books are my specialty, but I deal in other items if they cross my path."

"Did David collect?"

"He did at one time, but he hadn't bought much for some time, come to think of it. He knew people who were serious collectors. Contacts are everything in this business. I don't suppose you have an interest in antiques?"

"Sorry, no," Jayne said. "I . . . I . . ."

"What is keeping Donald?" Cliff glanced toward the door.

"He probably can't find the tea bags," Jayne said. "He's rather . . ."—she looked around the room—". . . disorganized."

Silence descended. Jayne had run out of conversation, and Cliff didn't seem to be in the mood for idle chat. Not once Jayne had told him she didn't buy antiques, anyway. Time for me to step in. I idly flicked through the book in my hands. "Is antiquing a lucrative trade?"

Cliff chuckled and reached for his whiskey. "No, not at all. But it is my passion and I'm lucky enough to be able to make a small living out of it."

"Donald has a particular interest in original documents by and about Sir Arthur Conan Doyle," I said. "Did he mention that Cliff?"

His eyes gleamed and he cradled his glass in both hands. "Yes, yes. He told me he appreciates such things. One of the many things Donald and I are finding we have in common."

"Isn't that nice," Jayne said. "Gemma, do you want me to go and help Donald with the tea?"

"No."

"Donald hasn't said in so many words," Cliff said, "but I get the impression he can't afford most of what he'd like to acquire. When I get home, I'll see what I can do for him. I might have some letters I'd be happy to sell to him at cost, in thanks for his kind hospitality."

"That's nice of you," Jayne said.

"It is," I said. "I might be able to help you with that, Cliff. I go to New York City regularly." Not entirely a lie. I've been to that city twice. Twice in the six years I've lived in America might be regular enough for some people. "Next time I go, I'll pay a call on you. My parents inherited a substantial number of letters from my father's family. The Doyle family."

Cliff's eyes almost popped out of his head. "You don't mean . . ."

"I told you I don't sell first editions or rare books at my shop, and that's true. The Emporium is strictly retail, but I have a side business dealing in and collecting letters written to and from English literary figures. You know the ones I mean: Austen, the Brontë sisters, Wilkie Collins. Sir Arthur Conan Doyle, of course. I spent a term at Sotheby's in London learning how to verify authenticity and provenance in private correspondence. I'd love to see what you're thinking of offering to Donald."

I turned a page of the book. Jayne sat forward and her mouth fell open. I gave my head a quick shake and flipped another page.

Cliff's smile died and he shifted in his seat. He took a hearty swig of his drink and then started to stand. "I . . . I'll check on Donald. He might need some help with the tea."

"He's perfectly competent," I said. "I've taught him all I know. About making tea. About handling and verifying historical documents."

Cliff ran a finger under his shirt collar, as though letting in some air. He took another hearty swig of his whiskey, switched on a bright smile, and turned his attention to Jayne. "Donald tells me you run a proper English tea room. I need to pay you a visit when I get a chance."

"That would be nice," she said. "It's next door to the Emporium."

I heard the clatter of the tea tray and a moment later Donald came into the room. I've taught Donald nothing about verifying old letters, but I had taught him to make a proper cup of tea. I was pleased to see the tray contained a teapot currently emitting steam, a cup and saucer, and small containers of sugar and milk. "I don't have any chocolate biscuits to offer you," he said.

Cliff leapt to his feet and cleared a space on the coffee table for the tray. I doubted he was always so helpful.

"Do you know, I just remembered an important engagement," I said. "Yup, gotta run. Come along, Jayne."

"What? You mean we're leaving? Now?"

"These gentlemen are obviously looking forward to watching Jeremy Brett bound across the moors shouting to Edward Hardwicke to keep up. We mustn't detain them any longer."

"But the tea," Donald said.

"Another time," I said. "I shouldn't drink caffeinated tea this late. If I do, I find it hard to get to sleep." I smiled at Cliff. "Good evening."

He cleared his throat. "I might have to change my plans," he said as I led Donald and Jayne into the front hall. "Go home earlier than expected." Behind me I heard his chair squeak as he dropped into it, and the clatter of the glass against the table as he picked it up.

"I attempted to delay the tea making," Donald whispered to me when we were out of earshot of his guest. "Not quite long enough for you to solve a three-pipe problem, but as long as I was able."

"Perfectly, thank you. Under no circumstances should you buy anything he's selling, no matter how appealing it seems. Have a nice evening."

I dragged Jayne down the steps and we got into the car. "I didn't know you know about authenticating documents," she said. "Although I shouldn't be surprised."

"I don't," I said. "And Donald knows even less than I do."

She switched the engine on and backed out of the driveway. "Why did . . . ? Never mind. You've always said you're not related to Sir Arthur Conan Doyle. Isn't that true?"

"Uncle Arthur has his opinion about that. My father has his. No need to confuse matters in front of non-family members. It was interesting, don't you think, that Cliff didn't leap at the opportunity to invite me to his place of business to examine what he has to sell?"

"You didn't give the man a chance, Gemma. You bolted out of there so fast my head's still spinning."

"I didn't have to give him a chance. I saw no point in lingering once I'd learned what I needed to."

"I'd ask what you learned, but I know better by now. Where are we off to now?"

"Home, I think. Violet and Peony will be starving and desperate to get outside."

"You don't have other avenues of investigation to pursue? I assume that's what we were doing at Donald's."

"I have plenty more avenues, Jayne. I said I intended to restrict my involvement to an advisory capacity, but somehow I seem to be involved once again. I can't help it if people like Miranda are eager to share confidences with me."

"What did Miranda have to say? Oh, never mind. I'll find out eventually."

"In the manner of Sherlock Holmes I will relax in my comfortable armchair and think it all over. He would have called this a three-pipe problem, but as I don't smoke, I'll have to come up with a better description. Also unlike Sherlock Holmes I don't have to send a wild pack of indigent boys scrambling across the city on my behalf or place ads in the classified sections of the newspapers. I have the advantage of the internet."

"Also unlike Sherlock Holmes, you won't be indulging in a seven-percent solution, I trust."

I smiled. "I won't even try to play the violin."

* * *

When I got home, I took a few minutes to greet my joyous dogs and then pulled one of Uncle Arthur's homemade casseroles out of the freezer and popped it into the microwave. While it heated, I got the dogs' leashes down from the hook by the mudroom door, grabbed my rain jacket, and we headed out for a walk.

The wind was building, the storm about to hit. Branches of the old trees swayed and the last of the leaves blew free to be tossed by the wind. I could smell the ozone in the air and the salt off the sea and a trace of someone's spicy dinner. A garbage can lid headed my way but rolled harmlessly past. Undergrowth rustled as small creatures headed for shelter.

Since getting a second dog, I've found my nightly walks are no longer pleasant intervals in which I can indulge in peaceful contemplation while I enjoy the quiet of a Cape Cod evening. When Peony goes one way, Violet goes the other. When Peony stops to sniff a bush, Violet charges ahead in pursuit of a scent only she can detect. More than once my legs have been completely tangled in leashes, threatening to topple me over. I took out my phone, put my earbuds in my ears, tried to control both leashes with one hand, and dialed Ryan with the other. "Ooof," I said.

"Gemma?"

"Yes, sorry. I'm walking the dogs and they're having a disagreement about which direction we should take this evening."

"What's up?"

I put my phone in my pocket and transferred one leash to my free hand. "I didn't get a chance to tell you why I went to Suffolk House in Irene's place . . . Oh, no!"

"What's happening?"

"A squirrel's crossing the road on a telephone wire. They haven't noticed it yet. If I'm cut off suddenly, it's because I've been dragged into the street directly in the path of an oncoming truck. If I don't get a chance to say goodbye, I love you, Ryan Ashburton."

He chuckled. "And I love you too, Gemma."

"I'm saved! For the moment anyway. The squirrel has disappeared into the foliage next to Mrs. Ramsbatten's house without making a giant fuss and daring the dogs to chase it. We are now carrying on down the street in a dignified, stately procession."

Ryan chucked. "As much as I love talking to you, I've got a mountain of paperwork to get through before I can knock off for the night. What's up?"

For a brief moment, I forgot why I'd called him. Something about exchanging our feelings for each other had derailed my train of thought. I loved Ryan, and I was confident in the depth of his feelings for me, but we'd traveled a rocky road to be together. We'd been on the verge of getting engaged a few years ago when I had, very foolishly, given him reason to believe I'd read his mind. It isn't always easy, or so I've been told, to be in love with a woman who appears to know what you're thinking. I told him I'd stop doing that, but he, wiser than I, knew I couldn't stop being myself, and if I did try, I'd end up resenting him because of it.

He'd quit the West London PD and taken a job in Boston. A few years later, he was offered the position of lead detective in West London. He came back and, whether we wanted to or not, we realized we still loved each other. Our relationship was now on an even keel, but we both knew it could tip over if I interfered in one of his cases to a degree he found unacceptable. Particularly if his partner or his chief, both of whom still had strong reservations about me and my observations, objected to that involvement.

Come to think of it, Ryan himself often had strong reservations about me and my observations.

Every time I was beginning to wonder if it was time to move our relationship up a degree, something happened, and we pulled back.

"Gemma? Are you there?"

"Sorry. I was thinking. I didn't get a chance to tell you why I'd gone to Suffolk House earlier. Irene was planning to go, but after the threats Daniel Steiner made against her and the paper, her editor ordered her to stay out of his way. She asked me to go in her place and meet the man."

"You couldn't just say no?"

I didn't answer.

"Foolish question. Do you think Steiner had something to do with Masterson's death?"

"No, I don't, although I suppose it's possible he knew David Masterson other than as a temporary renter of his house. Did you find anything about that?"

"As far as we can tell, they didn't know each other, and it seems as though they never met, not even online. Masterson rented the house through the property managers. Masterson lived in New York; Steiner's in Boston."

"Which is what I thought, but in trying to put a jigsaw puzzle together, one needs all the pieces." Squirrel incident averted, we walked through the quiet streets. It was still early enough that a few people were out. Cars drove slowly past and people walked their dogs. One of my neighbors, whose name I didn't know but whom I regularly saw walking a beautiful golden retriever, passed on the other side of the street. She gave me a wave. Violet darted in front of me and lurched toward her friend, while Peony swerved to sniff at a fire hydrant.

"Would you like a dog?" I said into the phone as I hauled them both after me. "Friendly, well trained."

"Anything else you need to tell me?"

"Yes, come to think of it. David was blackmailing Miranda."

"What?"

"Something about someone named Mark. David knew something about this Mark, whoever he might be, and Miranda was paying him to keep it quiet. She believed she had finished paying him, but David had other ideas and he made her come on his weekend."

"How on earth do you know that?"

"She told me."

I could practically hear him shaking his head. "Give me a sec." I heard papers rustling. "Miranda's son by her first marriage is named Mark Rennheim. He's a vice president at an investment bank in New York City. Not married. No children. No police record."

"That must be him. I wonder if his investment bank had any dealings with David."

"I'll find out. Anything else?"

I decided not to tell him, yet, about Cliff selling forged and/or stolen letters. That was still speculation on my part. "Not at the moment."

"In that case, I'll say good night, Gemma."

"Good night."

Our destination was the town park. When we arrived, I unfastened Violet and Peony and they charged across the grass, in different directions of course. I sat on a picnic bench, kept an eye on them in case I needed to pick up after them, pulled the hood of my rain jacket up, and thought.

I've sometimes wished I was rich—I suppose everyone does at one time or another. My mother's family is minor aristocracy, but nothing in the way of title, money, or land came down to her. She's a barrister, meaning a trial lawyer, and my father's a retired Metropolitan police officer. My grandparents had lived with us when I was young, and on their death my mother inherited our row house in South Kensington, an extremely fashionable neighborhood. Otherwise, we—my parents, my elder sister, and I—worked to earn our living.

Whenever I think it must be nice to be rich—to have unlimited funds, to do what you want, go wherever you want whenever you want—I meet people like Rebecca Masterson and Daniel Steiner, desperate to hold onto what they have, and I decide I'm happy with my life as a bookshop owner.

Daniel Steiner had, basically, threatened Irene and the *West London Star* against reporting that the house he was so desperate to unload had been the scene of a murder.

He'd blackmailed Irene: she hadn't come to Suffolk House this afternoon in pursuit of a valid story because she was afraid of running into him and getting into a confrontation. And then of incurring the displeasure of her bosses.

As I'd told Ryan, I didn't think Daniel had anything to do with the murder, although I was keeping all the options on the table, but it had made me realize that a lot of blackmail seemed to be happening at Suffolk Gardens House.

Miranda's son Mark has a secret. David was blackmailing Miranda to keep that secret secret.

Cliff might call himself a rare book and documents dealer, but if he was dealing honestly, I'd buy one of his letters and eat it. Did David know that? Had Cliff sold a forged or fake letter to David or to one of David's friends, using David as an intermediary? I thought about Cliff's words earlier: "If I wanted to play at being in England I would have gone to England." I took that to mean he hadn't particularly wanted to come on the weekend. He'd shown an obvious lack of concern over the death of his host. If Cliff was, as I suspected, dealing in fake or stolen books and documents, he had a lot to be blackmailed over.

As he'd said, contacts are everything in that business. As is reputation.

Kyle had had dealings with the law. Was there more to that story than what Ryan and the police knew? Had David known more than the police knew? Rebecca said she'd suggested Kyle come to the Cape, but had David planted the idea in her ear?

David had made his niece and nephew, Annie and Billy, do his bidding supposedly because of favors he'd done for them in the past, but more likely the threat of favors to come being withheld.

On the surface it seemed as though David had wanted to host a replication of a historic country house party, with Sherlockian elements to provide the entertainment. Donald, Uncle Arthur, and Jennifer had been invited to participate in the weekend because of what they were: lovers of Sherlock Holmes. Uncle Arthur had decided at the last minute to go to Spain, and sent Irene in his place. Jayne and I were there to work.

The only one whose reasons for being at the weekend were unaccounted for was Steve Patterson. Had he been invited for his knowledge of and interest in the Great Detective, or for more sinister purposes?

The best way to find out would be to ask him. Steve lived in Chatham, but I didn't have his address or phone number, and it was dark now. Not too late for me to ask questions, but probably too late to be invited into the man's home to kick back, enjoy a drink, and talk about whether or not he'd murdered David Masterson.

I became aware of a rapid drumming sound and realized that fat raindrops were bouncing off the hood of my rain jacket. I jumped off the picnic table and called to the dogs. They, eventually, came and we headed home.

* * *

I kicked off my sodden trainers, hung my dripping rain jacket up, and grabbed an old towel off the hook next to it. I did my best to wipe the dogs dry, and then they ran into the house to rub the rest of the rainstorm off on the living room furniture.

By the time I took my reheated casserole out of the microwave, it was cold, but I dished it up anyway and carried it and a glass of water to the rarely used home office at the back of the house. I put the tray on the desk and booted up my computer.

Steve Patterson, or perhaps the less frequent spelling of Paterson, is a mighty common name. I wish everyone had a name like Ebenezer Ferdinando Jones. Then again, if everyone was named Ebenezer Ferdinando Jones it would be hard to locate the particular person I was interested in.

It took a lot of time, but I finally narrowed down my search of Steve or Steven/Stephen Paterson/Patterson to the man I'd met this past weekend. He had no social media presence—nothing on Facebook, Twitter, Instagram, or any other common site. Whether he was deliberately keeping a low profile, or simply not interested in having one, I couldn't tell. But it's difficult, if not close to impossible, to keep oneself entirely off the internet. I found several pictures of him at a wedding. His niece had been married over the summer at a big splashy event in Harwich Port, and she created a public website to share details and photos of the engagement party, the showers, the ceremony and reception, as well as the honeymoon. She had, conveniently, been meticulous in labeling all the people who appeared in her pictures. Uncle Steve, full name Stephen LeFrancois Patterson of Chatham, Massachusetts, had not gone on the honeymoon but he'd been in the church, seated next to the grandmother of the bride, and gave a toast at the reception.

Conveniently (for me), my Steve Patterson had an uncommon middle name, probably his mother's family name. Once I had that, I was able to drill deeper and found that he was originally from Boston, but had lived in Chatham for twenty years. His wife was a high school teacher; they had two children, one of whom was a bit-part actor in Hollywood and the other a teacher in Boston. Steve's wife was still teaching, and Steve worked full time at a hardware store.

Hold on. Hadn't he been in the Marines? Semper Fi and all that? Hadn't he taught military history at some war college or other? That's what Donald said, and Steve had not contradicted him.

I dug deeper still, into places I was probably not supposed to venture. It didn't take long before I had what I needed and I backed out of those places, leaving no trace (I hoped) of my presence behind.

Steve had joined the Marines when he quit high school without graduating, and had spent ten years in the service. His career had been one without distinction but without disgrace either. He and his wife had then moved to Chatham and he'd started working at the hardware store, where he was still employed.

Nothing wrong with that. Nothing wrong at all.

But he was not a distinguished professor of military history, specializing in the Afghanistan wars of the nineteenth century.

Tsk tsk.

I picked my phone off the desk and dialed.

"Ummmm?" came a muffled voice.

"Donald, it's Gemma."

"Gemma! What's wrong? I'm on my way. Where are you?"

"I'm at home and nothing's wrong. Why do you ask? Oh." The clock in the bottom corner of the computer display said it was one AM. The congealing chicken casserole on the tray looked highly unappetizing. "Sorry."

"Let me switch on a light. There, that's better. How can I help?"

"As long as you're up . . . Tell me about Steve Patterson. Had you met him before this weekend?"

"No, and I wasn't aware he lived so close. I'm surprised that we've never met, but some people are more reclusive than others."

"But you knew of him?"

"Oh, yes. He's active in many of the Holmes online clubs."

"I searched them but couldn't find his name."

"As I recall, he calls himself SLPats. Not everyone uses their full name, particularly when it's one that might have been registered before. When David sent out the invitations for the weekend, he introduced us all to each other."

I, as a worker, not a guest, hadn't received the formal invitation. "As SLPats, is he well known in Sherlockian circles?"

"Moderately so. He's a specialist in Doctor Watson's military career, because of his own military service and teaching credentials. Didn't I mention that, Gemma? I'm surprised you've forgotten."

"I haven't forgotten, no. Thanks, Donald. Good night."

"Why are you—?"

I hung up. I drank the glass of water as I returned my attention to the computer, this time to search the message boards and online forums for SLPats. He did participate quite a bit and he did have something to add to the discussions. My own knowledge of the details of the Canon isn't that great, but it seemed to me as though SLPats's information and opinions were insightful and perhaps even valuable. Others on the discussion boards seemed to agree. I found a couple of articles he'd submitted to the journals of Sherlock societies and an essay in a book of Holmes-themed pieces produced by a small but respectable publisher. The short bio attached gave his online name only and mentioned that he'd been a professor of military history.

I leaned back in my chair. The dogs were curled up on the rug next to the desk, sound asleep. Peony's little legs moved as he dreamed he was chasing squirrels. Violet sighed and rolled over. Rain pounded the roof, branches scratched at the windows, and the old house groaned as it resisted the attempts of the wind to knock it over. This house had been built in 1756 and had weathered many storms, even by English standards, and it would weather many more. A car drove slowly past, splashing through puddles and kicking up rainwater.

Steve Patterson had no need to pretend to have a background in academe that he didn't. His knowledge of his field should have been enough, no matter where he acquired it or what he had done with it. But lies, once begun, take on a life of their own. He'd probably exaggerated his résumé when he first joined Sherlockian groups, trying to make himself sound important, and then, having started the lie, decided it was too late to back out. Instead, he'd dug himself deeper and deeper, exaggerating ever more.

How important was his status in Sherlockian society to Steve Patterson, aka SLPats?

Very important, I guessed. The deception would explain why he didn't socialize with Donald and his circle in person and why he hadn't gone to the BSI weekend: real historical experts, people with credentials, were going to be there.

Important enough that he'd pay blackmail money to David Masterson?

With that thought, I shut down the computer, woke the dogs, put them out for one last quick romp, dumped my chicken casserole in the trash, let the dogs back in, rubbed gallons of rainwater off them, and we all retired to our beds.

Chapter Sixteen

B efore I'd gone to sleep, I set my alarm for the unsuitable hour of eight AM. Unsuitable for me at any rate. Jayne would have been up for four hours by then and put in what for other people amounts to half a day's work.

I had a business to run, but I wanted to pay a call on Steve Patterson, and I thought my chances of finding him at home would be best in the morning. He wouldn't work at the hardware store seven days a week, but if he did intend to go to work today it likely wouldn't be until nine thirty or ten at the earliest.

The storm had raged throughout most of the night, but it had worn itself out by morning, and when I took a peek outside, the sun was rising in a clear sky. The street was awash with puddles as well as numerous small branches and leaves, but I could see no serious damage.

I put the dogs out and showered and dressed quickly. I had a glass of water for my breakfast and apologized to Violet and Peony for not taking them on a morning walk. I promised to get home during the day to do that, and I was in the Miata backing out of my driveway before eight thirty.

Early to pay a social call, particularly on someone you barely know, but if Steve Patterson didn't want my company, he shouldn't have gotten himself involved in a murder.

It was a pleasant morning for a drive. Midweek in late October the streets weren't busy with tourists heading to the beaches, and it took only a few minutes to get to Chatham.

Steve and his wife, who I'd learned was named Judy, lived on a street of small, nondescript houses, most of which appeared to have been built in the 1960s or '70s, on large lots. A clean Ford Explorer was parked in the driveway in front of the closed garage door. I pulled in behind it, got out of my own car, and checked out my surroundings.

Last night's storm had left a scattering of twigs, small branches, and freshly fallen autumn leaves on the lawn, but otherwise the yard was scrupulously maintained: leaves raked, grass mowed, bushes pruned, perennials cut back, annuals dug up for winter, flowerbeds turned over. The house itself boasted a new steel roof, and the doors and window frames appeared to have been painted within the last year or two.

I climbed the steps and knocked briskly on the door. I had no reason to be calling, so I'd decided not to bother coming up with one. I'd simply ask Steve if David had been blackmailing him.

The door opened and a woman peered out. "Good morning." She was in her late fifties or early sixties with gray hair cut short, washed and brushed but not styled, watery brown eyes, pink cheeks, and skin showing signs of age. She was considerably shorter than my five foot eight, and about thirty pounds heavier than she probably liked. She was dressed in a plain brown skirt, ironed white blouse under a black sweater, nylon stockings, and thick-soled brown shoes. The clothes were mass-produced, cheap but clean and well-maintained. Behind her, I could see a brown purse and a large, bulging tote bag on the small table in the front hall.

This was Judy Patterson, Steve's wife of more than thirty years, and the very picture of a high school teacher about to head off to work.

"Sorry to bother you," I said. "Is Steve at home?"

"No. He's not."

"If he's gone to work I can try and get him at Household Hardware." I dropped the name of his place of employment so she'd know I wasn't a total stranger or a door-to-door salesperson. If they even had such a thing as door-to-door salespeople anymore.

"Today's his day off," Judy said. "Can I ask what this is about?"

"We met this past weekend at Suffolk House."

She nodded. I decided not to ask this pleasant woman if her husband was being blackmailed and if so might he have murdered his blackmailer. Not because I was being sensitive to her feelings, but because it was unlikely she'd know. She hadn't gone to the weekend, even though it was close to home and being held at a place most people would have loved to visit. Even in this day and age, some Sherlockian societies try to maintain the aura of a men's club and frown on the presence of women, but that had not been the case at Suffolk House. David made Miranda come specifically so Jennifer wouldn't be uncomfortable at being the only woman. Easy to conclude that Judy hadn't gone because she wasn't interested in her husband's hobby.

"He's there now," she said.

That took me by surprise. "You mean Suffolk Gardens House?"

"Yes. I heard what happened on Saturday. A man died." She shook her head. "Terrible thing. Steve called to tell me about it before word started spreading around town, and he said he wanted to stay and finish the weekend. Man doesn't have a lick of common sense, not when it comes to Sherlock Holmes. I don't get the appeal myself." She studied my face, searching for signs of a lack of common sense.

"I'm Gemma Doyle. I was working there this weekend."

"Oh, yes," she said. "I recognize you."

"You do?" Good thing I hadn't pretended to be someone I wasn't. Despite being a keen Sherlockian, Steve had never been in the Emporium. Some consider our pastiche novels and games and puzzles and knickknacks to be beneath them, or at least not of any interest. I'd never seen Judy either.

"I've been to the tea room next door a couple of times. Some of the teachers at my school are regulars, and we celebrated the end of the school year there in the spring."

"That's nice to hear. Thank you. Uh . . . do you know why Steve's gone to Suffolk House this morning?"

"A few of the guests stayed on, he said. He went to see how everyone's doing." She glanced over her shoulder at her purse and bag. "I'm sorry, but . . ."

"You have to get to work. Thanks."

"I'm late as it is. I had a doctor's appointment and then I had to rush home to get some papers I forgot. Shall I tell Steve you called?"

"Not necessary." I started to walk away. Halfway down the steps I turned. "One more thing. I thought I saw Steve last week at the archery range. Was it him?"

She looked at me in genuine surprise. "Archery? Good heavens no. What would Steve be doing at a place like that?" She chuckled. "I might not share his love of military history or of Sherlock Holmes, or even understand those things, but otherwise, I'm a lucky woman. Steve's hobby's looking after the house."

"Thanks," I said as I skipped down the steps.

*　*　*

It was now nine o'clock. The Emporium opens at ten, and today was Ashleigh's day off. I could try to get to Suffolk House, interrogate Steve, call the police if I learned anything relevant—such as that he'd finally had enough, snapped, and in a fit of rage had murdered his blackmailer—and get to the shop in an hour, but that was unlikely to happen. Oh well, couldn't be helped. I'd just have to be late.

The Baker Street Business Improvement Association would not be pleased. They'd reminded me more than once that I was required to have the shop open at the same time as the rest of the stores on the street.

Sherlock Holmes, I thought as I drove out of Chatham, was a full-time consulting detective. I'm a shop owner who sometimes gets more involved in police cases than is good for her.

One thing I'd learned this morning: Steve was not a blowgun aficionado or practitioner. Blowguns and poisoned darts are not the same as bows and arrows, but I'd given Judy Patterson the opening to tell me if her husband enjoyed that sort of activity. She'd reacted only with surprise, and I believed she had a readable face. The property did look as though the owners spent a lot of time caring for it.

My route took me down Harbor Road, toward town. At the last minute, I decided if I was paying a social call I shouldn't arrive empty-handed, and I swung into Baker Street. I found a parking place in front of Mrs. Hudson's, which would be an unheard-of occurrence in the busy summer months.

At this time of the morning—breakfast rush finished, lunch and afternoon tea patrons still to arrive—the restaurant was quiet. A couple of students tapped at their computers while they sipped coffee, and in the window alcove, a group of thirty-something women laughed uproariously over a joke and nibbled at breakfast pastries. No lineup was at the counter. The wet streets and post-storm clean-up had kept many people at home this morning.

"Good morning," I said to Fiona as I studied the display behind the glass. "Quiet today?"

"Normal for the middle of the week at this time of year. Things will slow down for a while until the holiday shoppers get out there in force. Quite the storm last night, wasn't it? My neighbor had a tree come down. Missed her car by inches. Tea?"

I was about to say no, I wasn't going into the Emporium, when I remembered that all I'd had for breakfast was a glass of water. "Yes, please. In a takeaway cup. I'd also like eight muffins. Whatever assortment you want to give me."

"Morning, Gemma." Jayne's smiling, flour-dotted, hairnet-topped face popped out of the kitchen.

Fiona handed me two bulging paper bags and a takeout cup of tea.

"Someone's hungry," Jayne said.

"This isn't all for me. I'm popping around to Suffolk Gardens House."

"Lucky you," Fiona said. "Jayne says it's a fabulous place. Are you investigating that man who died there on the weekend?"

"No," I said.

"Yes," Jayne said.

"No," I said. "I'm simply paying a friendly social call. Want to come with me, Jayne?"

Jayne's eyes flicked to Fiona. "Can you and Jocelyn manage for a few hours? I've done most of the lunch prep. Soups are bubbling and Jocelyn's making sandwiches now."

Fiona indicated the nearly empty restaurant. "We'll be fine. Unlikely to have a big rush."

"I'd like to be back by one," Jayne said, "in time for tea." Proper afternoon tea service—good china, linen napkins, three-tiered cake stands bearing scones with jam and clotted cream, small sandwiches, delicate pastries—started at one and continued until closing at four.

"We won't be long," I said. "I'm going to drop these muffins off, ask if everyone's okay and enjoying their visit to West London, and oh by the way is anyone ready to confess to murder, and come straight back."

"Good thing you're not investigating," Jayne said.

"Investigating is a nebulous term. I have to get back to the shop anyway. I felt Maureen's steely gaze on me when I parked the car out front. She'll be on the phone to the BIA at one minute after ten to say I haven't opened on time."

"No, she won't," Fiona said. "She'll come in here first, asking if you're sick or something. Much innuendo will be placed on the word something. She'll then imply that she doesn't want to cause trouble for anyone but it's her civic duty to mention your absence to the other residents of the street. Whereupon she'll ask if we have any baking left over from yesterday that I can sell her at cut rate."

"To which you'll say no," I said. "Considering that by ten o'clock you have no leftovers going stale." We were referring to Maureen McGregor, owner of Beach Fine Arts situated at 221 Baker Street, who kept watch over Baker Street as though expecting organized crime to descend at any moment and set up operations inside a dress shop. Maureen has a particular dislike of me and the Emporium, not lessened in the least since I helped her out of a jam when she'd been suspected by the police of murdering a rival.

Jayne took my arm. "Peace in the home and in the business, Gemma, is sometimes worth paying blackmail to achieve."

That word again: blackmail.

"I'll pop into the back and tell Jocelyn I'm going out for a while, take off my apron. and comb out my hair," Jayne said. "I'll meet you out front."

I carried my paper bags and my cup to the car. Sure enough, Maureen was standing in the doorway to Beach Fine Arts, watching me. Beach Fine Arts sold nothing of the sort: they stocked mass-produced tourist trinkets as well as postcards and prints of Cape Cod scenes. I waved my tea container cheerfully and Maureen scowled.

* * *

I shook the last few bran muffin crumbs off my fingers as we arrived at Suffolk Gardens House to find the gates firmly closed.

"Are you going to climb the fence again?" Jayne said.

"Absolutely not. I have a rule to seek illegal ingress to a property only once."

"What does that even mean?"

"It means that in case I had to return, I learned the code." On my previous visit, I'd had the foresight to watch Kyle punch in the numbers to open the gates for the police on the panel in the house, and I hoped the same would work at this end. "Besides, I'm not dressed for climbing dusty, rusty gates today." I was wearing cream trousers and a blouse with a high collar and cream and blue stripes.

I punched in the code, the gates creaked slowly open, and I drove up the long driveway. The storm had passed through here: depressions in the pavement were full of water, more than a few tree branches had come down, and the lawn was littered with broken twigs and dead leaves.

We were halfway to the house when a car took the corner ahead of us at great speed, coming straight at us. It barely avoided my front bumper and the driver didn't so much as slow down to wave an apology.

"That looks like Donald," Jayne said, patting the approximate vicinity of her heart. "Where do you suppose he's going in such a rush?"

I'd also recognized Donald's rusty old clunker, and I slowed to watch as it faded in my rearview mirror. The car screeched to a halt at the closed gates and a man's arm protruded from the driver's window to punch the button. The person behind the wheel didn't wait for the gates to swing fully open before accelerating, barely avoiding scraping the sides of the car, and then taking the corner into the street far too fast, and disappearing.

Donald was, to put it mildly, a terrible driver. More than once I've feared for my life when he's been behind the wheel. But he isn't a fast driver. If anything, I often wished he'd hurry up.

"That's Donald's car," I said. "But he's not the one driving it."

I debated following Cliff, who I suspected had borrowed Donald's car, to find out why he was in such a hurry, but decided that would have wait, and we carried on toward the house.

The usual cluster of cars was parked outside. I left the Miata with them, sloshed across the courtyard, walked up the house steps, and rang the bell. A raindrop fell from the roof of the portico onto my head, but the door opened almost immediately, and Annie peered out. "Oh, it's you two. Again."

"Yup, me. Again. Was that Cliff tearing down the driveway just now? It was Donald Morris's car but Donald wasn't driving. It almost hit me."

She shrugged. "Yeah, that might have been Cliff. He was here earlier, don't know what about though." She made no move to step back and let me in.

So I took care of that myself. I held up one of the bags of muffins I'd brought. Jayne lifted the other with an awkward smile. "We thought you'd like a treat from our bakery." I stepped forward, pushed open the door, and walked past Annie. Two sets of luggage—a hard-cased matched set of suitcases in deep purple and a stuffed-full, tattered around the edges backpack—sat next to the door. "Are people leaving early?"

"Miranda's had enough, and so have I," Annie said. "Billy wants to stay on, so I'm getting a lift back to New York City with Miranda."

"I'm looking for Steve, and his wife told me he came here. Did he?"

"He's in the music room with the others. Least he was when I went by earlier."

"Do you know what he wants?"

One eyebrow lifted. "What's it to you?"

I wondered at the sudden change in Annie's attitude. She'd never seemed to care before what I or anyone else in this house was up to.

I smiled at her and said nothing. She shrugged and glanced away. She was dressed for traveling in a pair of well-worn jeans, the Bach T-shirt under a long sweater, and her Doc Martens. "No, I don't know. Don't care either. The gang's all here, you might as well join them. Your friend's here too."

"My friend? You mean Irene?"

"No, not her. David's friend. The fat one. Jennifer."

"Jennifer's not fat," Jayne said.

"Whatever. She's here. I don't know what she wants either. I'm going home. This is a nice house and all, but miserable company."

"You mean everyone's sad because of David's death?" Jayne asked.

Annie let out a bark of laughter. "No one's exactly mourning him, you know. I'm tired of Rebecca expecting me to fetch and carry, me saying no, and her pouting and putting on her grieving widow act. Which is now the grieving, *penniless* widow act. Serves her right." Her face lightened. "I've been called for an audition. I'm super excited about it. I have a good chance of getting the role."

"Good luck," Jayne said, "Broadway or film?"

"Neither. The Metropolitan Opera. I'm a mezzo-soprano and the role's a minor one, but if I land it, it'll be my big break. Who knows what will follow." Her smile grew and her eyes sparkled. Then the darkness descended again, and she shrugged, trying to look as though she hadn't pinned all her hopes on it. "I auditioned for the Met last year, and I did great. I was on fire, totally nailed it." She shrugged. "Sometimes talent's not enough, is it? It's who you know and who wants to do you a favor. Or who doesn't. But hope springs eternal, don't they say?"

"I'm sure you'll be great again," Jayne said.

"Thanks. I have to get to the audition first. If it all works out, look for me. My stage name's Ann Marie Masters. The others are in the music room. Go on in."

The sounds of a piano, being played extremely well, drifted toward us. Annie carried on down the hallway to the kitchen and Jayne and I went into the music room.

The music stopped abruptly as the pianist lifted his hands and swung around. To my surprise, Kyle was at the keyboard.

Five sets of eyes studied Jayne and me. I held up my bag of treats with a friendly smile. "Hi. We wanted to check how everyone's doing, and we brought some breakfast goodies from Mrs. Hudson's."

Billy leapt to his feet and practically snatched the bag out of my hand. "Great. Thanks." He peered inside. "Looks good." He took a blueberry muffin from the top, dropped the bag on the round table in the center of the room, and fell back into his chair. Jayne placed her own bag on the table next to a tray of coffee things.

"Thanks," Rebecca said. "Won't you . . . uh . . . have a seat?"

"Don't mind if I do," I said. "Where's Miranda?"

"Cliff needed to speak to her so they've gone for a walk outside," Rebecca said.

"Cliff? Do you know what it's about?"

"I do not. What business is it of yours anyway?"

I simply smiled at her and turned to Steve. "I called at your house earlier, and your wife told me I'd find you here."

Kyle swung around on the stool, settled his fingers on the piano keys, and began to play. Beethoven's *Moonlight Sonata*. To my uneducated ear, perhaps the most beautiful piece of music ever created. Kyle played it well. Very well. To say I was gobsmacked would have been an understatement. If Kyle was a classical pianist, and Annie was auditioning to sing at the Met, then it must have been Kyle's playing and Annie's voice I'd heard coming from this room over the weekend. Not a recording.

When I'd been told Kyle was a struggling musician, I'd assumed he played keyboards in an untalented garage band, accepting gigs in truck stops, underground clubs, and smoky bars that paid in food and drink and no one at the door examined ID too closely.

I'd assumed . . . The worst mistake of all. I'd assumed. I'd heard first-rate classical music coming from this room, and I'd assumed it was a recording. I'd seen no speakers in here, and I'd assumed they'd been tucked away when not in use.

The notes flowed around me; they caressed me. I let the music carry me away. Until a year ago, David had been a generous sponsor of the New York Philharmonic. Could that be why Kyle was here this weekend? Did Kyle want a job with that august organization or one similar? Positions as a classical pianist must be few and far between, yet highly desirable. Personal contacts and recommendations would count for a great deal. Rebecca had suggested Kyle join the party this weekend because she hoped David could help him get a job. Was it possible David was dangling the offer of a reference and asking Kyle to pay him, or he'd tell his contacts about Kyle's earlier legal troubles? No one in an underground garage band would object if Kyle had a police record. Such was probably a requirement to join. But the symphony might not care for it. Might not care for it enough to offer the position to someone equally talented, who didn't come with a rap sheet.

And Annie, excited about a chance to sing at the Metropolitan Opera?

My mind whirled.

"Good muffin," Billy said.

"Thanks," Jayne replied. Silence fell over the room. Steve got up and helped himself. "Jennifer?" he asked.

"Thank you. I haven't had breakfast yet." Steve handed Jennifer the one he'd selected for himself, tucked into a paper napkin.

"No need to make excuses, Jennifer," Rebecca said. "You can eat a muffin if you want one."

"I'm not—"

"How are you enjoying the Harbor Inn?" Jayne asked quickly.

"It's lovely," Jennifer replied. "Very nice, but I needed to get out so I called a taxi to bring me here. I had dinner by myself last night and enjoyed it, but generally I don't like eating alone in a restaurant. Every person I know in the entire state of Massachusetts is staying in this house. I thought I might drop in and, if not get breakfast, at least get some good conversation out of it."

I doubted friendly conversation was why Jennifer had come. She'd been hoping to learn what she could about David's affairs. The name and phone number of his lawyer, chief among them.

Rebecca stood up. "I don't run a charity kitchen. I'm going upstairs."

"Don't go on my account." Jennifer put the uneaten muffin on the table next to her and got to her feet. She wore a loose brown dress that fell slightly below her knees, a yellow sweater that had seen better days, and black shoes. "I know when I'm not wanted. I'll leave now."

Rebecca laughed. "Sorry if I'm not interested in your silly fantasy world, dear."

"It's too bad you and David had nothing in common," Jennifer snapped. "You could have learned a few things from him. He was so clever, so interested in everything." She choked back a sob.

"David's friends and family are not what I expected them to be either," Steve said. "Why don't you come around to my house, Jennifer? I'd love to show you my collection of memorabilia from the Second Afghan War. I'll give you a lift back to your hotel after."

Her face brightened. "I'd like that. Were you and David close? That's a subject he wanted to learn more about."

"Careful, Jennifer," Rebecca laughed. "We don't want any misunderstandings here. I hope war memorabilia's not a modern version of seeing my etchings."

Steve stiffened. "I'll have you know I'm a respectable married man. Your comment is insulting."

Jennifer burst into tears. She turned on Rebecca. "You're a horrible, horrible woman," she spat. "Just because you couldn't stay faithful to your wedding vows doesn't mean everyone else is like you."

"I don't think you—" Rebecca began.

"You had the honor of being married to the most wonderful man in the world, and you betrayed him, cheated on him, deceived him, disappointed him. He's dead and all you can do is snipe at the people who cared for him. The people who . . . who . . . loved him." She fumbled for a tissue in the pockets of her ill-fitting, baggy sweater, pulled out a worn and tattered one, and buried her face into it.

Jayne patted her awkwardly on the back, and murmured something along the lines of "there there."

"Jennifer," Steve said. "I'm leaving. Are you coming or not?"

Kyle continued playing and the beautiful notes washed over the room, quite the contrast to the storm that had suddenly been unleashed. I stood quietly in the corner. I'd interfere if I had to, but for the moment I was satisfied to stand back and watch. Although satisfied might not be the right word. Something was missing here, and I fought to pin it down.

A slow smile spread over Rebecca's face as understanding finally dawned. "Oh, good heavens. This is so delicious. Don't tell me my husband told you he was going to divorce me and run away with you. You poor pathetic creature. When I got here I wondered which one was the sad fool he was stringing along this time." She pointed a red-tipped finger at me. "I thought it might have been you at first, with your la-de-da English accent, that would impress David no end, and all your questions about things that don't concern you, but you don't strike me as a total idiot."

"Glad to hear it," I said to myself in my la-de-da English accent.

Rebecca turned her attention back to Jennifer. "I never even considered pathetic little *you*." She ran her eyes over the other woman's body and sneered. "Where did you get that dress? Your mother's closet?"

"You married him for his money," Jennifer sobbed. "As soon as you were married, he saw you for what you really are. A deceitful, penny-grubbing woman."

"Whatever," Rebecca said.

"Why don't I help you to the ladies' room?" Jayne said. "You can wash your face and . . ."

Jennifer ignored her. "The joke's on you, Rebecca. He changed his will last week. He left everything to me. Me!"

Rebecca's eyes widened and her jaw fell open. She stared at Jennifer for a moment before letting out a bark of ugly laughter. Her face twisted and all the pretense of moneyed boredom and sneering disinterest collapsed, leaving nothing behind but a small-minded, angry woman. "If that's true, which I very much doubt, you have a heck of a big shock coming your way." She gave Jayne and me her ugly smile. "Isn't that right, ladies? You were here. You heard what that detective had to say. Tell her. She won't believe me. Poor deluded thing."

Jennifer lifted her head and stiffened her shoulders. Her fists were clenched at her sides. Jayne threw me a panicked look. Steve took a step forward, ready to intervene if the insults crossed the line to a physical confrontation. Kyle continued to play, and Billy helped himself to another muffin, keeping one eye on the combatants in case he had to dodge blows.

"Never mind." Rebecca twirled her hand in the air. "I can't be bothered with you anymore. Get out of my house. This is my house, for a few more days at any rate."

Jennifer didn't move. The two women faced each other.

"Miranda," I said. "Where's Miranda?"

No one answered me.

"Cliff left at least fifteen minutes ago," I said. "Surely she would have come back inside."

"Why don't you let Gemma and me take you back to your hotel," Jayne said to Jennifer in a soft kind voice.

"That's a good idea," Steve said. "I can call you later. Maybe you can come around to the house for dinner. *My wife*," he threw a quick look at Rebecca, "would love to meet you."

The tension in the room shattered as though someone had thrown a glass against the wall. Rebecca dropped into her chair. Jennifer pulled herself away from Jayne and turned a questioning face to my friend. "What does she mean? About a surprise? I wasn't in love with David for his money, you know. I told him I don't need or want anything from him, but he insisted on writing me into his will as an indication of the depth of feelings he had for me. He loved me and wanted to take care of me. I did the same for him."

"You keep believing that if it makes you happy," Rebecca mumbled.

Miranda. I looked around the circle of familiar faces. All present and accounted for except for Miranda and Annie. Why hadn't Miranda appeared when Jennifer and Rebecca began yelling at each other? They were loud enough that anyone anywhere in this house would have heard, and Miranda was exactly the sort of person to want to observe every salacious detail.

Miranda and Annie.

Cliff had gone outside with Miranda, and he'd then sped away without bothering to pop his head into the house and say goodbye. He'd been driving a borrowed car far too recklessly for a narrow, private driveway. He'd either been in a heck of a hurry or in a blind rage. After he left, Miranda might have been upset enough to come inside and slip up to her room unnoticed. But where was Annie?

Annie the opera singer. Annie the poor relative. Annie expected to play the role of housemaid for her uncle and who knows what other humiliations in the past. If I believed, as I now did, that David had dangled the threat of a job recommendation withheld over Kyle, what might he have done to Annie? It didn't matter if he'd asked the Metropolitan Opera not to hire her. All that mattered was whether she thought he had when she didn't get the job last year.

"Billy," I said. "I need you go to upstairs and check Miranda's room."

"Why?" he asked.

"She might have come inside after Cliff left without telling anyone."

"So?" Billy said.

"Leave her alone," Rebecca said. "All Miranda ever wants is attention."

"She's not getting any by being upstairs in her room, is she?"

Everyone looked at everyone else.

"Who cares?" Rebecca said. "Why are you still here, Jennifer? Didn't I tell you to get out of my house? I'll call the police and have you removed if I have to."

"I'm leaving," Steve said. "Jennifer, do you want to come with me or wait for Jayne and Gemma?"

"Billy, check Miranda's room," I said. "I'd like the rest of you to stay here. Jayne, come with me."

"I don't take orders from you," Rebecca said to my rapidly retreating back. "I'll be in the morning room. I left my magazine there. The rest of you can do whatever you want. I'm beyond caring about any of you."

Jayne trotted after me down the hallway and into the kitchen. "You think something's happened to Miranda?"

"I think it highly uncharacteristic of her not to want to have a front row seat to Jennifer and Rebecca's quarrel." I opened the back door and stepped outside.

"What—?" Jayne said, but I held up one hand. The music room windows were open and the sound of continued arguing came from within. Kyle had stopped playing and his voice was among them. High in the branches of an ancient oak a crow called to another. Raindrops dripped from holes in the gutters. Otherwise, all was quiet.

Then a voice came from behind the hedge surrounding the kitchen garden. "You've misunderstood me." Miranda.

I put my finger to my lips and, taking care not to make any sound, walked down the path, dodging puddles drying in the warm sun. I sensed, rather than heard, Jayne behind me.

"I don't think so." Annie.

"We can come to an understanding. Let me assure you, I'm not lying awake at night worrying over who killed David. I'm glad to be rid of him. You did me a favor."

"You have a funny way of returning a favor, as you put it."

"All I'm asking for is a cut," Miranda said. "In exchange I won't tell the police about that nasty little dart I saw in your backpack on Friday evening."

Jayne threw me a wide-eyed look.

"Always snooping, aren't you?" Annie said.

"You never know when it's going to pay off. And this time, it did. I was so curious about the dart and the metal tube with it, I took a picture. Just in case it turned out they were important. That metal tube I saw looked an awful lot like the one the police showed us a picture of. They never actually said how David died. How he could have been murdered in the library in the middle of the day in the presence of that nosy Englishwoman and her ditzy baker friend . . ."

Beside me Jayne sucked in a breath.

". . . yet no one heard a thing and the killer got clean away. A dart. Such a small thing. So dangerous in the right hands. In your hands, Annie."

"I have no comment on any of that, but even if it's true, I've got nothing to cut you in on."

"Not at the moment, but you will. When David's estate's finally settled. That's why you killed him, isn't it? You knew he never intended to leave any more than required by law to Rebecca, leaving the bulk of it to you and Billy. It's only a guess, but I'm thinking you had plans for an accident for your dear Uncle David. A fall in the street maybe, directly into the path of an oncoming taxi. Such a tragedy. You thought you had time, but suddenly you couldn't wait any longer. You had to get it done before he contacted his lawyer and wrote in that ridiculous Jennifer."

"David had nothing but a mountain of debt to leave to anyone," Annie said.

"That news came as much of a shock to you as to the rest of us." Fabric rustled as Miranda moved. "I could read it all over your face. There'll be something. Maybe not as much as you'd been hoping for, but something. David wasn't a total fool, as you well know. He'll have kept some assets safe. Enough for you to share with me. Now, let's go inside. It's getting chilly out here."

"Whatever money I might, or might not, inherit from David, I'm not letting you hang that nasty accusation over me for the rest of my life, Miranda. You'll never let it go. Never."

I turned to Jayne, touched my finger to my lips again, and indicated making a phone call. "Police," I mouthed, pointing to the house.

She nodded and slipped away.

Piano music drifted out of the house once again. It was a different tune this time, something I didn't recognize. Still haunting, still beautiful. Above the music, I could hear the sound of Rebecca's voice. Still complaining.

The women in the kitchen garden had stopped talking. I heard a soft grunt as someone, presumably the older Miranda, moved. "Whatever you're thinking, Annie, I'd suggest you reconsider. I'm going inside. Time to say my cheery goodbyes and get out of here. That ride I offered you? Forget it. What are you doing? Annie? We can work this out!" Her cry was cut off.

Time for me to move. The iron gate screeched on its rusty hinges as I struggled to push it open. I burst into the garden to see the two women by the bench. Annie stood behind Miranda, holding Miranda's brightly colored scarf in her hands. The scarf was wrapped around Miranda's throat, her mouth open in a silent scream, her eyes bulging, her face flushed with fear. Her hands were up, clawing at the scarf, trying to pull it away, trying to get air. Annie's eyes also bulged, but with rage and a touch of madness as she tightened her grip.

"Annie," I yelled. "Stop that."

Miranda saw me and threw me a desperate panicked look.

Annie gave the scarf one last sharp twist, and let go. She stepped back and lifted her hands in the air. "This is none of your business. Go back in the house." Her voice was steady.

Miranda tore the scarf off and dropped to her knees, gasping, sucking in air.

I took a step forward. I held my own hands out, and I kept my own voice calm. "The police have been called. We'll go into town and talk it all over. I heard some of what you said. Miranda was going to blackmail you, wasn't she? I'll tell the police it was her fault."

Annie nodded. "I only want what's mine. I sucked up to him for years. Years. I didn't even care about his money. All I ever wanted was to sing on a big stage. To take my rightful place. He could have helped me with that. But he didn't. He could have put a word in for me last year. He said he would, but he didn't. He said I wasn't ready. I needed more time. Time! I'm running out of time. He promised to send me to Italy after Christmas, so I could spend a year in Europe, taking lessons from the best teachers, audition at the great opera houses, buy the right clothes, travel in the right circles. He'd provide me with introductions to all the right people." Tears welled in her eyes and dripped slowly down her cheeks. She made no move to wipe them away. "Miranda was wrong. I knew he was in serious financial trouble but I acted as though I didn't. I'm a good actress as well as a great singer. I fooled you too, didn't I? It came as no shock to hear that Uncle David was almost out of money. His offer to me was nothing but a sham. A pretense. A way of keeping me doing his bidding as long as he could. I had to get rid of him before all the money was gone. No one would be interested in any introductory letter from him if he was disgraced, ruined! And then he started making plans with that woman! He'd never even met her until last week and he was prepared to divorce Rebecca and marry her!"

Annie had killed David, but it sounded to me as though she didn't quite understand why, even to herself. A combination of things, probably: resentment at what she thought was him squashing her career hopes, humiliation at being forced to act the role of servant. Finally, his plans to marry the unassuming, pleasant Jennifer and dump the hated Rebecca, which would leave Annie without a role to play in his life, as much as she hated that role. It sounded as though David had hung the promise of future favors over Annie for years. She had to have realized, on some level, the grand tour of Europe was never going to happen.

All that didn't matter now. "I understand." I walked slowly toward her. I held my hands out. She looked at me. She smiled, ever so slightly, and took a step forward.

As Annie talked, Miranda had crawled away from the bench. The ground was thick with mud from last night's rain, drying slowly in the sun. Miranda's hands and knees were coated with the stuff and streaks of dirt ran across her face. She grabbed a wooden trellis, supporting nothing but dead vines, and hauled herself upright. "I didn't know anything about this," she yelled at me. "I was lying, stringing her along. I told her to go to the police and confess but she refused, so I had to trick her into confessing."

"Trick me!" Annie whirled around. "You used me."

That, I thought, was probably true. If Miranda had found a blowgun and a single dart in Annie's luggage, it was highly unlikely she thought the other woman was intending to practice in the woods. Miranda had known Annie intended to kill David. She'd done nothing to prevent it, and after his death she hadn't bothered to tell the police what she knew.

"We can talk about all that down at the police station," I said. "They'll be here any minute."

At that moment I heard the sound of sirens coming down the long driveway.

Annie hesitated. She glanced at me. I smiled at her.

"Gotcha," Miranda said, not bothering to disguise the triumph in her voice.

Annie turned and ran. I was standing in the middle of the path leading to the gate, blocking her exit. She charged at the ill-kept hedge and shoved her way through.

"Wait!" I yelled. "You can't get away. Annie! Let me help you."

I took off after her. Branches scratched at my face and tore at my clothes as I pushed my way through the foliage. I stumbled free and emerged onto the grass at the back of the house. Annie was running across the lawn, away from the house, down the slope toward the creek at the bottom of the property. Her long sweater streamed out behind her and her sturdy boots didn't falter. Two crows lifted off from a branch of a big old oak as she passed, and another cawed.

I ran after her. The grass and stones were slick from the rain and I'd dressed for a day at the store, not for chasing a killer, so I had thin-soled flats on my feet.

Last night's winds and heavy rain had blown the last of the autumn foliage off the trees, and the ones marking the boundary of the property stood stark and bare against the pale blue sky. Annie was heading for those trees. I didn't know where she was going, she didn't know where she was going, and I didn't know why I was chasing her. She was running in blind panic, and I was chasing her because my instincts told me to.

I flew past the statue I'd admired earlier, the bronze of a girl and her dog. So lifelike, I almost expected the dog to break off the game and join the chase. I could hear shouts from the police in the distance. I kept running, but the space between Annie and me was increasing.

Annie reached the woods and carried on without hesitation.

Footsteps sounded behind me, getting close, and I turned my head to see Jayne, who's a faster runner than I.

"Where's she going?" Jayne yelled.

"Nowhere. Everywhere. She doesn't know."

When I'd seen it the other day, the stream that runs through the bottom of the property had been calm and clear and serene. A gentle babbling brook, no deeper than the top of my foot. I didn't know what effect the rainstorm would have had on the water level or the speed at which the current moved, but I feared the worst.

I glanced over my shoulder again. Men and women were leaping out of the cruisers, but they were a long way away. Other figures huddled in a group at the kitchen door.

"Go back," I called to Jayne. "Tell the police not to let Miranda leave."

She spun on her heels without a word and headed back to the house.

Ahead, I could see Annie's red sweater moving through the line of trees. I called to her, but she didn't turn. She must have heard me, because she put on a burst of speed. She was younger than me, probably in better shape, and wearing better shoes. The distance between us was increasing but she had nowhere to go. This property was fenced. In some places the fence was broken or falling down, but it would take time to find a weak spot to break through, and time to get over or through it.

I heard the sound of rushing water, and I stepped out of the line of trees, gasping for breath. Annie had stopped at the edge of the flooded creek and was watching the fast-moving water, seeking the best place to cross. "The police have arrived," I said, my voice calm and steady. "Why don't we go up to the house and join them?"

She slowly turned to face me. "He wasn't a nice man."

"No, he wasn't."

The creek had risen with the rain and burst its banks. The water was no longer clear but dark with mud and debris, and I couldn't see the bottom. The water rushed over rocks and grass and swirled around the base of trees. Eddies flowed and whirlpools sucked water. Annie stood at the edge of the bank, her feet sinking into the mud.

She looked into my eyes. She touched her forefinger to her temple, and then she stepped backward.

Chapter Seventeen

I pulled off my shoe and then my sock. I gave the sock a good twist and watched muddy water drip to the ground. "That was cold."

Two officers led Annie away. Her hands were behind her back, her head down. She didn't protest and she didn't struggle.

"Be sure you get her into a pair of dry socks as soon as possible," I called after them.

"Why did you chase her, Gemma?" Ryan Ashburton crouched on the grass in front of me. "That was a foolish thing to do. She might have had a weapon, and you knew we'd arrived. We're not in the wilderness here. She wasn't going to get away."

"Pure instinct, I suppose." I pulled off my other shoe and sock and then I held one hand out. Ryan stood up and pulled me to my feet. I glanced at the stream. "I . . . uh . . . thought the water was deeper than it turned out to be."

Annie had taken two steps backward into the swirling water and sunk all the way up to her ankles. I'd taken one step, and held out my hand. She took it and allowed me to lead her to dry—dryish—land.

As rescues went, it had been a feeble attempt.

"I'm from England," I said. "We English tend to believe that in America you have mighty flowing rivers."

"We do have mighty flowing rivers," Ryan said. "We also have cheerful babbling brooks."

"In my defense, I'll point out that the mud in the water disguised the depth. The other day the water was perfectly clear. Sparkling even. I could see stones on the bottom and little fish frolicking about."

Ryan and I walked up to the house together. I held my shoes in my hands and tried to avoid stepping on small sharp rocks.

"Jayne told me not to let Miranda leave," he said. "Is she involved in this?"

"The extent of Miranda's involvement is to be determined, but at the least she knew far more about what had happened to David Masterson than she told you."

"Before we go in, can you tell me quickly what went on out here? You'll have to make a formal statement later."

I explained what I'd overheard and what I'd seen in the kitchen garden.

"Why did you come outside to look for them in the first place?"

"It seemed uncharacteristic of her that Miranda wasn't involving herself in the argument going on in the music room. Cliff had left in a heck of a hurry after going for a walk with Miranda. I thought I'd better check up on her."

"You thought Cliff had killed Miranda?"

"No, I didn't. He and Miranda had gone outside to talk in private, and they'd been seen leaving the house together by several people. He'd argued with Miranda and then departed in great haste, which had been observed by none other than me. If she was found dead shortly after, the police might come to the logical conclusion that he'd killed her. Meaning, it was the perfect time for Annie to make her move."

"How'd you know it was Annie?"

"When Jayne and I arrived at the house, Annie opened the door to us before my knock had so much as died away. She'd been in the front hall, standing at the window. I suspect she'd been lurking outside the kitchen garden, listening to Cliff and Miranda argue. When he left, she ran through the house to see what Cliff did next. He didn't come inside but walked around the house, got into his car, and drove away. She saw him leave, and I confirmed that he'd been driving fast in apparent distress. I would have made a reliable witness at his trial."

"You think she was thinking that clearly?"

"Oh yes. When I was trying to talk her down, first in the garden when she had Miranda by the throat, and then by the stream, of which the less said the better, I murmured all sorts of comforting words to the effect that I knew she'd been justified in killing David and trying to kill Miranda. Obviously, I don't believe anything of the sort. Not at all. She came here, on this weekend, with her blowgun and her dart intending to kill him. She did so, and she might have got away with it, considering the plethora of suspects. I've never known anyone to surround themselves with so many people who had reason to want to see him dead as David Masterson. But Miranda, the eternal snoop, had seen the blowgun and dart in Annie's luggage. I saw Miranda poking around in the morning room on Friday evening, when the others were in the drawing room. I believe she'd been in Jayne's room, the one who'd moved Jayne's ring that first night. She picked it up to check out the quality of the stone and didn't put it back properly. As long as nothing was taken, I let it go and I didn't confront her. I didn't think she'd be so bold as to actually open suitcases. That was obviously a mistake. I should have told you, so you could have asked if she'd come across anything in her snooping."

"In fairness, we did ask each of them, several times, if they'd noticed anything in the way of suspicious behavior on the part of the others, or if they had anything else to tell us. Miranda had plenty of opportunity to tell me about the blowgun. She chose not to."

"She let Annie know she'd found it. Exceedingly foolish of her, but greed has a way of overcoming instincts of self-preservation. Or so I've heard."

Ryan nodded. "That it does."

"Annie knew Miranda would hold David's death, his murder, over her head for the rest of her life, so Miranda also had to go. Until a few minutes ago, Miranda didn't out and out tell Annie that she'd seen, and photographed, the blowgun and dart, but Miranda's not all that bright. Annie became aware that Miranda knew, or at least suspected, what Annie had done. They were planning to drive back to New York City together; Annie probably intended to see to it that Miranda had an accident along the way. But then Cliff arrived, argued with Miranda, and left without anyone seeing Miranda again. The perfect fall guy."

"When did you know it was Annie?" Estrada asked.

"Not until it was almost too late. I made a serious mistake, and Miranda might have paid for that mistake with her life."

"Are you going to explain that?" Estrada asked.

"If I must. I took both Annie and Kyle at face value, and I didn't search far into their backgrounds. I came here, today, intending to confront Steve Patterson."

"Steve? Why? What did Masterson have on him?" Ryan asked.

"Nothing criminal, but enough to cause Steve enormous embarrassment among the people who matter to him. Let's leave it at that. I was wrong."

Estrada snorted. "That's a first."

"The first of which you are aware," I said.

"Okay," Ryan said. "You were wrong about Patterson. What happened today that made you suspect Annie?"

"She's an opera singer. Good enough to audition at the Met."

Estrada and Ryan exchanged glances. "So?" Estrada said.

"The blowgun has been worrying me a great deal. We know the weapon's easy enough to get. I'm assuming you had no luck tracing the one that was used?"

Ryan shook his head. "Nothing that would tell us who had bought that particular one."

"Or the strychnine?"

"Again no," Estrada said. "Will you please get on with it, Gemma. We don't have all day here."

"I wouldn't mind sitting out here all day." The kitchen step was warm beneath me, the sun shone on my face, the air was refreshingly cool and crisp. I wiggled my bare toes. "I love autumn in New England, don't you?"

Estrada growled.

"I knew Annie's in show business, but I thought she was an actor. I couldn't find traces of her career online, and so I assumed she had a stage name, which she does. I let it go and didn't keep searching. A blowgun can be difficult to use with precise accuracy, particularly one so small. In this case the dart had come through the tear in the screen of the door, crossed the twenty-five or so feet of the library floor, and hit the target in the exact spot intended. The side of his neck. Most importantly, the shot had to be successful the first time. I would have noticed a dart flying in front of my face and I would have turned to see what was going on."

"Get to the point, Gemma," Ryan said.

"I am getting to the point. If you'll both stop interrupting. Our killer must have practiced extensively. You searched, I'm sure, and found no trace of any of these people belonging to some sort of blowgun club, if there are such things, and I'm sure there are. No one around here had seen someone casually practicing shooting darts out of a blowgun. I considered briefly that they might have been archers, as the steady aim would be similar."

Ryan nodded, meaning he'd had the same thought.

"I'd initially concluded that the shooter was most likely a man, as men have greater lung capacity than women. But breath control can be learned, can't it? The shooter had to have, considering the small length of the blowgun and the distance the dart had to travel, extraordinary breathing power."

Ryan and Estrada glanced at each other and I saw comprehension dawn on them both.

"Such as a Met-worthy opera singer," Estrada said.

"Exactly. And that was why I suddenly realized I had to find Miranda. Because Annie, the opera singer, had been watching Cliff leave and she was not in the music room listening to everyone argue. As for where she got the strychnine, I'll suggest you contact farm and supply stores in Kansas and ask about purchases of wild animal control substances. Whether Annie had the idea of using the blowgun and dart back in the summer or not, murder has been on her mind for a long time." I pushed myself to my feet. "Shall we join the others?"

Chapter Eighteen

"So David was blackmailing them all?"

"Essentially, yes."

"Why would he gather together all those people who hated him for his house party?"

"Because he was manipulative and mean. Miranda said he liked making people dance to his tune. If I had to guess, I'd say he knew his power trip was coming to an end. He was running out of money, and out of excuses to keep borrowing, so he threw the last he had into making this grand gesture of playing host at a country house property."

We were relaxing on the deck of the Blue Water Café, gathered around a big table next to the railing. We had drinks in front of us, along with platters of calamari, bruschetta, and a bucket of mussels and clams. Below us, harbor seals played in the cool waters, and in the distance lights shone from boats bobbing at anchor. Heat lamps were turned on and we were bundled up in thick sweaters with blankets over our knees. Andy would be closing the deck after the weekend. He'd come out of the kitchen to join us and sat next to Jayne, holding her hand under the table. I grinned at Ryan and helped myself to a piece of bruschetta.

"We haven't asked Steve, Cliff, or Miranda what he had on them, as that appears to not be relevant to his death," Estrada said. "So why don't you tell us. If you know."

"Do you doubt I do?"

"Sadly, no."

I shook my head and helped myself to a crispy piece of calamari.

"I want to know why I'd been invited," Donald said. "And Arthur. David didn't even know us, not personally, much less have blackmail material on us."

"He might have been mean and manipulative," I said, "but David Masterson was, we mustn't forget, a Sherlockian. I believe the original idea for the weekend was to have a meeting of the like-minded in a mutually enjoyable environment. Then, once his financial world began crashing down around him, he decided it would be a nice idea to remind the others that he could ruin them if he so chose. As a bonus, Steve and Cliff do have some Sherlockian knowledge, so he could indulge his passion at the same time he made his victims squirm. We know Miranda was paying him off, and you'll find that Cliff was too. Ryan, you said David had unaccounted for deposits going into his bank account?"

Ryan nodded.

"The blackmail payments. Steve doesn't have the kind of money that would help David out of his financial difficulties, probably not Cliff either. It wasn't about the money for David. It was about holding the threat of disgrace and ruin over their heads and making them dance to his tune. You'll likely find that some people who weren't at this weekend were also being blackmailed.

It's entirely possible David's victims thought they were finished paying up, but blackmail never stops, does it? The blackmailer gets greedy and can't let go of the pressure."

"As I tried to tell my editor when he said we were to keep mention of Suffolk Gardens House out of the paper," Irene said. "He wouldn't listen to me, but it became a moot point after the chief of police's statement about the events surrounding David's death and Annie's arrest, didn't it?" She chuckled. "I wish I could have seen Daniel Steiner's face when he heard it on the radio. Naturally, the paper printed the chief's statement in full."

"Let's hope that was sufficient to dissuade Steiner from taking up the life of a blackmailer," Donald said.

"If you've decided those matters are irrelevant to the case against Annie, then I'll keep what I know to myself," I said to Ryan and his partner. "It's mostly speculation anyway." Miranda had been paying David so he wouldn't reveal what he knew about her son, Mark. I have no interest in finding out what Mark's secret is, so I hadn't looked into him, and I wouldn't ask Ryan if he knew. David might not have been blackmailing Annie but he did enjoy holding the promise of helping her with her music career over her head, and he was intending to do the same for Kyle. The only one of them who seemed to owe nothing to David was Billy, although he resented having to play the poor relative.

"You might drop a word to your friends at the NYPD to look into Cliff Mann's antique business," I said. "It's not entirely above board. Cliff came back to the house to ask Miranda to give him a letter he'd sold to David, which David had given to his mother and after her death to Miranda as a memento. A letter supposedly written by Emily Dickinson."

"That would be nice to have," Jayne said.

"Not in this case," I said. "Supposedly is the operative word. I can't see Miranda as a collector. When David died, the first thing that crossed Miranda's mind would be that she could now sell the letter. That would require it being examined, and Cliff couldn't have that. They argued about it, and Cliff stormed off." I remembered Friday night, when I'd heard someone telling David they wouldn't have come if they knew "he" was going to be there. I now believed that had been Miranda, complaining about Cliff. Even before David's death, Cliff had been pestering her about wanting that letter back.

"Jennifer?" Jayne asked. "What about Jennifer? You saw her earlier, Gemma. What did she have to say?"

After Annie'd been arrested and the others had given their statements, Jayne and I had been allowed to return to town and our businesses. Steve had given Jennifer a lift back to the Harbor Inn. Shortly before closing she came into the Emporium and we'd chatted while she browsed.

"Annie's role this weekend, initially, was to play the housekeeper. In that position, she put the towels in the bathrooms, made the beds, tidied the rooms."

"Wouldn't help in the kitchen," Jayne muttered.

"Which meant she was in and out of people's bedrooms. She and Billy came in Billy's car, and they got to the house on Friday before the guests arrived. Annie would have been expected to ensure the rooms were ready and in doing so, she would have realized, almost immediately, that David and Jennifer had slept together the night before. Once she knew that, she would have wanted to know more. The walls in that house might as well be made of paper. Annie listened to David and Jennifer making plans for their future. Annie knew David had told Jennifer he was going to divorce Rebecca and marry her. I believe he intended to do that, and Annie must have believed it also."

"Why?" Jayne asked. "I mean, why do you believe it? He was a scoundrel."

I'd watched as Jennifer browsed my shop. She picked up everything and selected what she liked, without looking at the price tags. She didn't spend a lot of money on herself—her clothes, shoes, and purse were serviceable, but not new and not particularly attractive, although of good quality—but clearly she could afford to indulge her passions whenever she wanted. Period clothes of the quality and detail she'd brought for the weekend are not cheap. Her earrings had been gold, and the diamonds in the jewelry she'd worn to the Saturday dinner were genuine. She'd given me an address in Beverly Hills to have her purchases sent to. "Your parents' home?" I asked her.

"Yes. I've decided to go to London after all. To take the trip David and I intended to take together. Maybe I'll spend some time in Europe too. After that, I'll go back to California and back to working at my dad's publishing company." She was having dinner at Steve's that night, she told me, where they'd have a lively spirited discussion about the Second Afghan War and Doctor John Watson's part in it. Tomorrow she'd be gathering all her courage around her and booking a flight to England. I gave her the contact information of my friend Grant Thompson, who'd recently moved to London to be with my older sister, and suggested she give him a call. Grant was a true Anglophile, and he'd be delighted to show an American first-timer the sights of his beloved adopted city.

"Jennifer," I said now, "is financially comfortable. She's not mega-rich by the standards David and Rebecca tried to maintain, but well enough off not to need to work for an extended period. Her family live simply, and they taught her to live simply, but they have a great deal of money. When Jennifer told me she'd rewritten her will to mention David, I wondered why a single, childless woman of her age with a job in publishing and a rented flat would even have a will, and so I checked into her. You can be sure David did the same. Yes, he intended to divorce Rebecca, who'd rapidly run through her own inheritance, and marry Jennifer and her trust fund. Annie had been intending to get rid of David when and if the chance presented itself, but she realized that if she was to get anything from him, she had to act now." I looked between Ryan and Estrada. "Am I close?"

"Annie's not talking," Ryan said. "But we'll get her. We have the pictures Miranda took of the blowgun and the dart in Annie's luggage. We've no proof, yet, that Annie put those things there, but we'll get it."

"The NYPD have found mysterious holes in the walls in the corridor of her apartment building," Estrada said. "Tiny holes about the size of a dart. Her apartment itself isn't very big, nowhere near the size of the library at Suffolk House. Neighbors say they've wondered what she was doing out in the hallway at night."

"The dress she wore as the housekeeper was baggy enough to conceal the blowgun," I said. "Slip it down the side, tuck it into her knickers, secure it with the belt, and no one would notice. Annie had no need for a hollow walking stick or ladies' parasol. As for why she used a blowgun in the first place, please let me know when she confesses. I'm very interested in that."

"Do you suppose, Gemma," Donald asked, "she was making a direct reference to *The Sign of Four*?"

"I believe so. If not the book itself, some reference to Holmes at any rate. David's mother was an enthusiastic patron of the arts, and she donated a lot of money to theatrical and musical companies. David did not. David spent his money on Sherlock Holmes first editions and Sherlockian country house weekends. I suspect Annie resented his devotion to Holmes and she wanted to express her contempt for that passion. She really is a very confused young woman."

"Don't tell me you feel sorry for her," Estrada said. "And you hope we go easy on her?"

"Sorry for her? Not in the least. Plenty of confused young women are out there, and they don't go around killing people and attempting to frame others. I thought she was genuinely grieving for David, but I now believe I was mistaken. An opera singer is also an actor, and she's a good one."

I took a sip of my wine and glanced around the table at the faces of the people I loved and cared about. Even Louise Estrada. "So, Jayne. Andy. Let's talk wedding plans. If Suffolk Gardens House is still available in the spring, it would be a lovely setting."

"I am never, ever stepping foot in that place again," Jayne said firmly.

"Perhaps we could use it for the January sixth dinner." A gleam popped into Donald's eye, and he rubbed his hands together. "It will be even more atmospheric in winter. Roaring fireplaces, drafty halls, creaking floorboards. Dark moonlit nights."

"Count me with Jayne," Ryan said. "I'm not working in that kitchen while you and Arthur entertain your friends, Donald."

"I have no particular desire to go there again, myself," I said. "But I have one last detail to tidy up. I trust you're all free Sunday at nine?" I smiled at everyone. No one smiled in return.

Chapter Nineteen

"Careful there!" I called. Violet and Peony danced around the newcomer, sniffing at everything.

I stood in the mountain of debris scattered across my lawn. Yards and yards of bubble wrap, heavy blankets, packing tape, Styrofoam peanuts, cardboard. I stroked my cheek lightly as I thought. "Maybe it would look better under that tree."

Ryan Ashburton leaned his hands against his knees. "Absolutely not," he gasped. "We're not moving it again, Gemma."

"But—"

"No buts," Jayne said.

"If I can't claim my back injury as work-related, I'm going to sue you." Louise Estrada put both knuckles in the small of her back and leaned against them with a groan.

"Okay," I said.

Andy Whitehall peered at me from behind the wheel of the forklift. "You mean we're done? Thank heavens. Sorry about those bushes, Gemma. It's been a while since I drove one of these."

My neighbor Mrs. Ramsbatten had pulled a garden chair out of her shed and set it up on her lawn, where she sat drinking iced tea and cheering us on. Heads had popped out of nearby houses to watch and more than a few people wandered over to offer the benefit of their advice. A rental truck filled my driveway, and the forklift had dug up a good part of the lawn, destroyed some flowering bushes, and barely avoided taking out the steps to the mudroom. My friends were exhausted and dirty, Louise Estrada was threatening to sue me, and my dogs were wary.

I was delighted.

The bronze statue of the little girl and her dog sat in the center of the back yard. Next week, I'd buy a bench to put next to it. I'd create a pleasant oasis where I could sit and read on a warm summer's day. I'd done my research into the sculptor and the cost and value of similar bronze work before calling Daniel Steiner and offering to buy the statue. I'd gone in low, giving my opening bid, expecting he'd drive a hard bargain. Instead, he'd said, "Come and pick it up any time. But you have to bring your own crew."

I'd gathered my "crew," rented a truck and forklift, and we'd spent most of Sunday morning packing the thing up, moving it, and unpacking it.

"As fun as this has been," Jayne said, "not, I have to get to Mrs. Hudson's."

"It's unlikely crime stopped in West London while you moved your piece, Gemma," Estrada said. "So I have to go to work too."

"Lemonade first?" Leslie Wilson came out of the back door bearing a pitcher tinkling with ice and a platter of homemade chocolate chip cookies.

Everyone gathered around and helped themselves. We sipped and munched and studied the statue.

"I almost expect them to move," Andy said at last.

"Violet wants to join in the game," Jayne said.

"At first, I thought you were nuts getting that thing," Louise Estrada said. "As though you wanted some sort of memento of what happened at the house. But I have to admit, it suits your garden."

Ryan draped his arm over my shoulders. "It suits Gemma."

"You have mud on your cheek." I wiped it away, and we exchanged smiles.

"Thanks for the lemonade and cookies," Andy said to Leslie. "Jayne, if you're ready to go I'll drop you at the tea room."

"Thanks. Mom, do you want a lift?"

"No, thank you, dear. I'll enjoy the walk." Leslie carried the tray back into the house and came out with her purse.

"Catch you later, Detective," Estrada said to Ryan. She gave me a nod and what might, barely, have passed for a smile.

"Donald," Jayne called, "are you coming?"

"What?"

"We're leaving now."

"Okay. Goodbye."

"Perhaps I need a lift home after all." Leslie linked her arm through Donald's. "I'll go for my walk later. You can take me. Let's leave Gemma to enjoy her statue in peace."

"I think Louise and I are getting on much better now," I said to Ryan when we were left alone to admire the statue.

He dropped to the ground, grabbed my hand, and pulled me after him onto the soft, cool grass. Violet had given up waiting for the bronze ball to come her way and found a real one under a bush somewhere. She dropped it next to Ryan, and he obliged her. Peony joined in the chase.

Ryan and I leaned against each other and looked at the statue for a long time. "There's something about it," Ryan said. "It's mesmerizing."

"It speaks to us of our own childhoods, I think. Freedom and fun and happy memories."

Peony dropped the ball in my lap, and I tossed it into the bushes. They scrambled after it.

"Did you have a happy childhood, Ryan?"

"I did. We always had dogs. I remember Nipper in particular. What a fun little guy he was." The edges of his mouth turned up and his ocean blue eyes looked at something far, far away. "Memories. I wonder, when I'm old and gray, what memories I'll have of you. Getting yourself in trouble and chasing criminals, most likely."

"Is that all?" I asked.

His eyes came back into focus and he grinned at me. "I certainly hope not." He cleared his throat and glanced away. "Perhaps, Gemma, it's time for us to talk about making memories together."

I put my head on his shoulder. "I'd like that." I studied the statue. The girl's bronze eyes caught the sun, and almost seemed to have a twinkle in them.

"Sorry, sorry. Hope I'm not interrupting. Forgot my keys."

Ryan and I pulled apart as Donald bustled around the corner. "I'm sure I had them in my pocket, but I must have put them down somewhere. Gemma, have you seen my keys?"

Ryan pushed himself to his feet with a groan. "I'll help you look."

"I don't mean to disturb you. They must be around here somewhere. I searched the front of the house already."

I stood up. "Don't worry about it. It's not as if we were talking about anything important."

Ryan might have muttered something rude, and I gave him a warm smile. Let Donald fuss: Ryan and I had plenty of time to talk about important things.

Acknowledgments

I started this book at the beginning of March 2020. I was staying with a friend in a hot, distant country for a month and I intended to get the first draft finished over that month. That would be about 70,000 words. Three weeks later I had 6,000 words and was on a plane home, having been called back, along with all the other traveling Canadians, by our prime minister. The rest of the book was written in quarantine, and then in lockdown, and over the very strange summer and fall. It took me longer than usual to write this book, mainly because of all else that was going on, even though I myself was going nowhere. Someone said that writing is largely done by the subconscious, and if your subconscious is otherwise occupied it can be hard to keep focus on the story.

I believe that's true, and I know so many writers and other artists who've been struggling in one way or another in these plague times. Fortunately, we writers, unlike stage actors or musical performers, can work at home in blissful isolation.

Over this past year, I've missed traveling to bookstores and conferences and missed meeting so many people in person. Fortunately, we've had Zoom and the like to keep us connected and communicating.

Acknowledgments

Let's hope that by the time you're reading this our lives are somewhat returned to normal and we can meet again.

I'd like to thank my good friend Cheryl Freedman, who read the manuscript with her keen mystery-lover's eye and provided much-needed gentle correcting. Also Sandy Harding, the best editor a writer can have, the crew at Crooked Lane Books for believing in Gemma and the gang, and to Kim Lionetti, my marvelous agent.

Thanks to Robin Harlick, Barbara Fradkin, Mary Jane Maffini, and Linda Wiken, who provided humor, support, and friendship when we were all so far apart. And, as always, my marvelous daughters, Alexandra, Julia, and Caroline.

Special thanks to Mike Ranieri, the Myers of the Bootmakers of Toronto, for the title.